One-Night Stand . . .

He caught her eye and tossed a hundred-dirham chip onto the table. Twenty-eight. She matched his bet. They lost. Philip shrugged, gathered up his chips, and got to his feet, nodding toward the bar. She smiled and made her way through the crowd to join him. To celebrate their meeting they drank champagne; they danced in the nightclub; they returned to the tables and an hour later they were tiptoeing past the dozing night porter and up the stairs to his room. Philip hung up the "Do Not Disturb" sign and locked the door behind them. And while she drew the curtains to shut out the electric-blue glare from the floodlit pool, he opened the bottle of Moet et Chandon that he had bought from the barman at the Casino.

There she was, superbly naked with him on the crisp white sheets, blonde hair cascading over his stomach, lips cool and damp, hands gently caressing the inside of his thighs . . .

Philip snapped out of his reverie to see that the gates had been raised and the old Arab was beckoning him on. The Porsche jolted over the tracks and out onto the open road. My God, Philip thought, settling into a steady cruising speed of eighty-five, it was a music hall joke, a Feydeau farce; the one-night stand that wasn't—but what was it and why?

Other Pinnacle Books by Peter Townend:

OUT OF FOCUS
ZOOM!
FISHEYE

TRIPLE EXPOSURE

(QUEST #1)

by Peter Townend

PINNACLE BOOKS   LOS ANGELES

TRIPLE EXPOSURE

An original Pinnacle Books edition, published for the first time anywhere.

ISBN: 0-523-40163-9

First printing, November 1979

Cover photograph by Jacqueline Marsall

Printed in the United States of America

PINNACLE BOOKS, INC.
2029 Century Park East
Los Angeles, California 90067

FOR
JUAN-MANUEL
"Excellence, je m'appelle Figueras."
ERFOUD 1967

CONTENTS

TRIPLE EXPOSURE

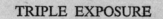

Prologue

After Fkih ben Salah the road runs northeast, fast and true through the vast olive grove that sprawls across the plain of Beni Amir. Pulling out to avoid a tiny donkey almost totally hidden beneath a load of freshly cut lucerne, Philip Quest took the Porsche up through the gears, then settled back and let the car drive itself. Both windows and the roof were open, the rush of the wind taking the edge off the heat of the sun, which was already high above the peaks of the Middle Atlas. He had made good time for the hundred and twenty-odd miles from Marrakesh, and at this rate would have no problem in getting to Tangier with a couple of hours in hand to have a bath, change, and relax before dinner. He shook his head, smiling, as he recalled the last dinner party in Tangier, a fortnight ago: various consuls and their wives, the Episcopalian minister, and the two middle-aged English ladies who ran a home for stray dogs in Fez. But that would hardly be Billy's style tonight; at least with him one could still recapture some of the old glamour of Tangier in the halcyon days before the Moroccan Independence. Gone now forever from the harbor were the war-surplus MTBs with their cargoes of cigarettes for Spain, guns for Algeria, gold, penicillin, and narcotics for wherever there was a profit to be made. The International Credit Bank of Panama (S.A.) was now the American Library; and the Mar Chica that used to serve the most vicious absinthe in the Mediterranean now proudly advertised "TEA AS MOTHER MAKES IT!"

Chapter I.

From Ticino to Tangier

Every morning at 9:26 the Trans-Europ-Express No. 74, the *Roland*, leaves Milan on its journey northwards to Basel and Bremen. After crossing the Swiss frontier at Chiasso, it stops for two minutes at Lugano before starting the long climb up the valley of the Ticino to Airolo and the St. Gotthard tunnel through the Alps. Standing by the bookstall with its racks of postcards and kaleidoscopic shelves of chocolates, the girl in a white fur hat like a dandelion gone to seed shivered and thrust her hands more deeply into the pockets of her ankle-length suede coat whose collar was turned up against the wind that swept across the lake. At precisely 10:39 the train slid to a halt and the few passengers climbed down onto the low platform: a group of expensively dressed Italians, the inevitable pair of nuns, some out-of-season tourists, and, just as she was about to give up hope, the Brigadier. He was a bluff, hearty man of about fifty. His sandy hair was cut short, his clipped moustache yellowed with nicotine, his cheeks purple with broken veins. He wore a brown tweed cap and a matching overcoat with raglan sleeves. He carried a scuffed pigskin briefcase and there was a copy of the *Daily Telegraph* tucked beneath one arm.

He was almost too good to be true, the girl in the white fur hat thought as she walked to meet him; all that was missing was a shooting stick. She smiled at her joke and then the Brigadier's hand was fumbling toward the peak of his cap and she was steering him out past the buffet into the station forecourt. The metallic blue BMW was sandwiched between two taxis, parked at an angle of forty-five degrees to the curb. She backed out expertly, flashing a smile at a policeman, while the Brigadier launched into a tirade against the breakfasts served by Alitalia. She drove in silence down to the lake which the wind had whipped into a flurry of gray-white waves. The clouds swirled down from the mountains and a solitary steamer, deserted except for the crew, rocked against an empty landing stage. Part of the road was being dug up, and the single-lane traffic was at a standstill.

"Christ," she said, gazing at the tossing fronds of the bedraggled palms that lined the lake. "It's a miracle they survive. It's a miracle anyone survives in this bloody country. Chocolates, watches, cuckoo clocks . . ."

"As a matter of fact, practically all the cuckoo clocks come from Germany, from the Black Forest. But you must admit there are certain other . . . er . . . advantages that Switzerland has to offer." He glanced out of the window and pointed a gloved finger toward the plate-glass windows and the polished steel of the Credinvest Svizzero. "Such as banks, for example."

A squall buffeted the car, bringing with it the first drops of rain. "Did you know," the Brigadier went on, ignoring her silence, "that here in Lugano, a town of some twenty-five thousand inhabitants, there are more than forty different banks? All highly discreet, of course, and no questions asked when a Milanese industrialist lays down fifty million lire on the counter

2

and pays it into his numbered account. It was once estimated, you know, that the equivalent of three million sterling—sterling, mind you, not lire—was smuggled across the border at Chiasso every day. Every day," he repeated. "It's brought a whole new way of life to the criminal classes of Milan. Some of them even make ten or more runs a day, choosing their times and their frontiers, changing cars and so on."

"Please, Brigadier, I only came to collect you because Thami's got a cold and can't leave the house. And you've got all day to talk money with him. One thing I will tell you, though. There's been a hitch."

"Hitch?" The Major turned around in his seat to face her. "What sort of hitch?" She sighed and drummed her fingers on the leather-covered rim of the wheel. "Last month in Grenoble. You must've read about it in the papers." The Major nodded slowly and rubbed his moustache. "Yes. Bad business that. Someone got killed, didn't they?"

"He was a nice boy, too. One of the best." She eased her foot from the clutch pedal and the car moved forward, only to be stopped again a few yards further on by an old man in a Loden coat shuffling across a pedestrian crossing with his arm outstretched. The heater whirred and wipers ticked monotonously as they battled with the rain that had now settled in for the day. She watched sourly as the steamer cast its moorings, gave an ironic blast on its siren, and churned off down the lake.

"And the . . . er . . ." the Brigadier ventured.

"Not a penny, not a cent, not a sou."

It took them twenty minutes to cover the half mile to Lugano Paradiso and the tires screamed as she whipped the car across the oncoming traffic, missing a trolley bus by inches, and up the narrow road that snaked up the side of Monte San Salvatore to the village of Pazzallo. They were now in the clouds and visibility was cut to ten yards, the car a cocoon of warmth in a world of dirty gray cotton. A high stone wall appeared on the left side and she slowed down

3

and turned into a short graveled driveway barred by a steel gate which swung upwards as she hit the horn with the flat of her hand three times. Leaving the car in the garage, she led the way through the dank and dripping garden along a flagged path between two rows of gloomy cypresses toward the low pink-washed house with its Moorish arches and mock-Spanish ironwork covering the windows.

The rain drove against the picture window of the overfurnished living room and the wind lashed the flooded terrace into an angry sea. Left alone, the Brigadier stood by the log fire that hissed in the central fireplace, warming his hands, wondering if he would ever finally close the deal.

Upstairs in her bedroom Thami Fouquet's mother had fallen asleep and was snoring gently. In her day, which had lasted more than fifteen years, Rose Osborne, *La Rosa d'Angleterre*, had been a name to conjure with; first as a young woman at Madame Albertine's in the Rue Debarcadére, and then in her own establishment on the Quai Voltaire. Blonde, delicately boned, with a superb skin and body, she epitomized the European ideal of an English beauty. But beneath the cool facade there flared a depraved and genuine sensuality, made all the more erotic by the contrast with the gray-eyed elegance of her appearance. Seeing her sipping a White Lady at the Ritz, even connoisseurs found it impossible to believe that this was the same women whom they had watched pleasure three men simultaneously on the mirrored dais at Madame Albertine's, or whom they had held in their own arms as she writhed and moaned beneath them. And then came the summons from El Glaoui, the Pasha of Marrakesh. She refused; he must come to her. His pride forbade it, but eventually a compromise was reached and they met for the first time in the Hotel de Paris in Monte Carlo. Whether or not the child, her only child, was his, no one ever knew. But Rose Osborne believed it and he was christened Thami and given the surname Fouquet, in honor of the café on the Champs-Elysées where Madame Albertine would treat the girl who had earned the most money during the previous week to a bottle of champagne after Mass on Sunday morning.

Once the body of the man sitting at her bedside had been all muscle, but over the years it had softened and run to fat so that he now weighed almost two hundred and forty pounds. The nose, broken by one of his mother's girls when, aged thirteen and on holiday from his preparatory school near Tunbridge Wells, he had forced himself upon her anally, had lost its high bridge and had gradually spread across his face. The features, darkly handsome as a young man in his twenties, were now, at fifty-two, blurred and coarsened and bore little or no resemblance to the silver-framed photograph that stood among the array of cosmetics on his mother's dressing table. The gray hair was cropped close to the skull, and he affected a beard clipped to the same length to conceal his sagging jowls. The ears were small and neat, without lobes; and the whites of his puffy eyes were shot with yellow. It was a cruel, vicious, arrogant face; a face that he admired and cultivated as befitting a son of the House of Glaoua, a true-born Pasha. He wore an open-necked white silk shirt, dark blue flannel trousers, and a green, the color of the Prophet, dressing gown of the finest cashmere.

He touched the button of the gold Pulsar on his wrist and the bright red numerals flashed out 11:31 on the ruby screen. He had heard the car arrive but the Major could wait, as it was fitting that a messenger should wait upon a Prince.

It was six months ago, after long negotiations conducted by go-betweens, that they had first met at Shannon when the Brigadier had escorted him across the tarmac to a single-engined airplane, a four-seater Cessna, which was ready for takeoff. Although it was night, the windows of the cabin had been blacked out, a detail of which Thami Fouquet with his passionate belief in the theory of 'need to know' thoroughly approved. They were airborne for some two hours, then landed on a grass strip beside a long white beach. The air was soft and echoed with the subdued hum of a generator that provided the power to light the strip. There was a half moon and a chain of rocky islets stretched out into the calm waters of the bay like basking whales. A Land Rover took them over the field to a solid stone-built house where he slept in a comfortable room. And in the first light of dawn the exercises began, when a ten-man team in inflatable Zodiacs appeared out of the mist and landed in a cove hemmed in by towering granite cliffs. All day long the silence was punctuated by the rattle of small arms' fire; a bazooka attack destroyed a rotting pillbox; cliffs were scaled; a sentry was stalked through the heather; and at midday lunch was served from a Fortnum and Mason hamper. They left the same night, and by lunch time the next day Thami Fouquet was back in Switzerland, impressed by what he had seen, arranging the first down payment with his bankers in Zurich, and wondering where he could raise the balance of half a million dollars.

For the past twenty years, ever since the official closing of the French brothels by the *Loi Marthe Richard*, times had been hard for Thami Fouquet and his mother. There was too much freelancing and amateur competition; there was too much protection to be paid to the police and the Union Corse. And now that *U Capu*, his old friend Dominique Sanguinetti, was dead, he was being squeezed dry by his successors as they carved up the Corsican's empire among themselves. There was no way that he could raise the money there; nor, as a matter of principle, would he even consider the Italians. But a blow even harder to bear had been the closing down of his operations in North Africa: the first in 1969 when all his and his mother's properties in Morocco had been confiscated; and then when Gaddafi came into power in Libya and in a crusade of Islamic puritanism banned

6

liquor and the time-honored profession of keeping a brothel.

Grenoble, where all his problems should have been solved, had proved a disaster: a cashier and a woman bystander dead, and Mohammed shot down on the Boulevard Gambetta to die surrounded by a ring of policemen's boots, coughing out his life on to a greasy wet pavement on a Monday morning a month ago. His mother stirred in her sleep and he pulled up the slipping eiderdown and smoothed back a tendril of lifeless gray hair that straggled across her sunken cheek. Moving surprisingly lightly on his feet, he crossed to the windows and drew the curtains. As he was doing so, the rain driving against the glass triggered the memory of his last visit to Telouet, the Glaoua Casbah that stands on a plateau 8,000 feet high in the Atlas mountains. It was a day of racing clouds and sunshine, of sudden squalls of sleet whipping down from the surrounding peaks. The snows had already begun to melt and the river ran high, carving its course between banks of brilliant emerald turf. He halted the car on the last rise and stared through the windshield at the crumbling majesty of the palace that never would be finished, the decaying relic of a dynasty that was said no longer to exist. The almond trees were in blossom and the sky was full of birds; the kestrels soaring on the wind, and the storks flapping around the nests that they had built on every tower. It was then that he had made his vow.

Closing the door softly behind him, he went downstairs to join the Brigadier.

Philip Quest took one hand from the wheel and fumbled for a tipped Casa-Sport from the packet on the seat beside him. He had placed it between his lips and was reaching for the dashboard lighter when his thoughts were shattered by the sudden banshee wail of sirens. Their images blurred by the red dust that coated his near side view mirror, the sun glinting on the chrome of their headlights, three motorcycles in

7

echelon hurtled up behind him, unswerving, holding the crown of the road. As Philip took his foot from the accelerator, the noise rose to a screaming crescendo and then the leader of the three was drawing alongside and angrily waving him to the right. Philip caught a glimpse of teeth bared beneath a thick moustache, a white gauntlet and a sub-machine gun slung over one shoulder, then the Porsche was slewing off the pock-marked asphalt at seventy miles an hour and he was fighting to regain control as it bucketed across the stony strip of waste ground that lined the road.

The three motorcycles roared on past without slackening speed, followed seconds later by a phalanx of another dozen. Philip hit a patch of deep sand and skidded sideways toward an outcrop of rock hedged by prickly pears. Then, as the car slid to a lopsided halt with a dreadful clang of hollow steel, six black Lincoln Continentals with blacked-out windows swept on up the road toward Oued Zem. More motorcyclists brought up the rear. A helicopter clattered low overhead, a monstrous mechanical dragonfly chasing its own shadow. Then the cavalcade had vanished over the next shimmering ridge and there was silence except for the shrilling of the cicadas and the tick of cooling metal.

"And may Allah rot your balls in Hell!" At last Philip stopped swearing, unfastened his seat belt, and climbed out of the car. After examining the chassis, it seemed that the only damage was to the coachwork where the impact had buckled the panel of the far door. He wondered how he was going to explain it to his insurance company. Still, half a minute or half a mile earlier and it would've been even money on his ending up wrapped around an olive tree. He wiped his greasy hands on a bunch of withered grass, then maneuvered the battered orange car back onto the road.

The headache that had been nagging him all morning ever since he had woken alone in his room at the Saadi had not got any better, and he thought long-

8

ingly of the cool turquoise water of the hotel pool beneath his balcony, of bottles of beer frosting in a silver ice bucket. The road breasted yet another rise, then dipped, and beside a bridge over a stagnant green river he saw a solitary low concrete building on whose front was a familiar red and white sign which bore the only written words that he knew in Arabic.

A CTM bus timetable was nailed to the blue-painted door. He paused to inspect it; just two buses a day, to and from Casablanca. The cement-floored room was dark and seemed deserted; a counter on one side, a few metal chairs and tables, a motionless fan hanging from the ceiling. He walked over to the counter and as he approached a small boy popped up from behind it. He wore a patched striped djellaba and his head was shaved except for a pigtail which sprouted from his crown. He was, Philip guessed, no more than eight years old.

A fly settled on a sore at the edge of the boy's mouth, but he made no effort to brush it away, gazing wide-eyed at Philip as if he were a visitor from another planet.

"*Ça va?*" Philip grinned the traditional greeting and scanned the shelves of unfamiliar bottles, all sickly greens, pinks, and oranges. "*Alors,*" he shrugged. "*Un Coca . . . Non, deux,*" and held up two fingers.

The boy, still staring fixedly at the black patch over Philip's left eye, jumped, ducked back down behind the counter, and came up again with two dusty bottles and a glass.

Philip nodded his thanks and drank. It was tepid, sweet and sticky and he wondered whether to lace it with some of the Scotch that he had in the car. It would either be kill or cure and for once he thought that it might be 'kill'—and he still had some three hundred miles to drive. At the far end of the bar there was a plastic plate heaped with hard-boiled eggs and he suddenly realized that he was hungry. He took one, shelled it, dipped it into a saucer of coarse rock salt, and as he munched it his glance caught the two

9

pictures hanging on the naked wall at the back of the room; two large framed photographs, tinted and retouched, of Mohammed V who died in 1961, and of his son, the present King.

Philip turned back to the boy. "*C'etait lui*," he gestured with his half-eaten egg, "*qui vient de passer?*"

The boy said nothing.

"*Les motos* . . . vroom . . . vroom." He mimed a motorcyclist. "*Les voitures grandes comme ça.*" He stretched out his arms. "*Le Roi* Hassan . . ." He did his best to imitate the expression captured by the royal photographer in Rabat. "*Il y'a un quart d'heure . . . Helicoptère . . .*"

The boy's face broke into a wide grin and he clapped his hands delightedly at Philip's antics. He jerked his head up and down like a lunatic puppet and pointed at the photograph. His mouth worked, but no sound came from his lips. And Philip realized that he was dumb.

Driving north again, Philip thought of the fat American tourist in the Djemma El Fna in Marrakesh who had almost been lynched by a group of water-sellers for photographing them, then turning away without paying them their 'fee.' It had cost him a twenty dollar bill (they refused to accept dirhams) before they would let him go. Once Philip had loved Marrakesh; but now not even the snow on the High Atlas orange in the sunset, nor driving around the ramparts in a horsedrawn carriage watching the stars come out one by one could make up for the thousand grasping hands and whining voices, the wheedling pimps and the police-informers, the air-conditioned charabancs and the fifth-rate hashish. Then, he had despised the modern town outside the walls but on this trip there was more of the innate dignity and honesty of the pre-Sahara in the wide boulevards of Gueliz than in all the souks of the *medina*. And so it had been with the boy who was dumb. "*Ça fait combien?*" Philip had asked. With his fingers the boy had indicated one-dirham-fifty, and Philip had handed him

10

a five-dirham note, smiled, and left. But just as the car began to move, the boy came dashing out across the pitted tarmac, djellaba flapping around his scarred matchstick legs, and pressed a fistful of coins into Philip's hand.

"*Mais non. Pour toi.*"

But the boy shook his head, the pigtail swishing around his ears, gave a little hop, and started to imitate Philip imitating a helicopter. His arms were still flailing, his body still spinning, when Philip lost him in the rear-view mirror.

The glare was intense and Philip exchanged his eye-patch for his dark glasses. The silver-green of the olive groves had given way to the slag heaps and the gaping open sores of the mines of the Plateau des Phosphates, a blinding landscape of naked eroded desolation where only scorpions and lizards lived. Silos and draglines stalked the skyline like prehistoric monsters and the sun burned orange through a sultry pall of yellow dust. A choking crawl through the streets of Oued Zem behind a convoy of trucks taking the phosphate to the railhead did nothing to improve his headache or his temper; and on the outskirts of the town the level-crossing gates were closed. It was then that the events of the last half hour finally caught up with him, and Morocco turned sour in his mouth.

He had allowed himself to be persuaded to take the assignment after a long and liquid lunch at Chez Victor. At first he had protested that he knew nothing of fashion photography; it wasn't his line, it didn't interest him. "Come off it," Maclean, his London agent, had told him. "Don't be such a snob." Who did he think he was—Cartier-Bresson? And if Lichfield could photograph mackintoshes, then he could damn well photograph caftans. The money was good, very good; and as long as he remembered to put film in the cameras, he couldn't go wrong. It was a cinch; a holiday in Morocco, all expenses paid. And, he had added with a lecherous grin, perhaps the bonus of a bit on the side. Philip had looked out at the umbrellas scurrying along a rain-lashed Wardour Street and asked for another armagnac to help him make up his mind.

The three models and the team from the magazine were to fly to Marrakesh, then rent cars to take them over the mountains to the Gazelle d'Or in Taroudant. But Philip chose to be independent, and took the car-ferry *Patricia* from Southampton to Tangier where Billy Paterson and his boy friend had a house. He stayed a few days with them, and then it was time to work. (He already knew that Gazelle d'Or by repute; the most luxurious, secluded, and discreet hotel in Morocco, and he made a private bet with himself that he would see someone he knew within twenty-four hours of his arrival. In the event, he won his bet that same evening when he went into dinner; and after that "Monsieur le Comte et Madame" had all their meals sent into their bungalow.)

It took him the best part of a week to get the shots that the Fashion Editor and the Art Director wanted, posing the girls not only in and around the hotel, but in the souk of Aoulous and at sunset on the beach of Agadir. The motorized Nikon and the Hassleblad gorged themselves on roll after roll of Ektachrome; and on the principle of the champanzees and the typewriters something was sure to turn out. But it was back-breaking work; long periods of tedium waiting for the light or the wind, only to lose the decisive moment because a camel decided to take a bite out of the model's shoulder. In the evenings he was too tired to make even token passes at the girls; anyway he found none of them particularly attractive, no matter how well they might photograph, and if they wanted to think him queer, then let them.

And so, when it was time for them to fly back to England with their suntans and their silver bangles, he said his goodbyes and made his way to Ouarzazate and the banked mud casbahs and the palm groves of the Draa, feeling that his money and his freedom had been well earned. Luck was with him and he missed the coach tours which turn the Grands Hotels du Sud that sand like forts guarding the pre-Sahara into Towers of Babel. And luck was still with him on his first night at the Casino in Marrakesh when he walked up to the roulette table and dropped a fifty-dirham chip on thirteen, and heard the croupier intone, "*Treize, noir, impair et manque.*"

The antiquated tank-engine, leaking steam from every pipe and valve, which had been shunting the phosphate-streaked hoppers, now hissed to a halt in the middle of the level crossing. Philip raised his hand to hit the horn, then let it fall back into his lap. *Mektoub*, it was written; and there was nothing he could do to change the will of Allah.

By the end of the evening he had won the equivalent of four hundred pounds, only to lose most of it the next night, playing a complicated progressive system on the columns. That left him one more night to cover his expenses and pay the bill at the Saadi. He spent the day sunning himself by the pool, then treated himself to a splendid dinner at La Petite Auberge. He drank a bottle and a half of red Chaudsoleil. Then the *patron* invited him to join him for a glass of *marc*, so that it was nearly eleven o'clock and he was feeling his drinks before he finally left the restaurant.

The Casino was crowded and he waited at the bar until there was a seat at his usual table. He decided that it would be too boring to try to play to any system, and staked solely on the even chances as his fancy took him. Almost at once he hit a winning streak and could do no wrong. After awhile he became aware that a blonde girl in a red dress standing on the other side of the table was riding his luck; when he backed red so did she; when he stayed off the table she followed suit. He caught her eye and tossed a hundred-dirham chip onto twenty-eight. She matched his bet. They lost. Philip shrugged, gathered up his chips, and got to his feet, nodding toward the bar. She smiled and made her way through the crowd to join him. To celebrate their meeting they drank

13

champagne; they danced in the nightclub; they returned to the tables and an hour later they were tiptoeing past the dozing night porter and up the stairs to his room. Philip hung up the 'Do Not Disturb' sign and locked the door behind them. And while she drew the curtains to shut out the electric-blue glare from the floodlit pool, he opened the bottle of Moet et Chandon that he had bought from the barman at the Casino.

The gates were slowly being winced open. Philip threw away his cigarette and made a silent vow: never again champagne on top of whisky on top of *marc*. To hell with losing, or rather chucking away, all the money he had won. It served him right for being so flash, plastering the table with hundred-dirham chips *en plein*. No, it was the dreadful fiasco of what followed in the hotel. There she was, superbly naked with him on the crisp white sheets, blonde hair cascading over his stomach, lips cool and damp, hands gently caressing the inside of his thighs . . .

"*M'sieu! Vas-y!*"

Philip snapped out a reverie to see that the gates had been raised and the old Arab was beckoning him on. The Porsche jolted over the tracks and out onto the open road. My God, Philip thought, settling into a steady cruising speed of eighty-five, it was a music hall joke, a Feydeau farce; the one-night stand that wasn't. No wonder she hadn't stayed for breakfast.

The Villa Gharbi—so named after the prevailing wind that blows in from Cap Spartel where the Atlantic rollers boom into the grottoes of Hercules—stood in a forest of mimosa high on the mountain above Tangier. A long L-shaped house, it had been built in the twenties by a French admiral who had made no concessions to Moroccan architecture, and from where he sat in the window seat of Billy Paterson's bedroom Philip looked down over the Straits of Gibraltar to the Spanish coastline that was not blurred in the evening haze.

14

"It's too awful about your car," Billy Paterson was saying, "but you can't really blame the dear darling King." He was lying supine on his canopied four-poster bed, hands folded across his stomach, as motionless as a Crusader on his tomb. Two slices of cucumber covered his eyes; his face glistened under a layer of cream and a hairnet held the waves in his bright orange hair tightly in place.

"I don't see why not. It was his gorillas who forced me off the road."

"You must try and understand his problems. All this business with Spanish Sahara, that dreadful Oufkir . . ."

"Come off it, Billy. Oufkir's been dead for years now."

"And serves him right, too. Dreadful man. Shooting himself was the only decent thing he ever did."

"I've always wondered about that," Philip said. "Just how can you manage to shoot yourself six times at point-blank range? You know, I've heard it on pretty good authority that Hassan himself did the shooting."

"Absolute nonsense. He'd never do a thing like that. And if he did, he'd have done it out of kindness."

"Rather like putting down a mad dog?" Philip suggested with a smile.

"Exactly. Putting him out of his misery. But even worse than Oufkir, there's that unspeakable Colonel Gaddafi. I'd been asked, you know, to the party."

Philip did know. It had been on July 10, 1971, and the King had given a party at Skhirat, on the sea outside Rabat, to celebrate his forty-second birthday, inviting most of the foreign ambassadors and the diplomatic corps. At a given moment insurgent officer cadets surrounded the palace and opened fire with bazookas and machine guns; officially ninety-two people died and more than a hundred were injured. And within an hour Colonel Gaddafi's Radio Libya was on the air, joyfully proclaiming that the rebels were in command and promising support to the Moroccan people in their fight for freedom. By a miracle the King was unharmed, and gave the job of crushing the revolt to General Oufkir, who himself, a year later, was to plan the perfect crime when three Moroccan F-5 fighters attacked the King's Boeing 727 over the Mediterranean. But once again Hassan survived, and Oufkir died that night.

"Talking of parties," Billy Patterson said, "what about Bobo Corviglia?"

"What about him?"

"My dear, you haven't heard? I thought it was the talk of *le tout Marrakesh*."

"It may have been, but none of it reached my shell-like ear. Who is he, anyway?"

"Was, my dear, was. He was gathered on Monday. Fell out of a window at his own party, his annual ball. The full scene, ostrich feathers, tiaras and all. He didn't invite me, of course, and even if he had I wouldn't have gone." He sniffed loudly. "Really too common, calling himself 'Prince.' No more a Prince than I'm Burt Reynolds. Still, *de mortuis* and all that, I suppose. But he was the most crashing snob." He sighed. "But what's the time?"

Philip glanced at the stainless steel Rolex on his wrist. "Nearly seven. Time for a drink." Billy Paterson sat up and removed the semicircular slices of cucumber from his eyes, put them in his mouth, and began to eat them. "I must say you're looking almost too well." He drew the folds of his black silk kimono across his hairless chest, picked up the telephone from the orange lacquer bedside table, pressed a switch, and told Achmed in pidgin Spanish to bring up the drink tray. Then he took a Kleenex and wiped the cream from his face, all the time prattling on about his feud with Bobo Corviglia, a story that Philip had heard a dozen times before.

There was a discreet tap on the door and Achmed, in white gloves and a black-tasseled fez, shuffled into the room with a silver tray.

"*Gracias.*" Billy Paterson swung his legs off the bed

16

and said to Philip, "Be an angel and make us some Martinis while I have my bath. By the way, we're dining with a divine American girl—you'll adore her."

The previous night's fiasco was too fresh to Philip's memory, and privately he doubted it. Nor did he want a Martini, especially one made with gin. He poured himself a weak whisky, mixed Billy's drink, then took the glasses into the bathroom and sat down on the lavatory.

"Divine," Billy Paterson said and returned to studying the bags under his eyes in the magnifying shaving-mirror. "Good for another year or two, I think. Then back to that charming little man in Lausanne. So clever and not really that expensive. I know you rather like it and it's all very dashing and piratical, but perhaps he could do something about your eye."

Philip shrugged. "They did once try to give me a glass one. But apparently the muscles had atrophied. Anyway, it kept on dropping in the soup."

"Or down some lady's cleavage—somewhere even more intimate, knowing you." He leaned closer to the mirror and plucked a hair from his nostril. "I wonder what's going to happen to his jewels. There was one diamond pendant that was said to be worth God knows how many hundreds of thousands of dollars. Rather too vulgar for my taste, of course, but then his whole life was."

Philip was lost, and said so; tired after the long day's drive he was unable to keep up with his host's constant grasshopper changes of subject.

"Why, that hideous Bobo." He drained his glass and shuddered. "Now close the door and let Madame continue her *toilette* in peace. We're seeing Adolfo and Ellen-Ann at the Parade at eight and no doubt you don't want to make too long a night of it if you're catching the boat tomorrow morning."

17

Chapter II.

Rushworth

"Look, Phillip, it's Saturday and the banks are closed. There's a lot of very professional villains around these days and to them that safe of yours—whatever your insurance company might say—is just another kiddy's piggy bank. So do yourself and me a favor and let me look after it for you."

Charlie Thomas was a quick, nervous man with restless brown eyes, a high forehead and a shock of thinning black hair. Philip had first met him at a floating chemin de fer game in the days before legalized gambling. He had then been working in his father's shop, learning the jewelry business, and losing heavily. It was the year that Joey Pegrum had been found in a Soho car park with his right hand sawed off after welching on a debt, and Philip, riding high on what was left of his inheritance, had lent Charlie £5,000. The money had long since been repaid, but Charlie had never forgotten and was one of the handful of men in the world to whom Phillip would willingly entrust his life.

"Right," he said, "and thanks."

The strongroom locked, they talked for a few more minutes, then Philip left the shop and walked thoughtfully down the quiet street, away from the gasoline fumes and the stalled traffic that was jamming the Earl's Court Road. The dustmen had been on strike when he had left for Morocco, and now they were on strike again. The black plastic bags were piling up against the area railings; the pavements were littered with crushed red-and-white cartons from the take-away Kentucky fried chicken shops; and in the gutters the cherry blossom had formed miniature drifts around the discarded cans of Foster's and Coca Cola. A sheaf of parking tickets sprouted from the windshield of a Dormobile with Dutch tourist plates and two flat tires; on its dusty side the legend LONDON-SINGAPORE-SYDNEY OR BUST was stenciled in dark green paint. It was a part of London that had always depressed Philip; beetling red brick Victorian squares, one-roomed basement flats where the lights burned all day, cars with wire coat-hangers instead of aerials, African students and beefy girls in anoraks shouldering bright orange rucksacks. But today he hardly noticed it, his thoughts a thousand miles away.

Back in his top floor flat in Paulton's Square, he took a can of beer from the icebox and walked through into the bright high-ceilinged sitting room that overlooked the square, an oasis of green in a desert of brick and concrete. He drank directly from the can and with his index finger traced the scratch that he had made that morning on the window pane. It was a beautiful, cloudless day; the King's Road was crowded, and the engines of the planes on their approach to Heathrow had already taken on the curious muted drone of high summer. After a while he went through into the bedroom and began to pack his old Louis Vuitton holdall for the weekend.

Philip Quest had long outgrown the extreme dandyism that he had affected while up at Oxford—pink linen suits, leopardskin trousers, Spanish capes. Now all that he wanted from his clothes was that they should be comfortable. From time to time he might buy half a dozen shirts from Turnbull and Asser or Deborah Clare, but usually he dressed in levis, polo-necked sweaters, and casual jackets, often leather or suede. From time to time he ordered some suits from his tailor in Hertford, but he disliked ties and less than a dozen, mainly all misguided Christmas presents, hung in his wardrobe.

He zipped up the bag and then took the two battered aluminum cases of camera equipment and a tripod from the darkroom. On a sudden impulse, he dropped to his knees and slid back the door of the cupboard beneath the enlarger where he kept his stocks of printing paper. He pushed the yellow boxes aside, then spun the dial of the combination lock of the small Chubb safe which the previous tenant of the flat had built into the wall. The only objects that it contained were his father's gold Fabergé cigarette case, which Philip never used, a few trinkets that had belonged to his mother, the plain brown envelope that was his Survival Kit, and a box that had once held fifty Larranaga cigars. Philip sat back on his heels and lifted the lid.

A light film of oil glistened on the blue-black steel of the automatic. It was a Walther PPK, chambered for a 6.35-mm cartridge, which he had bought as a souvenir during a drunken evening in Hamburg while he was doing his National Service. For so short a barreled gun, it was surprisingly accurate and, although it was unlicensed, Philip sometimes used to take it with him when he went shooting, and once—by a sheer fluke—had won a £100 bet at 10-1 by bringing down a rocketing pheasant stone dead. And in the evenings pistol shooting made a change from billiards or bridge. The neat serrated butt fitted snugly into his palm. He checked the action and the clip, worked the slide to and fro, them at last put it back in the box and closed the safe.

All the way from the Chiswick flyover to London

Airport the traffic on the westbound lane was restricted to two lanes. The sky was hazed with fumes and Philip gazed enviously at the cars on the far side of the crash barrier zipping freely into London while he crawled forward in second, sandwiched between an oil truck and a bus bound for Cardiff. Trying to separate the grains of fact from the cloud of theories, guesses, and conjectures that whirled around his brain, he failed to notice the truck's brakelights flare until the last second when he brought the car to a squealing halt seemingly only inches from the mud-splashed differential. To hell with it, he told himself. It was a beautiful day, he was going to spend the weekend with a beautiful girl, and even traffic jams, unlike diamonds, didn't last forever. And Monday was another day. Absorbed by the memories of his last night with Jackie, now more than a month ago, he almost overshot the turnoff, Exit 13, for Newbury, and fifteen minutes later he had crossed the hump-backed bridge, jangled over the cattle-grid, and the gravel of the winding driveway was crunching beneath his tires.

A pair of black swans regarded him suspiciously from their island on the small lake, edged with rushes, on his right; to his left the landscaped park ran down to a line of elms and willows that marked the course of the river, and then, on top of a slight rise, Rushworth came into view. As always, Philip slowed down and shook his head in delighted amazement. Where else, except perhaps in California, could one find such a magnificent monstrosity? Between them a mad architect and the mad third Viscount Ardale (who had later died of apoplexy while laughing at a dirty joke), had anticipated Disneyland by a century and a half, marrying Palladio to Neo-Gothic, and Tudor to Nicholas Hawksmoor. He coasted on down the drive between banks of massed azaleas, then brought the car to a halt beside the worn stone steps that led up to the East portico.

Burford, the white-haired butler, appearing almost before he had turned off the ignition, allowed Philip one of his fractional smiles and informed him that Miss Jackie was at the pool. Leaving him to deal with the luggage, Philip made his way across the flagged terrace and the freshly mowed grass to the mellowed brick wall that sheltered the pool. Her splendid body the color of caramel and glistening with oil, one knee drawn up, she lay on a wicker chaise longue, naked except for a ragged straw hat with a scarlet ribbon that was tilted down over her eyes to shade her face from the sun. As always, Philip's breath caught in his throat. 'A tigress in heat,' someone had once described her, and he stood for a long moment admiring the animal beauty of the full firm breasts, the flat stomach, and the long tapering thighs. One languid hand moved from the arm of the chaise lounge and curled gently over the neat dark triangle of hair that Philip knew so well. For a crazy instant he was tempted to rip off his clothes and throw himself on top of her, then out of the corner of his eyes he caught sight of Lord Ardale approaching from the river.

Philip swore and turned to greet his host. Behind him he heard a low laugh and realized that while he had been watching Jackie, she had been watching him. "For Christ's sake," he said over his shoulder. "Here comes your father. You're not in Mustique now." Then he was shaking hands with Lord Ardale who was wearing his inevitable rusty tweed suit and the yellowed panama hat which he religiously took out of his cupboard every year on the first of May, come rain, come shine. They chatted for a few minutes about the weather and the fishing, an obese golden Labrador panting at their feet, then Lord Ardale excused himself and wandered away toward the stables.

"Honestly, Philip," Jackie said when he returned to the pool. "I've never known you so prudish about clothes before." Now demurely draped in a towel, she was standing by the umbrella-shaded round white wooden table, pouring Pimms into two glasses from a tall frosted jug.

23

Philip shrugged. "After all, one's father . . ."

"Well, it's about time he got used to it, especially now that Moronsay's a nudist camp."

"What? Moronsay? I knew you'd rented it to someone but I thought it was for the stalking and the fishing. But a nudist camp! Who the hell wants to go prancing round naked in Scotland, on a God-forsaken island in the Hebrides?" "It's a lovely island," she countered. "And it's got the Gulf Stream." "And ten million mosquitoes, no doubt." He took the proffered glass and raised it to her. "Hello, darling. It's good to see you."

"Good to see you, too."

"Missed me?"

She made a vague gesture with her hand. "Once in a while. Every now and then."

"Bitch." Philip put down his glass and pulled her to him, feeling the warmth of her body beneath the towel, looking down into the deep blue eyes that sparkled with a mocking challenge. "Bitch," he said again, and then her arms were around his neck, her mouth melting into his.

It was Philip who broke the embrace, backing away unsteadily. "A swim," he said. "It's the only way."

"Till later."

"Till later."

No one else was staying that weekend. Lord Ardale, a widower, had withdrawn into one of his silent moods and seemed unaware of their presence in the paneled dining room, concentrating all his attention on the overcooked roast lamb, followed by tapioca pudding, and drinking bottled beer while Philip and Jackie finished two decanters of white Burgundy, their feet touching beneath the table. After lunch, while Lord Ardale snored in front of the television in his study and Jackie sunbathed by the pool, Philip tried to work. An architect friend of his was writing a book on English follies and had asked Philip to help with the illustrations. But as he stood with his Hasselblad and tripod in the marble-floored rotunda beneath

24

the cupola decorated with frescoes depicting the Battle of Waterloo, he realized that his mind was a thousand miles away. And then there was a chance remark that Jackie had made that morning; that tomorrow Piers de Salis was coming to lunch.

Abandoning his equipment and any idea of work, Philip strolled out to the orangerie, sat down on a carved stone bench, and lit a cigarette. De Salis had been a contemporary of his at school but he had never really known him until, as a National Service subaltern in the 17/21st, he had been posted to a camp near Hanover where he found de Salis already established as the junior bon vivant of the Mess. Philip's job was driving tanks, de Salis' Intelligence and in their ample free time they drank together, gambled together, whored together. Then, when Philip was demobbed, de Salis stayed on and they lost sight of each other for a number of years while Philip traveled around the world pursuing his career as a freelance photographer and journalist. And then one night, by chance, they had met at a dance in Belgrave Square; neither of them had married and the friendship—like all good friendships—resumed from where they had left it. "Sitting behind a desk in Whitehall, liasing with the Foreign Office," was how de Salis defined his present job at the Ministry of Defense; a statement from which Philip drew his own conclusions, and asked no questions.

He had last seen de Salis two days earlier at the Clermont. There, over a quiet pre-dinner game of backgammon before the Club was invaded by Americans from the Playboy, de Salis had brought up Morocco in an innocent enough way and Philip had told him about his trip, about Taroudant, and then, rather sheepishly about the debacle in Marrakesh.

"And the girl, was she worth it?" de Salis asked, refusing the double and pushing the board aside.

"Worth what, for God's sake? I told you, I never even got it in. Bang, out like a light. I've never felt such a fool in my life. And then when I woke up, of

25

course my first thought was that I'd been rolled. But there was nothing missing, not a thing. Obviously she got pissed off and left. Now let's drop it. It's bad enough having to live with, let alone talk about it."

But that had been on Thursday, and it was only this morning that he had gone round to his garage in Old Church Street to see if work had started on repairing the buckled side door of the Porsche. A mechanic told him that Ian was in the yard at the back and he picked his way across the oil-stained concrate floor, squeezing between a Ferrari with its front axle jacked up by an engineless Aston-Martin. The door had already been removed for the panel-beater and everything was under control. As Philip turned to leave, Ian, a chunky Scotsman in his early thirties, reached into the pocket of his spotless white overalls and handed him a flat metal tin the size of a salmon fisherman's fly-box.

"Here," he said with a knowing grin. "You'll be forgetting your own name next. Best hash in the world, isn't it, the stuff from Chechaouen?" He jerked his head toward the workbench against which the door was propped. "Pretty smart place to hide it, too. I suppose there's always a risk, but what'd life be if you didn't take risks? And it's not as if you were bringing half a ton of it in. For personal use only, eh?" He winked and patted Philip on the arm. "So how about us getting together next week and finding out if it's as good as they say?"

Philip, at a total loss for words nodded blankly, turning the tin in his hand. Then Ian was gone, bawling across the yard, "Come on, lad, get your finger out! You're not at British bloody Leyland now!"

Back in Paulton's Square, the tin, though sealed with solder, posed no problems, Philip's Black and Decker ripping through the thin metal in a matter of seconds. Inside it was a package wrapped in oilskin, and inside the oilskin a folded rectangle of chamois leather, lumpy to the touch. His mind flashed back to Tangier, to Billy Patterson chattering away in the

26

bathroom; and even before he opened it, he knew what he would find. He stood staring down at the pool of white fire that seemed to light up the whole room and after a while picked up the telephone and rang Charlie Thomas, and fifteen minutes later the door of the musty jeweler's shop was pinging shut behind him.

"So here you are! I've been looking for you everywhere. And I thought you said you had to work!"

Philip came back to the present to find Jackie standing over him, silhouetted against the afternoon glare. "I know, I did. But somehow it just didn't work out."

She came and sat down beside him, dressed in the same clothes that she had worn for lunch—blue jeans cut off at the knee—and looked into his face. "What's the matter, darling? I've never really seen you like this before. Trouble?"

Philip bit his lip. Trouble there certainly was, he could scent it like a stag. But of the why, how, when or where, he had no idea. And anyway, it was not for her. He managed a smile. "Just tired, that's all. Morocco really took it out of me."

"All those lovely, oh-so-glamorous, wet-lipped models?"

Philip snorted. "Plastic titless wonders, every one of them. And dykes, too, into the bargain."

"Poor Philip." She marched her fingers stealthily up his thigh. "How about a beautiful, relaxing massage?"

"Relaxing?"

"Well, it will be later. It's been a long, long time."

"Yes," he said, drawing her to her feet. "Much too long."

In the evening Philip fished, borrowing one of her father's old Hardy split-cane rods. There was a hatch of large Dark Olives and he landed five fine trout before it was time to return to the house and change, strolling back through the water meadows, the sun gilding the tops of the elms. He watched a kingfisher skim low across the river in a darting flash of electric blue, and suddenly realized that thanks to the joy of rediscovering the magic of Jackie's body and the thrill of the sudden swirl of water as a trout rose to take his fly, that a whole hour had passed without his once thinking of de Salis or Bobo Corviglia's pendant.

There were guests for dinner. The candles were lit; the glass, the silver and the conversation shone; and over the port even Lord Ardale came out of his shell, telling stories of his gambling days in Monte Carlo before the war, and taking in good heart the endless jokes about the nudist camp on Moronsay. Then, joining the ladies in the Chinese drawing room, they all played *vingt-et-un* with a maximum stake of 10 pence and Philip won two pounds. Shortly after midnight, the guests departed and Lord Ardale said goodnight, reminding Jackie to make sure that all the lights were off before they went to bed.

Sprawled on the oyster satin cushions of the sofa, Philip stubbed out his cigar and smiled across at Jackie. She was standing by the fireplace, black hair swept back into a chignon, looking as beautiful as he had ever seen her in the white caftan embroidered with gold that he had bought for her in Casablanca. One question had been nagging at the back of his mind all evening, but to ask it now would be to break the mood.

So, instead, he asked, "Your room or mine?"

"Mine. It's got that mirror."

A breeze ruffled the curtains and a strip of moonlight wavered across the floor. The room smelled of lavender and furniture polish, of Jackie and *Je Reviens*. She lay beisde him with her head in the crook of his arm, her breath warm upon his ribs. A barn-owl hooted and from the stables came the faint snicker of a horse.

"That's one thing you won't get me on in the morning," Philip murmured drowsily. "Bloody animals! Who was it who said, 'Uncomfortable in the middle and dangerous at both ends?' "

28

But the only reply was a faint snore. Gently Philip disengaged his arm, kissed her lightly on the corner of her mouth, collected his dressing gown from the floor, and went back to his own room off the corridor known as Bachelors' Row. He smoked a last cigarette by the open window, the warm night air heavy with the scent of wisteria, gazing up at the stars, then went to bed, to sleep badly and wake in the small hours from a dream in which he saw himself dead, lying on a beach while the sea lapped around his feet, Corviglia's diamond pendant flashing white on the bloody remains of his own shattered chest.

Chapter III.

The Big Zero

Twelve hundred miles away in Africa, after the third session in as many hours, the heat and stench of sweat and roasted flesh was appalling. It was a square room, windowless, with roughly whitewashed walls, lit by a single fluorescent strip hanging from the high ceiling. The floor was cement and in one corner a tap dripped insistently into a bucket. In the middle of the room stood a bed, without a mattress or springs, but covered with a fine wire mesh on which the naked body of a woman was stretched, wrists and ankles manacled to the frame. She lay face down, her head free, the long darkened and matted blonde hair brushing one of the cables that was connected to a panel in the wall. One of the three men in shirtsleeves standing over her mopped his forehead on his arm, then removed the cigarette from his mouth and casually ground it out on her left buttock. She did not move, and he shrugged, gave an order, then left the room, followed a few moments later by the others, the steel door clanging shut behind them.

For one glorious minute when she surfaced into a

pool of silence and darkness, Tania Berger believed that her prayers had been answered and that she was dead. The threshold had been crossed; time and pain no longer existed. She was floating effortlessly high above the chestnut forests and the deep blue lake, the snows of the Matterhorn flaming pink in the rising sun.

A drop of water pinged into the bucket; a muscle twitched in her thigh and with the hideous knowledge that she was still alive, the agony returned. She opened her mouth to scream and the movement, slight though it was, seemed to rip all the flesh from her bones and once again the world exploded and she cartwheeled down into a pit of merciful oblivion.

It was now five days since the two plainclothes policemen, tieless and in shiny synthetic suits, their eyes hidden behind steel-rimmed dark glasses, had walked up to her table in the bar at Menara airport outside Marrakesh. Without a word, completely disregarding the frightened stares of the other passengers, they had dragged her to her feet and frog-marched her to a small office behind the *Douanes*. Her dark wig had been torn from her head and the man in a khaki uniform sitting behind the desk had taken one glance at her American passport and contemptuously tossed it aside. Then she was bundled out of a side door and into a black Mercedes which drove off at top speed across the tarmac to the military side of the airport. Her final clear memory of the outside world, as she was pushed up the steps of the drably painted DC3, was of the morning Trident to London, now waiting to board, shimmering in the sun.

The flight lasted an hour and a half, during which she was raped four times, by the two plain clothes men, the pilot, and finally the co-pilot.

From the airport she was taken in an ambulance to a large modern villa standing in its own grounds on a quiet street lined with acacias and Judas trees between the Cîté Universitaire and the Rabat Hilton, where she was carried down to one of the reception cells in

32

the basement. They left her alone in the darkness for four days, bringing her a bowl of soggy couscous and a mug of tepid water every morning. And then, on the Saturday night, the interrogation began.

But when, after the third session on the Toaster, she had still not talked, Leroy Papich, with thirty years of experience behind him, decided to pull the plug. If they went on like this, he warned them, they would turn her into a mindless vegetable in a matter of hours. Then they began to argue about priorities, but by nine o'clock the next morning Papich had roused the Ambassador who made a formal request to the Minister, and Tania Berger was handed into Papich's custody for twenty-four hours.

"Tania?" A distant voice was calling to her out of the clouds. "Tania, can you hear me?" Her eyes flickered open, but were unable to focus on the face that was looming over her, blocking out the light. The room was seesawing up and down and her fingers scrabbled for a grip on the rough blanket to prevent herself being catapulted to the ceiling.

"Easy now, easy," the soothing voice continued. She felt a stab of pain in her arm and a cool towel mopped the sweat from her temples. The nausea gradually receded; the room rocked gently to a standstill and swam into focus. A languorous warmth crept up from her toes, cradling her, cosseting her. She gazed wide-eyed around her: white-tiled walls, white ceiling, white washbasin; trees and a patch of blue sky framed by a barred window, birds singing and sunlight blazing on a skein of purple bougainvillea. She seemed to be in the hospital, lying in a narrow bed, the whole of her torso from her neck to her hips a cocoon of bandages. Why? she wondered. And who was this man in a bright red sport shirt and a plaid madras jacket who was sitting beside her? Not a handsome face, the nose and the chin were too heavy. But a nice face, a kind face. He reminded her of her father. He smelled nice, too, of talcum powder and eau de cologne. She smiled at him, and he smiled back. It was a kind smile and made her feel comfortable and protected.

"Hello," she whispered.

"Hello there," he replied. "How're you feeling?"

"Mmm," she murmured. "Marvelous. Snug as a bug in a rug."

"Feel like telling me about it? Not too tired?"

"Drowsy, yes, but wonderful . . . and thirsty."

"Here, let me." He poured out a glass of Oulmès and held it to her lips. Some of the water ran down her chin and he dabbed it dry with the towel. "Better now?"

"Thank you. You're very kind."

"Now, where were we?"

There was a fresh C-120 cassette in the portable Sony on the table beside him and he had already prepared a second syringe. He sat down and smiled into the still beautiful eyes in the once beautiful face that was now set in a vacant grin. He switched on the recorder and gently, as delicately as a safe-breaker picking a lock, began to probe into the recesses of her brain.

An hour later, the tape recorder slung over his shoulder, he nodded to the uniformed policeman on the gate and crossed the street to his car, an old Ford station wagon with Virginia and CD plates. After locking the cassette in his office safe at the Embassy, he glanced through a few routine reports, then decided that he had earned himself a drink. Not caring for the French pavement cafés, he drove over to the Hotel Tour Hassan where, in spite of the aggressively Moroccan atmosphere—intricately carved woodwork, low divans heaped with cushions, acres of polychromatic tiles—the barman stocked Old Grandad and knew how to mix a passable whisky sour.

Leroy J.—the J stood for nothing, like the S adopted by Harry Truman—Papich was a second-generation American of Polish extraction who had been born in the steel town of Gary, Indiana. He was now fifty-six years old. Joining the Marines when the

34

United States entered the war, he was soon singled out by the newly formed OSS and parachuted into France where he won the *Croix de Guerre* for the part he played in the 'Alpha' network of agents which operated in the mountains around Clermont-Ferrand. It was there in the Auvergne that he developed his gifts for kidnapping, torture, and murder, talents which in time would take him to South America, to Laos and the CIA-directed Armée Clandestine in Vientiane under the nominal leadership of General Vang Pao, then on to Saigon where he ran an immensely profitable side line dealing in Chinese heroin.

Most of the men in the wartime Office of Strategic Services came from Ivy League colleges and there was more than a grain of truth in the joke that the letters OSS stood for "Oh So Social." The CIA continued this tradition, zealously fostering the public relations image of a clean-living crew-cut St. George purging the world of the dragons of Communism. But then a certain Director reasoned as follows: It is a well-known fact that the CIA does not employ homosexuals; therefore if a man is a homosexual he cannot be working for the CIA. And so it was that Leroy Papich was launched on his spectacular career. The pendulum soon swung back as the security risks became alarmingly apparent, but by then Papich was too well ensconced and too valuable, and he had already dealt with a Russian attempt at blackmail in a way that had chilled even the most hardened veterans of the service.

But then, when he was fifty years old, his superiors at Langley decided to pull him out of the field and sent him back to school at "The Farm" outside Williamsburg, Virginia, to groom him for his new career in the Diplomatic Corps. But Embassy life was not for him, even though Wagner had been transferred with him. He champed at the bit and fretted through the Middle East, longing for the night patrols in the jungle, feeling again the barrel of his M3A1 leap in his hand as he clamped down on the trigger and unleashed a screaming hail of death in the first light before dawn.

The bar was dark, cool, and almost empty. From the central courtyard came the shouts and laughter of a group of German tourists playing makeshift water polo in the recently built pool. Papich lit a filter-tipped Camel and gestured to the barman to bring him another drink. And then Arafa entered the bar. A tall, extremely handsome man with gleaming black hair and the profile of a hawk, the Hollywood thirties ideal of a desert sheikh, and wore an immaculate white shangtung suit and black and white shoes. The waiter in a fez and baggy trousers who had been chatting to the barman leaped to attention. Arafa gave his order and pointed at Papich's corner table.

Papich made a halfhearted effort to rise to his feet, but Arafa waved him back with a brusque gesture of one manicured hand. Then he himself sat down, selected a Casa-Sport from a gold cigarette case and lit it with a matching lighter. He blew out a long plume of smoke, and tapped his fingers on the inlaid rim of the table. He neither looked at Papich nor spoke to him until the boy had poured out his beer, salaamed and backed away. Then he raised his eyes and said in his accentless sibilant English, his voice as cold as steel, "Well, Mister Papich, I believe you owe me some explanation."

"Hell, Hamid, I'm sorry but how was I . . ."

"I said 'explanation.' The apologies can come later."

Papich swallowed and chewed the knuckle of his thumb. "Well, like I said to your boys last night, they were killing the goose that lays the golden eggs and she hadn't even started laying. Jesus, Hamid, there's interrogation techniques and interrogation techniques. And your way, no one was getting nowhere, but fast. So, O. K., you weren't around so we discussed it, and this morning I got the go-ahead from your Minister. There's nothing wrong in experimenting, nothing to be ashamed of, trying out something new if the old ways don't work out." He caught Arafa's look and spread his hands. "So it didn't work out. Obviously this new stuff doesn't mix with morphine. But hell, I was only giving her the dose that your own doctor advised."

"What does that fool know about ordinary Pentothol, let alone the new concoctions your friends dream up in their laboratories back in Virginia? Go on."

"Well, she was conscious, and everything was going according to plan, when suddenly," he snapped his fingers, "pouf, like that! Here one minute, gone the next. Her heart stopped beating and by the time I'd got the doc it was too late. There was nothing he could do except pull the sheet up over her face." He grinned. "But at least I'll be able to give the lab boys a first-hand report on their new wonder drug. The big zero."

Arafa did not smile. "For two thousand years, Mr. Papich—or should I address you by your correct title? For two thousand years, Mr. Cultural," he underlined the word with sugared irony, "Attaché, our civilization in the Maghreb has grown and flourished without the need of any help from parvenu Colonials. Unfortunately, recent economic circumstances have forced us to relax our standards and accept outside aid and you, to use your own imagery, are one of the crosses we now have to bear. My duty is the security of my King and country—a concept that you might find difficult to understand. But enough of that. The old ways are best, and in the end we would have made her talk." He sighed. "You got nothing from her, nothing at all?"

"Not a thing. As I said, I was just establishing some kind of rapport—you know, the soft stuff after the hard—when up roll her eyes and that's it."

Eyes hooded, Arafa was staring into the middle distance, fingering his smoothly shaved chin. There was a long pause broken only by the clink of glass from behind the bar. Then at last he spoke. "This Berger woman was Thami Fouquet's whore and Thami Fouquet is one of the pack of jackals" and now he looked directly into Papich's eyes, "who prowl and skulk in the shadows, never daring to show their cowardly faces. She was his confidante, she shared his secrets, and no doubt schemed with him against the King. What was she doing in Marrakesh? How did she enter the country unnoticed? Where else had she been? Who were her contacts? Who among us? What murderous plot is Thami Fouquet planning now? Yes, Mr. Papich, we have our sources, too, though doubtless not as comprehensive as yours. But myself, I place far greater faith in the loyalty of men that I know than in all your hundred computers and satellites and so-called wonder drugs. And now what Thami Fouquet's whore could have told us, no one will ever know."

"O.K., Ha . . . Captain. So I blew it. I admit it and I'm sorry. You wanted an apology and now you've got it. So why don't we make up for it in some way? Hell, with the kind of clout we've got I'm positive we can arrange something. You want Thami Fouquet, we'll get him for you. Put him on ice and deliver him right to you here in Rabat."

"The Bay of Pigs, Mr. Papich. Such a happy choice, both geographically and metaphorically. However, as I am sure that even you have discovered in the nine months that you have been a guest of my country, here we do not eat pig. Nor," he continued, rising to his feet, "do we employ pigs to protect us from the jackals sniffing at our heels." The waiter was already by his side and he spoke to him in Arabic. He glanced down at Papich who had not moved. "Please by my guest now for this one last time. Your Ambassador spoke to my Minister on the telephone this morning, but I shall be dining with him tonight in Skhirat, so do not be surprised if, in the very near future, you are declared *persona non grata*. Goodbye, Mr. Papich. I cannot say that it has been a pleasure. And if I can be of any assistance to your career, I will recommend, in writing, to you superiors that your next assignment should be the purveying of your own particular brand of culture to the penguins in Antarctica."

Leroy Papich watched him go, his smile broadening as the tall figure disappeared. The waiter, sensing the atmosphere, hovered uncertainly, flicking his napkin at specks of invisible dust. Papich pointed at his glass. "*Encore.*" And when his drink arrived, he raised it to the empty chair.

"In a pig's ass, you snot-nosed bastard! I'm already on my way."

"But I don't understand it, dear. It's six weeks now that the Rolls has been in that garage. Surely it doesn't take all that time to get a new whatever-it-is? Why, in the old days they used to send a mechanic out from England on the train, and I can't believe that things have really changed all that much, in spite of what the papers say. I remember once in Biarritz—or was it St. Jean de Luz?—when Bunny . . ."

But Thami Fouquet was no longer listening. All morning he had had to endure his mother's endless complaints; her corset was too tight, one of the under-managers at the bank in Lugano had been positively rude to her, last night's veal had been grossly over-cooked; and as for the Rolls-Royce, he had sold it two months earlier to a Marxist-Leninist publisher in Milan. He rose to his feet and crossed to the stone balustrade of the terrace that was dappled by the sun that filtered in through the vine-covered pergola. A thousand feet below him a hydrofoil carved a curving white furrow in the placid waters as it swerved to avoid a flotilla of orange-sailed dinghies tacking across the lake toward the Italian enclave of Campione. From where he stood he could easily make out the long modern building on the water's edge that was the Casino, and where all the profits from the sale of his mother's car had evaporated in one murderous night's game of chemin de fer.

"And speaking of that," his mother now was saying, "any news of Tania? Such a sweet child and it's so unlike her not to send me a card. Where was it you said she was going?"

Thami Fouquet did not turn around. "France, to stay with friends. But she should be back any day now."

"I do hope so—for your sake, dear. You've been like a cat on hot bricks all week. Now how about giving your poor old mother another glass of champagne?"

The call came through after lunch, while his mother slept. It was a personal call from Gibraltar. The line whined and crackled against a multilingual murmur of background voices and he chewed his knuckles as he waited for it to clear, once again smelling the incense that was always burning in the dingy back room of Habibi's shop in Main Street. There was a click and a girl said, "You're through now, caller, Lugano."

Kittani wasted no time; he spoke in Arabic, concisely and to the point. Yes, stage one had gone according to plan. But the heat was on in Marrakesh, Arafa's men had taken Tania at the Airport, and he himself had been forced to go underground until he could get a fishing-boat out of Essaioura. That was why he had not called before. He knew nothing about the others, And the merchandise? The last time he had spoken to Tania she had sensed that something was wrong and was working on a contingency plan. She had been checking up on an English photographer who was staying at the Saadi and driving back to London later in the week, and had mentioned him as a possible courier. His name was Quest, Philip Quest.

The distant voice died and a low-pitched whistle echoed in his ear, rising and falling like the wail of an ambulance. He angrily banged the cradle for the operator, cursing until he was reconnected. But Kittani could tell him little more, and it was with a hand that suddenly seemed as heavy as lead that he finally replaced the receiver. His shoulders heaved and he began to rock to and fro, endlessly repeating Tania's name, blinking back tears that he had not shed for

40

over forty years, praying that she had died quickly and cheated Arafa of his sickening pleasures, remembering the life that they had shared together.

The afternoon wore on; a few harmless white clouds appeared high above the placid chocolate-box landscape beyond the picture window. At last, now drained of grief, Thami Fouquet returned to the present. Life was for the living and all was not yet lost. Corviglia's death had rated a paragraph in an inside page of the *Herald Tribune*; it was described as an unfortunate accident and no mention had been made of any missing jewels. Nor had Kittani heard any whispers either from the Moroccan underworld or from his brother-in-law's cousin who was an Inspector in the Sureté. That Tania, with her sixth sense for danger, should have tried to smuggle them to London herself, was unthinkable. Therefore, logically, she must have used the Englishman, Quest.

The ormulu clock on the mantelpiece chimed six. Almost simultaneously a bell shrilled in the kitchen. He blinked and pushed himself to his feet. It was time to take his mother her evening glass of champagne.

Chapter IV.

Jump Shot

"Double?" Ankles crossed, one hand on his hip, Philip Quest was leaning on his mallet like an Edwardian masher at the seaside. A high brick wall, espaliered with peach trees, surrounded the croquet lawn; there was no breath of air and the afternoon heat was intense. They had been playing now for the best part of an hour, a hard, tough game with no quarter asked or given. They spoke only to offer, accept, or refuse a double; or to mutter an automatic, grudging "Shot." They were as far removed from the popular image of elderly clergymen pottering around a vicarage lawn as are the joint leaders in the last round of the Open from the weekend golfers hacking around a municipal course. As if by osmosis the manicured Berkshire turf had become the green baize of the Clermont.

Piers de Salis flicked his cigarette butt into a flower bed and walked slowly around the hoop to study the lie of the balls. He was dressed with careless elegance in white cream flannels, a pale blue silk shirt, a red scarf loosely knotted at his throat. Whistling tunelessly between his teeth, he squatted down on his heels

43

and drew an imaginary line with his mallet. The sun caught his sleek blonde hair and for the first time Philip noticed that he was going bald.

"Absolutely," he said as he got to his feet. "I suppose you realize what you're doing?"

"Side bet?"

"A tenner you won't make it."

"You're on. Now watch this." His weight thrown forward, feet apart and knees slightly bent, Philip adjusted his grip. One final sighting glance, then he locked his wrists and swung the brass-rimmed mallet head down through a quarter arc. It was a perfect jump shot. The red ball rose sharply, easily clearing the three others that lay blocking its path, then dipped and homed in like a guided missile, shaving the white paint on the underside of the hoop, and the game was won.

"You bastard!" De Salis shook his head. "So how much does that make it? Seventy?"

"Eighty. You're forgetting that last tenner."

"Ay God! I could've spent the weekend in Paris for what today's cost me."

"Another?"

"So likely. With the winning streak you're on? Perhaps later."

Philip shouldered his mallet and they made their way to the summerhouse, a miniature painted pagoda in the far corner of the lawn. On the table was a portable icebox from which he took cans of beer, passed one to de Salis, then sank back into a deep wicker chair and reached for his cigarettes while de Salis untied his scarf and mopped the sweat from his forehead that was already beginning to redden from the sun.

Philip looked at his cigarette, then at de Salis, and made up his mind. "All right, Piers, let's have it."

"What? Have what? Surely you don't want to settle up now?"

"Oh, for God's sake," he said impatiently. "That can wait—it always has. No, I know you well enough after all these years to be able to tell when you've got something on your mind. And I also find it . . . well, rather uncharacteristic of you of all people, my dear Piers, to ring up Jackie and more or less invite yourself to lunch. She told me so herself. After all, it's not as if we haven't seen each other for a couple of years. A couple of days, in fact, at the Clermont where, I seem to remember, you showed an almost unhealthy interest in my trip to Morocco."

Now de Salis was folding his scarf into a neat square and tucking it into his hip pocket, eyes averted from Philip's questioning stare.

"And especially," Philip continued, "in that girl in Marrakesh." He paused, giving de Salis a chance to speak; and, when he did not, he slammed his beer can down upon the table, making the ashtray rattle and his lighter roll onto the floor. "Look, Piers, let's stop pussyfooting around. You come clean with me and I'll come clean with you. O.K., you're right, something odd did happen in Marrakesh—but just how odd I didn't find out till yesterday when . . ."

"When what?" de Salis prompted, his face expressionless in the semidarkness of the summerhouse.

For a long moment Philip hesitated, gazing out at a white dove that was strutting across the grass. "When what?" he said at last. "When I found that someone had planted about a quarter of a million pounds' worth of diamonds in my car. Diamonds that were stolen from an old queen in Marrakesh called Corviglia. A pendant, to be exact. And putting two and two together, it can only have happened on my last night there—when I picked up that girl at the Casino and took her back to the hotel. Where, as you know, I passed out cold, something that hasn't happened to me for years. Right, so I'd been mixing my drinks, but I ought to know my own capacity by now. No, there's only one logical explanation as I see it—she slipped me a Mickey Finn. It all ties in. I've got special burglar-proof locks on the Porsche and I only had one set of keys with me, which I had on me all the time. And there were no signs on the car of anyone having tried

45

to jimmy the windows or any of that sort of thing. So there I am dead to the world; she lifts my keys, takes the car off somewhere, a simple job any mechanic could do, and there's the car back in the parking lot in the morning. It's the kind of set-up one reads about in the papers all the time: innocent tourists abroad being used as unwitting couriers. Mum, Dad, and the kids having two weeks holiday in the sun, then driving back to Wolverhampton or wherever sitting on top of a small fortune in heroin. The first night back, their car is stolen, the stuff's collected, and the car turns up in a side street around the corner. Only with me, it wasn't drugs, it was diamonds. As easy as falling off a log—except for the King and his bloody bodyguards riding me off the road. Luckily it was only the coachwork that suffered. But then I go round to my garage yesterday morning and they've got the door off and there between the panels was this box containing Corviglia's diamond pendant."

"You seem very sure it's his. How do you know?"

"Billy Paterson in Tangier couldn't stop talking about it."

"And where is it now?"

Philip grinned at him. "Safe."

"And what are you going to do with it?"

Philip spread his hands. "I honestly haven't the faintest idea. Finders keepers? The early morning flight to Antwerp tomorrow?"

"For God's sake, Philip," de Salis said angrily, "be your age. You really believe that you'd be allowed to get away with it?"

"One can always try."

De Salis got to his feet and stood staring out at the sunlit lawn, his hands plunged into his pockets, jingling his loose change.

Philip spoke to his back. "All right, I've told you my story. It's your turn now. It's the girl your interested in, isn't it? That oh-so-casual invitation to have a drink at the Clermont was just an excuse so you could pump me about her. Come on, out with it. You can forget the Official Secrets Act with me."

"Can I? I wonder. The girl, yes. But first of all we'd better make absolutely sure we're talking about the same one. So let's go up to the house and get it over with. I've got her picture in the car."

Sitting on the bed of Philip's spartanly furnished room in Bachelors' Row, de Salis took a buff-colored cardboard folder from his briefcase and extracted a 8 × 10 glossy photograph. "It was taken about a year ago. I know it's not very good, still . . ." He handed it to Philip.

"Too much grain, out of focus, and underexposed."

"We can't all work for *Vogue*," de Salis remarked dryly.

"Far from it, it's just the kind of thing they'd splash across a double-page spread."

The photograph showed a girl sitting on the terrace of a café that looked like the Flore in Paris. It was obviously a cold day as she was wrapped in a dark coat with the collar turned up around her ears and wearing a fluffy white fur hat like a dandelion gone to seed. Her elbows were resting on her folded hands. She seemed to be gazing straight into the camera lens, but the eyes were dead and unseeing.

"She's certainly very beautiful." He crossed to the window and held out the photograph at arm's length. "Yes," he said at last. "That's her. God, what a wasted night! So, who is she? She looks vaguely Slav. A mysterious Russian Countess, the leader of quote An International Gang of Jewel Thieves unquote? But if it were as simple as that I don't see what it's got to do with you and . . . well, whatever you people call yourselves these days."

De Salis replaced the photograph in the folder. "Her name, her real name, is Tania Berger. Born in Dusseldorf in 1946, G.I. father, German mother. She started as a dancer and a singer in various sleazy continental nightclubs. When she was nineteen, in Munich, she shot and killed her lover who was also her ponce. Both barrels of a shotgun at point-blank range, cut him in half. She claimed she thought he was a burglar, and got away scot-free. For a while she drifted on the fringes of the underworld, then she came across a certain Thami Fouquet who picked her out of the gutter and did a Professor Higgins on her and now has her eating out of his hand." He tapped the folder on his knee. "That's it in a nutshell. Not only beautiful, but tough, dangerous, and clever. Ten years ago what they used to call a gangster's moll, but today a terrorist—or be even more fashionable, an urban guerrilla. I must say, Philip, you really do pick them."

"Come off it, Piers. You know as well as I do that she picked me up." He smiled wryly. "And I thought it was my dashing looks and irresistible charm. And now here I am, the patsy, the mug, the sucker. Still, it's early days yet."

"I'm afraid not. In fact, it's later than you think. Much later."

Philip looked up, startled by the sudden seriousness of de Salis' voice.

"Look," he continued, "as you yourself said just now, this isn't a simple matter of a few stolen diamonds, though I wish the hell it were. Tania Berger is on our list and that means that when you were spotted with her in Marrakesh questions were going to be asked about you. And, Philip, I have to tell you that as far as one of my superior officers is concerned, you could be run over by a bus and he'd stand there and spit on what was left of you."

Philip stared at him open-mouthed, at a total loss for words.

"Webb-Walker," de Salis said. "Wanker Webb-Walker."

And then Philip remembered, and he was seventeen again, with two passions in life, cricket and the slim, boyish body of the violet-eyed Laura Webb-Walker, thirty-five and his housemaster's wife. It was the Lord's match and he was seven short of his century in an inning which *The Times* correspondent was to describe as one of the best exhibitions of schoolboy batting that he had ever seen. But the hands of the clock on the Pavilion stood at five to four, and at four o'clock he was meeting Laura in a changing room in the Royal Tennis court. The game was as good as won so he pushed the ball to short extra-cover, called for a run, stumbled, and was yards short of the crease as the wicket was broken. Laura was waiting for him, wearing a yellow dress, her pants already in her bag. The door would not lock, but they had taken even greater risks before. Her lipstick tasted of strawberries and her hands were expertly unbuttoning his flies. Then she was lying back on the table, her high heels digging into his buttocks and she moaned and bit and writhed. "Yes, Philip, yes! Now, darling! Come!" He heard a vague noise behind him but by then it was too late and he was exploding into her as her husband pushed open the door. There was no public scandal, but his school days ended then and there. An announcement was made that a severe attack of food poisoning had forced him to withdraw from the match by which time he was drinking whisky in the Refreshment Room at Victoria Station, waiting for a train to take him home to Sussex.

"I know it was a long time ago," he heard de Salis say, "but I'll bet you he's been brooding about it all these years. When the report from Morocco came through, those piggy little eyes positively lit up and one could almost see him rub his hands with glee. I honestly think if I hadn't been there, he'd have had the Special Branch pick you up the minute you got off the boat."

"But on what charge?"

"He'd have thought of one. Let's face it, you've been mixed up in some pretty bizarre goings-on in the past few years. Spain, Sardinia, and then that Rommel business in Corsica. So far you've always managed to keep on the right side of the law. But as far as Webb-Walker's concerned, the dividing line between

49

you and a common criminal is very thin." He held up a hand as Philip began to protest. "No, you said you wanted my side of it, and now you're getting it—or rather the official side. In all these . . . er, adventures you've come out ahead."

"I suppose," Philip said bitterly, "you call losing my eye 'coming out ahead'?"

De Salis counterattacked immediately. "You didn't exactly lose financially, did you, when Buccaneers Incorporated recovered Rommel's treasure? Two percent of how much was your cut?"

"Mind your own bloody business!"

"Relax, I'm only trying to show you how Webb-Walker's mind works. When that report comes in . . ."

"And just how was I recognized?" Philip demanded. "Don't tell me I'm on one of your lists, too."

"When you enter a Casino," de Salis explained as if to a child, "you produce your passport, they take the details and check them against their little black book and make you out a card. So a ten dirham note into the outstretched palm . . ."

"O.K., I'm with you. Go on."

"When that report comes in, Webb-Walker asks for your file. And before you start yelling about police states and invasion of privacy, remember that in Whitehall's eyes you're still Quest P., 2nd/Lieutenant, and the Army likes to keep its tabs on its officers even if they're no longer on the Active List. They never know when they might need you again. Anyway, he laps up the gory details and his day is made: Quest P., well-known—for the want of a better word—adventurer in cahoots with a beautiful blonde terrorist who is the mistress of Thami Fouquet. And honestly, Philip, knowing your track record, can you really blame him for the conclusions he formed?"

Philip shifted his weight on the uncomfortable high-backed chair. "No," he said. "I suppose not. So whether I like it or not, I've really landed myself in this one, haven't I? So while we're about it, tell me who this Thami Fouquet is I'm meant to be working for."

De Salis reopened his folder, shuffled through a sheaf of papers, and passed Philip three typewritten sheets that were stapled to a photograph.

"Wouldn't much fancy meeting him in a dark alley," he said as he rose from the bed. "I've got to pee. Where is it?"

"Right, then second on the left." He glanced at the photograph. "Nor would I. And let's hope I don't have to." He lit a cigarette and settled down to read.

"A nice character," Philip commented when he had finished the last paragraph of stilted officialese. "Does he really believe he's the son of El Glaoui and the rightful Pasha of Marrakesh?"

"Apparently."

"And what actually happened to El Glaoui? All I seem to remember was that he was a great friend of Churchill's."

"He was, and I suppose his finest hour was in 1953 when, with the help of the French, he managed to get the then Sultan, Mohammed V, kicked out and sent off to exile in Madagascar. Of course, things being what they are in the Arab world, two years later the situation was reversed and he got kicked out. And that, in spite of the Sultan's promises to the contrary, was the end of the House of Glaoua—imprisonment, exile, confiscation of property, and God knows how many executions. But one must hand it to the Sultan; he allowed El Glaoui to come home to die."

"Charming."

"But it wasn't till about 1970, when his properties in Morocco were confiscated, that we first heard of Thami Fouquet flirting with the various organizations planning coups in Morocco. Oufkir didn't want to know—luckily for Thami. The MSU, the banned Moroccan Student Union, doesn't want to know. They're essentially Maoist and to them he stands for capitalism and everything they hate. And as for Colonel Gaddafi, the Big Daddy of them all as well as a lunatic Islamic puritan, he wouldn't even soil his hands to talk on the telephone to Thami, let alone meet him. Even the Polisario in the Sahara weren't interested. So Thami had to go it alone."

"Rather him than me," Philip said. Once again his ears were filled with the scream of sirens and the clatter of the helicopter as the Porsche—lurched and bucketed off the road in the wake of the royal cavalcade. "He's certainly going to have his work cut out."

"As a matter of fact, he's chosen his time well. You don't read much about it in the Press, but there's plenty going on in Morocco. Pliny was right: *Ex Africa semper aliquid novi*. For the last fifteen years there's been a sporadic war on the Algerian border. Then there's Gaddafi's propaganda war. There've been abortive uprisings among the tribesmen in the High Atlas—the old Glaoua country. Bombs in Rabat and Casablanca; trouble in the desert over who really owns Spanish Sahara." He gathered up his papers and replaced them in his briefcase. "Now say you wanted to mount some terrorist operation. What's the first thing you'd need?"

Philip nodded slowly. "Not just a common theft."

"No more than that ballsed-up bank job in Grenoble was. You can buy one hell of a lot of terrorism for a quarter of a million pounds and still have plenty of change left in your pocket. Ever since before Christmas there've been whispers on the grapevine that Thami's in the market for a small private army, perhaps no more than a properly equipped twenty-man strike force, for a one-off job of his own. But the lack of cash has been holding him up—and these people don't accept post-dated checks."

"These people?" Philip frowned. "What people?"

"The professionals who provide this kind of service—anything from sub-machine guns and bazookas to second-hand Centurions, perhaps the very same ones you used to trundle around Germany, and if you want and can afford it, the men to work them. Ever since the Renaissance recruiting mercenaries and hiring them out has been a way of life. And recently, look at Katanga and the Congo. You'll remember the Watchguard affair, David Stirling and all those ex-SAS boys getting in on the private army game. As you know, HMG viewed the whole set-up with distinctly jaundiced eye—too much potential embarrassment politically, so they pulled the shutters down, made them toe the line. And they did. But the demand still exists and the game goes on. And this is where I come in. After Watchguard and the Angolan fiasco it looked as if the bottom had dropped out of the British market. But I believe it's starting up again. It's back to Edgar Allan Poe and *The Purloined Letter*. Where better to hide a letter than in the letter rack?" He paused and studied his nails.

"Go on," Philip prompted him.

"Thanks to you, Thami's bankroll is now in London. Not Zurich, Paris or wherever, but in London where they planned it to be. Stages one and two completed. And now it's all systems go for stage three, the pick-up." De Salis paused and stroked his chin. "So what they're looking for is an orange Porsche, registration so-and-so, that's usually parked in Paulton's Square. As you said, as easy as falling off a log—the only trouble that it isn't there and hasn't been since the day you got back. Right?"

"Yes. It's been in the garage around the corner in Old Church Street."

"And how soon could it be back on the road?"

"Sometime tomorrow," Ian said. "They were already respraying yesterday."

"I wish my garage was that efficient," de Salis said sourly. "Anyway, give me the address and I'll have someone round there first thing in the morning." He caught Philip's puzzled glance and explained. "From the minute that car's back on the road, it's going to be under twenty-four hour surveillance. And not only that. It'll be bugged internally. You can fix that with your friend Ian; say the stereo needs overhauling or something. Then . . ."

"Look," Philip interrupted, "what exactly are you getting at? O.K., X comes along, steals the car and drives it off to some quiet place where he can take the door to pieces and remove the diamonds. But what happens then? You move in and arrest him?"

De Salis hesitated. "I doubt it very much. I'm not interested in the little men, the ones way down at the bottom of the ladder. I want to get to the top."

"And when he finds the diamonds are gone . . ."

"He'll report back for instructions, but we'll be breathing down his neck and with any luck we'll be another rung up the ladder. We'll be dealing the cards by then and forcing their hand. And no one's going to write off a quarter of a million pounds, let alone Thami Fouquet."

It was then that Philip understood how it felt to be a goat staked out in a clearing to await the tiger. "I suppose you realize," he said slowly, "that the trail leads straight back to me."

De Salis nodded. "Don't worry, we'll be looking after you. And, Philip," it was as if he were reading his thoughts, "you can forget any idea you had of hopping over to Antwerp. I hate to think of the interpretation Webb-Walker would put on a move like that. But play it my way and you're off the hook."

Philip stared at his shoes. "It's sheer bloody blackmail, that's what it is!"

"It's hardly my fault if you choose to get involved in . . ."

"Choose?" Philip snorted. "That's one hell of a fine word to use. And just what choice have I got now?" he waved de Salis down as he started to speak. "Sweet fuck all." Through the open window came the sound of voices and the rattle of the trolley as it was wheeled out on to the terrace. "Tea," he said sourly. "Another hour and a half till drink time. Sunday, bloody Sunday!"

Chapter V.

Rhinestone Cowboy

Piere de Salis left for London before dinner, but Philip and Jackie stayed on for the cold cuts and salad, then drove up together in Philip's rented Volkswagen. She had come down on Friday by train, having lent her Mini and her flat in Fulham to a friend for the weekend, and was to spend the night in Paulton's Square, a plan which Philip saw no good reason to change, and de Salis had agreed with him. "So long as everything's squared for my man to start work at eight." There was little traffic and they made good time along the M4; and as they turned off the King's Road he noticed that the lights were on in Ian's flat above the garage.

Philip pulled over to the curb. "You go on home, darling, and take the car. I won't be long. I've got to see someone and I might as well get it over with now. Got the keys?"

"Honestly, Philip," she said as she rummaged in her bag. "I've hardly seen you all day. First Piers, and now this."

Eventually she produced the keys of his flat and he

kissed her on the cheek and climbed out of the driver's seat. "See you in a minute." The noisy thump of the engine echoed in the empty street, and then she was gone. The night was hot and sultry, the stars invisible through the reddish glow of the sky that veiled the city. He pressed the bell set into one of the large double wooden doors that were painted the royal blue of the Chelsea Football Club, then stepped backwards into the road. A window opened and a head appeared.

"That you, Ian? It's me, Philip Quest."

"Oh, hello, Mister Quest," Ian's wife answered. "Sticky, isn't it? There's thunder about. I can feel it in my bones. But if you want Ian, you'll find him down at the pub. And tell him not to forget that it's tonight that play he wanted to watch on BBC 2."

Philip thanked her and walked down toward the river. The doors had been wedged open and he spotted Ian in the far corner of the Saloon Bar, playing darts. It was one of the few pubs in Chelsea that had so far escaped the plague of jukeboxes and one-armed bandits, of 'Music Lights' and go-go girls, of hideously patterned carpets and artificial red-shaded candles on plastic paneled walls dripping artificial wax. It was a pub to drink in, standing at the bar, leaving the few cigarette-scarred tables to the Chelsea Pensioners with their sticks and medals and pints of mild and bitter.

Philip ordered a large whisky and chatted with the landlord until he caught Ian's eye and guestured toward him with his glass. They had a couple of drinks together, then Philip left, Ian promising that the car would be ready by midday and that he would give Philip's friend any help he needed.

The street door was on the latch and taped to it was a card on which was scrawled in orange ink: THIRD FLOOR—THAT'S WHERE IT'S AT. COME STRAIGHT ON UP. BARRY. Philip grinned; the Australian architect who lived in the flat below him was giving yet another party. He stood aside as two young men, identically dressed in black

56

leather, arms around each other's waists, came lurching down the stairs toward him.

"Ooh, kinky," one giggled, pursing up his bright scarlet lips. "I've never had a one-eyed man before. Isn't he lovely, dear?"

"You bitch! You common little tramp!" his friend shrieked and dragged him staggering out on to the pavement.

The front door was ajar. The sounds of the party behind him, Philip dropped the cases that he had taken from the car in the hall, then paused uncertainly. None of the lights in the sitting room was on. "Jackie?" he called, glancing at his watch; he had been with Ian longer than he had intended. Perhaps she had gone downstairs to the party; as a decorator she had worked with Barry on several houses. In the kitchen the refrigerator clicked and hummed into life, and a sudden draft ruffled the hair on the back of his neck. But as he began to turn toward it he caught no more than a blurred glimpse of a figure looming over him before the arm descended and his skull exploded into a ball of white fire. He felt his knees folding beneath him like hinges, heard the crack of his forehead hitting the parquet floor, then all was silence.

When Philip recovered consciousness, he found that he was slumped in the old buttoned leather armchair that had been dragged over to the desk. A triphammer thudded rhythmically down on his cortex and he could taste the bile, bitter in his parched mouth. He gingerly raised his hand to his temple and his fingers came away sticky with blood. The Anglepoise lamp, the only light in the room, had been tilted until it shone directly into his face so that all he could see of the man sitting behind the desk was a loudly checked tweed-covered arm and a hairy hand. And any illusions that he might have held that this was simple house-breaking and had nothing to do with Corviglia's diamonds, were scattered to ashes by the gun that the hand was holding. It was a professional's gun, a Colt

Python revolver, a .357 Magnum which could stop a car engine or blow a man's head clean off his shoulders. Behind him, a lighter—a Zippo by the sound of it—snapped. He slowly looked around. Sprawling on the sofa, legs crossed to reveal elaborately tooled high-heeled cowboy boots, wearing a beige suede safari-suit, a second man was drawing on a cigarillo. He had thick wavy brown hair and at first glance was almost excessively handsome; but then Philip noticed the yellowish eyes set too close together beneath the long curling lashes, and the thin rat-trap of a mouth.

He raised his cigarillo in salute. "Glad you could join us." His voice was American, high-pitched and slightly nasal. "Welcome back."

A sudden blast of heavy rock from the flat below made the windows rattle and there were screams and shouts of protest before the volume was turned down.

"Sounds like quite a party," the man behind the desk said, as if regretting that he was not there.

Philip fought to clear his throbbing head. He pushed himself upright. "Look," he blustered, "what the hell's going on here? Who are you and what are you doing in my flat? And where's Jackie?"

"Jackie?" the man on the sofa said. "The kid with the boobs? She's back there in the bedroom having a laydown. She's not feeling too well." He giggled. "She tried to kick against a prick."

"Don't you worry about her," the man behind the desk said. "Play your cards right and you'll soon be tucked up in bed together, as snug as bugs in a rug."

"All right," Philip said. "Take what you want and get out. Not that there's much worth stealing. A few cameras, lenses, that's all. A bit of cash, but not much."

"Listen, son," his voice was pained, "you've got us all wrong. We don't want to take anything that belongs to you. Why, that'd be stealing. It just so happens that you've got something that rightfully belongs to us."

"I've got . . . You must be out of your mind. I've

58

never seen you—not that I can see you now—or that drugstore cowboy over there before in my life. You're crazy! Stark, staring, raving mad!"

"Boy, you watch your mouth!"

Philip swiveled around to face him. "And sod you too, shitface."

"Easy, Wayne. Let me handle this." He spoke as if he was calming a skittish colt. He had never once raised his voice, but Philip could detect an underlying current of menace beneath his calm and knew that it was him, and not the loud-mouthed fashion plate on the sofa, that he had to fear.

"What do you mean?" Philip asked. "Rightfully belongs to you?"

"She didn't tell you?"

Philip sat very still. "She? Who?"

"Who Why Tania, of course. Tania Berger, your friend Tania from Marrakesh."

"Tania from Marrakesh?" His nails were digging into his damp palms. "I don't know any Tania from Marrakesh."

"But she says you do. And I say you do. And this says you do." The ventilated rib running along the barrel gleamed as he raised the revolver and thumbed back the hammer. Philip held his breath and felt his stomach contract as he watched the cylinder slowly turn and lock into place. The double click seemed to echo through the whole room. Reason and logic told him that only a madman would pull the trigger, that dead he was worthless, but all the same a drop of sweat trickled down his spine and his flesh crawled as the single monstrous eye stared unwaveringly into his.

"For God's sake," he protested. "You've got to believe me. The only girl I know in Marrakesh was some tart I picked up last week at the Casino. I was drunk and took her back to the hotel and passed out. When I woke up, she was gone. And that's the truth. I swear it."

"And how much did she roll you for?" the man on the sofa taunted him.

Philip ignored him, willing the lie to be believed, gazing bewilderedly into the darkness behind the glare of the lamp. Then, at last, he breathed again as, using both thumbs, his hidden inquisitor lowered the hammer and laid the gun on the desk.

"All right, son, I've listened to you, now you listen to me. I haven't got the time so I'll give it to you straight. This tart of yours used you. She used you to smuggle some stolen property out of Morocco, property that was stolen from me. She and her friends stashed it in your Porsche, so if you'll just hand over the keys and tell us where it is, we'll be on our way and in half an hour we can all go home to bed. It's the easy way. No cops, no sweating it out in a Moroccan jail, good night. We'll forget you, you'll forget us." He pushed the bunch of keys that had been in Philip's pocket into the light. "VW, but no Porsche. Come on, son. Give."

"But I can't . . ." Philip swallowed hard. "I mean, I haven't got them. And anyway the car's not here."

"Not here?" Not here in London?"

"No. It's in Yorkshire."

"Yorkshire?"

"Yes," Philip said. Now that the first, and highest, hurdle had been cleared, he was approaching the others with ever-increasing confidence. "I lent it to a friend who was going up there for the weekend and who . . ." He was about to invent a reason for lending his car, but stopped himself just in time; so often it was unnecessary embellishment that belied the lies. "Well," he spread his hands, "he won't be back till tomorrow."

"What time tomorrow?"

"I'm not sure. Around lunch time, he said."

The ensuing silence seemed to last an age and Philip wiped his palms on his trousers. A car door slammed in the square and a woman laughed.

"She-it," the voice behind him complained. "We've got to stick around in this lousy town another twelve hours?"

The fingers drummed a brief tattoo on the scuffed green leather. There was a squeak as the chair was pushed back and for the first time Philip saw his inquisitor face to face. Although not much above average height, his shoulders were those of a Miura bull. He had a tanned, outdoor complexion which was surprisingly smooth, and eyes the color of faded blue denim. His black hair was touched with silver and cut *en brosse*, and any Hapsburg would have been proud of his jaw. His white shirt bulging over his belt showed the beginnings of a paunch.

Looking down at Philip, he rubbed the side of his fleshy nose and the stone set in the heavy gold ring that he wore on the little finger of his left hand flashed blood-red as it caught the light. Then he turned away and said, "Get the girl and bring her out here so's he can kiss her good night."

"Now wait a minute . . ." Philip began.

"No. You listen to me. You, son, are putting us to a lot of inconvenience. So fair's fair. Deliver the goods and you'll get her back. And anyway she'd be no good to anyone tonight. Just look at her."

Philip watched tight-lipped as Wayne dumped her on the sofa. Her skirt rode up; she was naked from the waist down. And then he saw why; her black lace bikini pants had been stuffed into her mouth. Her head lolled drunkenly; her eyes were closed; her ashen cheeks streaked with mascara. Philip struggled to restrain himself; but by now he was in far too deep. He cursed that night in Marrakesh, he cursed de Salis, he cursed himself.

"O.K., so she's a mess now but tomorrow lunchtime she'll be fine, just fine. Simple sedation, that's all. And that's the way we'll keep her until we're on *our* way. A slight hangover when she wakes up, but she won't remember a thing. Nor, if you've any sense, will you. Just write it off as a bad dream that never happened."

The nickel-plated handcuffs that Wayne had produced when they were left alone in the flat bit cruelly into his flesh, and he clenched and unclenched his fists to keep the blood circulating in his numbed hands. He lay on the sofa, face buried in the cushions, feigning sleep. Guests were noisily leaving the party and he realized how little attention the sight of Jackie being carried down the stairs would have attracted. He thought longingly of the Holland & Holland 12 bore in the hall cupboard, of the Walther in the safe; but they might as well have been on the moon.

"Hey boy! You asleep?"

Philip hunched his shoulders and settled deeper into the cushions.

"Hey, boy! I'm talking to you."

Yawning, Philip rolled over and sat up. "So? What am I meant to do? Stand up and salute?"

Boots resting on the desk next to Philip's portable Sony, on which some disc jockey was babbling the usual inanities, he was leaning back in the swivel chair, tapping the ash from his cigarillo on to the floor. He had taken off his jacket, revealing a black leather shoudler holster. "Refresh my memory for me, will you?" The mean eyes were small and calculating. "You mentioned something about cameras and lenses, but it wasn't that that grabbed me. Something more . . . tangible." He grinned, showing small, pointed teeth. "Like cash?" With his heel he indicated Philip's wallet, lying open in front of him. "But this here's chicken-shit, seven pounds and a Swiss ten-franc note. No, boy, I somehow don't reckon that was the cash you were talking about."

"For God's sake, you rhinestone cowboy, stop calling me 'boy'!" As he spoke, he rose to his feet.

The boots thumped to the ground, the chair skidded across the parquet, and the gun jumped like magic into his hand, the hammer at full cock even before Philip had reached his full height. Philip froze, as much through sheer admiration of the speed of his draw. "It's all right," he said calmly. "I only want to go to the lavatory—the can, the john."

"O.K. but don't do that again. It makes me nervous," the thin lips twisted into a sneer, "boy." He gestured with the gun, the twin of the colt that Philip had faced earlier. "On your way."

One of the first lessons that Philip had learned in unarmed combat was that a man with the muzzle of a handgun pressed against his body can knock the gun away before his opponent can pull the trigger. But it was only too obvious that Wayne had studied at the same school. As they walked through the bedroom, he allowed Philip plenty of space, making no attempt to crowd him and laying himself open to a mule kick to the groin, knee, or shin. He waited in the doorway while Philip flushed the lavatory then turned to examine himself in the mirror above the basin. He grimaced and splashed cold water over his face, washing the dried blood away, the handcuffs clinking against the porcelain.

"I was reading a fascinating article the other day, by a psychiatrist," he said to Wayne's reflection. "Something about the size of a man's gun increasing in inverse proportion to the size of his cock. Phallic compensation, I think he called it. Police Specials, Browning Hi-Powers, even Lugers—they're O.K. But once you get up into the Magnums, boy, have you got a problem. You're in a real . . ."

A deafening crash drowned the rest of his words. He flung himself to the floor as the mirror disintegrated into a thousand lethal slivers and the ricochet whined around the tiled bathroom like an angry hornet before embedding itself into the ceiling. A shower of plaster fell into the bath and the acrid fumes of burned cordite hung motionless in the silence.

"On your feet, boy. On your feet." A muscle twitched in his jaw. "You talk real dirty, boy, and if there's one thing I hate it's boys like you talking dirty."

Philip did as he was ordered, the broken glass crunching beneath the soles of his shoes.

"So let's get down to the nitty-gritty." Once again the vulpine grin. "The cash, boy. Now just how much have you got stashed away, and where?"

Philip leaned against the basin. "You really think I'm going to tell you."

"You will, boy, you will. We've got a long night ahead of us and by the time I'm finished with you you'll be kicking yourself—if you can still move your legs—for not telling me now." The narrowed eyes looked Philip up and down. "You've got nice teeth, boy. How about them for starters? Dentists here as expensive as they are back in the States?"

Philip lowered his gaze and shrugged helplessly, opening his hands in a gesture of defeat. "It's not that much. About two thousand pounds."

"How much is that in real money?"

"Three and a half thousand dollars."

He gave a low whistle. "Hey, not bad. And where d'you keep this little nest egg?"

"In the safe. Do you think I'd leave it lying around?"

"And where's the safe?"

"In the darkroom."

"So what are we waiting for?"

Once again he kept his distance, following Philip across the hall and waiting while he pushed open the door and flicked on the lights. It was a square room with one blacked-out window; waist-high work-benches ran along two walls, a set of stainless steel sinks along the third. The floor was covered with black and white linoleum tiles. In the center stood a table heaped with photographs, magazines, and sheets of color slides.

Philip led the way over to the big Durst M601 enlarger. "It's under there. Clear the muck out and it's built into the wall. The combination's forty, three to the left; ten, five to the . . ."

"Uh uh. Serious accidents have happened to friends of mine while opening unfamiliar safes."

Philip knelt down and slid back the cupboard door.

"Nice and easy now. Anything I don't like the look of—see how you like the look of your kneecap taking off on a walk on its own."

His movements restricted by the three steel links separating the handcuffs, Philip began to remove the boxes of printing paper and stack them neatly to one side. Wayne was squatting down on his haunches behind, and at an angle to him, so that he could peer over his shoulder. Philip reached into the back of the cupboard for the serrated knob and dialed the combination. Even if he had not been manacled, and even if the Walther had not been in its box, his chances would have been a million to one against. The tumblers fell into place and he eased the door open. His fingers closed over the thick brown manila envelope and he straightened up and offered it to Wayne who had risen with him and was now standing by the table.

"And other friends of mine have had their hands blown off. Open it."

Philip sighed. "Suspicious son of a bitch, aren't you? And nice company you keep, a whole bunch of basket cases." He had already measured the distances and the angles, and as he began to tear open the flap, he moved half a pace back, his left foot brushing the stacked boxes, the heel slightly raised. An inch more, then he stamped down on the rubber-encased heavy-duty switch that was set into the linoleum. The glaring fluorescent tubes on the ceiling went out, plunging the room into a darkness that was total except for the dim orange glow from the safelight high on the wall. Head down, fists clenched, arms outstretched, Philip launched himself through the air.

The gun belched flame; the blast singed his hair; glass shattered. Then Philip was upon him, fists driving into the unprotected solar plexus, his weight and impetus sending them both crashing to the ground. Philip scrabbled at his groin, found his testicles, gripped, squeezed, and twisted with all his strength. Wayne screamed, a thin, animal scream, bucking and writhing as Philip fought to hold him down, increasing the pressure, twisting harder. His gun arm flailed wildly and the heavy barrel caught Philip a glancing blow on the side of his head, opening up the cut on his temple. A curtain of blood poured down over his eye, but still he did not let go. Now Wayne's screams and struggles were growing weaker. With a single fluid movement, Philip relinquished his grip and jumped astride him, pinning his elbow with his knee and clubbing at his wrist. The revolver skidded across the floor and Philip dove for it, cannoning into the table and knocking it over. After groping frantically in the chaos of fallen photographs and the gloom, his fingers were touching the checkered wooden butt when he heard the rasping breath close, too close, behind him. He kicked out blindly, but connected with nothing. He spun around in a half crouch and there, incredibly, was Wayne, his teeth bared in a rictus of agony, swaying on his knees like a wounded bull, the upraised knife gleaming a hellish red.

This time Philip left nothing to chance. He pivoted on his hip and swung. The edges of his interlocked hands smashed into the grinning face between the nose and mouth. Bone cracked and great gouts of blood spurted from his nostrils. The knife clattered harmlessly to the floor. Then, falling as slowly as a factory chimney, he toppled sideways, twitched once, and lay still.

Drawing in great gulps of air, Philip hung his head while the adrenalin ebbed from his veins and the pounding of his heart returned to normal. He was suddenly very aware of the reek of chemicals and his stomach heaved. He picked up the revolver and stuck it into the waistband of his trousers, then climbed unsteadily to his feet. He wasted no time searching Wayne's pockets for the key to the handcuffs; he would never succeed in unlocking them by himself, and it would be at least an hour before he regained consciousness after the double blow that the Japanese so aptly called *shuto*, or knifehand.

In the doorway, he paused and took one final look at the spread-eagled figure, motionless on the floor.

"Don't say you didn't have it coming to you . . . Boy!"

The whisky burned his throat, as did the first cigarette that he had smoked since leaving Ian in the pub, a thousand years ago. He switched off the Sony in the middle of a Radio One commercial for Radio One and pulled back the sitting room curtains and opened a window wide. The storm that had been building up all evening was about to break. Lightning flickered in the west and the first heavy drops of rain fell through the sultry air to splash upon the dusty pavements. The tops of the plane trees began to sigh and a newspaper swirled and cartwheeled past the silent cars parked in the deserted street. He flicked his half-smoked cigarette out into the night. The wind caught it and whipped it away, a miniature comet trailing a plume of glittering sparks. Then he reluctantly turned away to the telephone on the desk and dialed the number at Egerton Terrace.

De Salis answered on the seventh ring, his voice furred with sleep.

Some thirty seconds later Philip replaced the receiver and sat staring at the china jar which had once held a pound of the finest Beluga caviar and in which he now kept his pens and Magic Markers, but seeing nothing. After a while he walked stiffly into the bathroom, wincing at the mess, snapped open a vial of Vitamin B_{12}, mixed it with water and drank it down. Then the buzzer sounded. He pressed the button to release the catch on the street door and stood out on the landing and watched de Salis come running up the stairs, the shoulders of his trench coat dark with rain.

"God!" de Salis said, staring at him in horror. "What the hell's been going on?"

Philip managed a wry grin. "You ought to see the other guy."

"What other guy?"

"The one who's out cold on the darkroom floor." He held out his hands. "The key's in his trouser pocket."

When de Salis returned to the hall, his face was set and strained.

"You certainly took your time," Philip said, massaging his aching wrists.

"Is it any wonder?" He ran a hand over the blonde stubble on his chin. "This one's in spades, doubled and redoubled. When you said trouble, you didn't know what you were talking about. First of all, he's dead. Yes, Philip, dead. I'm no doctor but it looks as if you got his philtrum. And secondly, I know him. His name's Morollo, Wayne Morollo, among other things a professional hit-man who enjoys his work. I could tell you stories about him and his boss-cum-boyfriend that'd make your hair stand on end. Batman and Robin, they like to call themselves, the blue-eyed boys of God's gift to the free world, the CIA."

Chapter VI.

A Busy Day for Buggers

The rain was still gurgling in the gutters when Philip awoke shortly after seven o'clock and a cheerless gray light edged its way around the curtains. Out on the King's Road he could hear the soggy hiss of tires as the early morning commuters from the suburbs drove into work. It was on a day like this, he recalled, that he had lunched with Maclean and accepted the Moroccan assignment. Exhausted though he had been, he had slept badly, a thousand disjointed images like the glass fragments in a kaleiloscope jostling around his brain, but refusing to settle and form a stable pattern. He propped himself up on the pillows and lay listening to the rain while the projector of his memory reran the film of the previous night.

"Curiouser and curiouser," had been de Salis' first reaction to Philip's story.

"No wonder you took them for a couple of hoodlums who'd got to hear about the diamonds and decided to muscle in on the act."

"I suppose it is the diamonds they're after," Philip

interrupted. "No one actually mentioned the word as such. I mean, if as you say they're CIA . . ."

"And they are, Philip, believe you me."

"Well then, couldn't it be something to do with Thami's plotting against the regime? Information like a list of the people they can count on, or a timetable of the King's movements on a certain day, or the plan of some building they intend to blow up."

" 'Could be,' " de Salis admitted. "Like God, the CIA moves in very mysterious ways."

"But surely," Philip objected, "you can find out what they're up to. Damn it all, they're our allies, aren't they? Ring up whoever's in charge here in London and ask what the hell's going on. Just who do they think they are, rushing around with guns, kidnapping people? Tell him that you at D. I. 6 or whatever it's called have got it all under control and will they kindly bugger off and stop queering your pitch. Hell, how would they like it if you carried on like this in Washington or New York? They'd bung you in jail so fast your feet wouldn't touch the ground."

"Point taken. But you try ringing up the Embassy and asking for the head of station. Of course I can arrange it, but not at this moment. I'll have to go through the proper channels. And then it's odds-on we'll get the same old treatment. 'Neither confirm nor deny,' that's the motto of the CIA. What's more, Papich—the late unlamented Morollo's boss and the one who took Jackie away with him—is a fully accredited diplomat: Cultural Attaché in Rabat. And if chauffeurs of emergent African countries can get out of paying thousands of pounds of parking tickets by pleading diplomatic immunity, just figure out for yourself how strong his official position is. And then," he nodded toward the sitting room door, "figure out your own position. Whatever the circumstances, Philip, he's dead. And you killed him. I know of half a dozen countries who'd be delighted to pin a medal on you for what you've done tonight. Unfortunately, the United States of America doesn't happen to be one of them."

Philip refilled their glasses, then ripped the cellophane from yet another pack of Gitanes, his third that day.

De Salis sipped slowly at his drink, swirling the ice around and frowning at the wall while Philip flexed the bruised edges of his hands and picked at the dried blood beneath his nails.

"But that's tomorrow," de Salis broke the silence. "And our immediate problem is back there in your darkroom. So we'd better get moving before he gets too stiff to handle."

"Moving? Moving where?"

"Wake up, Philip. Don't tell me you're going to have him stuffed and put him in a glass case over the mantelpiece. "We've got to get him out of here."

"But . . ." Philip was genuinely puzzled. "But can't you . . . can't your department for the want of a better word as I still don't know the name of the people you work for . . . Can't they handle this? I'd have thought they were used to this sort of situation. They, or the police, the Special Branch . . ."

"The police?" De Salis gave a short laugh. "You must be joking. You'd be helping them with their inquiries till the tea came out of your ears. Then there's the Press. Of course, one can slap a D-notice on them but the word still gets around. I personally haven't got the pull. To sort this one out, we'd have to get Webb-Walker out of bed, and, for all I know, the Prime Minister out of bed, too. And, just think of what I'd have to say to Webb-Walker: 'Awfully sorry to disturb, you, Sir, but I've got a slight problem. Quest's just killed a man in his flat. Morollo—you know, Sir, that chap who's with the CIA in Morocco.' And as to using my people, it's straight back to Webb-Walker again."

Philip held up his hand. "All right, Piers, all right. Your point taken, too."

"No, for the moment we've got to play this one

very close to the chest. Keep a very low profile, as our transatlantic friends would say."

"O.K., then. But where? The river? The foundations of some flyover on a motorway."

De Salis shook his head. "We're not the Kray Brothers. No, I've a friend who owes me a favor who's a past master at dealing with problems like this. I'll ring him now and tell him I'm on my way."

"I?" Philip asked. "Come off it, Piers. We're in this together. You're sticking your neck out for me and the least I can do is come along with you. Anyway, how are you going to fit him into the Morgan? Sitting in the passenger seat, with a face like that?"

"Fair enough. Thanks. And we can talk on the way."

Together they checked the dead man's belongings. His suit came from *Rex, Men's Apparel*, at the Beverly Hills Hotel and triggered off memories for Philip of whisky sours in the Polo Lounge and the bellboy who was a fifty-year-old dwarf. The pockets revealed nothing more than a crocodile Hermes wallet stuffed with one hundred dollar bills, a few dirhams, a Virginia driver's license, various credit cards, and a Polaroid of an Arab boy grinning into the camera with the biggest erection that Philip had ever seen; a ribbed gold Zippo lighter and a tin of Schimmelpenninck Duet cigarillos. On his wrist, on a gold bracelet, he wore an Omega watch whose black face showed not only the day of the week but also the phases of the moon.

"He certainly liked the trimmings," de Salis remarked. "The Golden Boy, his friends used to call him. One can see why. No, that's enough. He won't have a radio in a secret compartment in his heel. You can forget the Dick Tracy stuff. Why bring out your electronic gadgetry on a job like this? He won't be carrying any identification papers either." He replaced the wallet in the pocket of the jacket. "So let's get going."

72

"And what about this?" Philip picked up the Colt and hefted it in his palm. "God, it weighs a ton."

"Two and a half pounds, to be exact. I'll take care of it. Ugly brute, isn't it? Not the pleasantest of guns to have shoved in your face."

"No," Philip said. "It wasn't."

Now that the party was over, there was a free space in front of the house. Philip maneuvered the Volkswagen into it, then cut the engine and pushed the front seat forward. Leaving the door next to the pavement open, he rejoined de Salis in the unlit hall.

"All clear," he whispered.

Then, as if they were supporting a drunk, arms around his waist and gripping his wrists across their chests, they marched him to the car, the toes of his boots scraping on the glistening flagstones, and bundled him on to the back seat. While de Salis man-handled him into position, Philip ran back inside for the blanket, handed it to de Salis and climbed in be-hind the wheel. As the passenger door slammed shut and he reached for the ignition, he found that his hands were shaking and damp with sweat.

"Are you all right?" De Salis asked, his face pale green in the glow from the lamp twenty yards down the square.

"Reaction setting in, I suppose. No, I'll be O.K. once we get going. Which way?"

"Wandsworth Bridge, on to the Kingston bypass, and I'll direct you from there. And take it very calmly. No going through lights even on the amber. No speeding, nothing. This is just the time of night when the traffic cops are on the prowl, bored and looking for anything to break the monotony."

Except for a few occasional trucks, throwing up great sheets of spray, the roads were almost empty. The windshield wipers clacked and squeaked; the air-cooled engine hammered on relentlessly as they chased along the tunnel of their headlights. The car had developed a rattle and they had to raise their voices as they talked. From time to time Philip would

73

glance instinctively into the rear view mirror as if to reassure him that Morollo was not sitting up, listening to their conversation, but all that he could see was a fold of tartan blanket. Once off the A3, Chessington Zoo was no more than a cluster of bedraggled flags flapping in the wind, and the looming mass of Box Hill invisible against the sky. Past Dorking, they skirted Abinger Forest, then branched off to the right on the Bognor Regis road.

BUCKS GREEN 2, a signpost read. De Salis glanced out of the window. "Only about a mile now. There'll be a wall on the right and then the gates. That's it."

Philip changed down into third, braked, and brought the car to halt in front of a tall pair of wrought-iron ornamental gates, on which there was a sign painted in black and white: HYES EXPERIMENTAL GRASSLAND RESEARCH INSTITUTE. Pulling up his collar, de Salis got out and hurried across to a small lodge where a light burned in a downstairs window. Philip caught a glimpse of dark uniform and a peaked cap, then de Salis was back beside him and the gates were opening.

The asphalted drive curved up between sprawling clumps of rhododendrons and ended in front of a rambling Victorian mansion built of the same red brick as the lodge. Twin carriage lamps, converted to electricity, cast feeble pools of yellow light on either side of the porch. Leaving the blanket behind, they carried Morollo to the house and sat him down, propped against the wall, an oversize guy for whom November the fifth would never come.

"You wait in the car," de Salis said. "This is my pigeon."

Philip nodded and turned away. Tonight de Salis was breaking all the rules but still the principles of "need to know" held good. A distant bell jangled. The door open; a black silhouette appeared. The door closed again and Philip was left alone with the rain dripping from the laurels, idly speculating as to the true nature of the research that went on at Hyes, then

74

realizing that he would never be told and that he did not give a damn.

Fifty minutes later they were back in London and de Salis was squeezing himself in behind the wheel of his latest toy, one of the two current British production cars with a character of its own, a hand-built Morgan Plus 8, finished in British racing green.

"When this is all over," de Salis said, "I'll take some leave and race you down to Monte Carlo. First one into the bar at the Hotel de Paris and loser pays all—drinks, food, and rooms for a week."

"You're on." Philip patted the long, low louvered hood and straightened up. "And Piers . . . thanks."

De Salis' reply was lost in the boom of the exhausts. He raised a hand in salute and Philip watched his brakelights flash as he turned into the King's Road, then he let himself into the house and wearily climbed the stairs for a shower and bed.

At half past eight, now shaved and dressed, Philip took his fourth cup of coffee into the sitting room and rang the garage. Yes, Ian answered, the stereo bloke was already working on it and said it was a piece of cake. Philip said that he would see him later and his next call was to his cleaning lady, Mrs. T, telling her not to come in today. He was starting to sweep out the bathroom when the buzzer sounded. "Yes?" he said into the speaker.

"Mr. Quest?" a metallic voice answered. "We've come to see about your phone. Major de Salis said you'd been having a bit of bother."

"Come on up."

There was two of them, one middle-aged and wearing steel-rimmed glasses, the other young and bald with bushy ginger sideburns. Both wore dark blue overalls and carried heavy leather satchels.

"Morning, Sir," the older one said. "Not as nice as it has been. All right for the farmers though."

"Sorry?"

"The rain, Sir. Been praying for it, my brother-in-law told me."

"Yes," Philip replied. "Yes, of course." He showed them into the sitting room and asked them if they wanted some coffee. They refused; they had a busy day ahead of them. The younger one was already unscrewing the baseplate of the telephone while his colleague unstrapped his satchel, and Philip left them to their work.

He had finished the bathroom and was running the mop over the darkroom floor when the older man poked his head around the door and said, "Well, that's it then. All fixed. The most important thing to remember is for us to get a trace you've got to keep on the line for at least three minutes. At least three, but the longer the better. And don't worry about bug detectors. What we've used is the very latest model, an anti-anti-bug, you might call it. Well, cheers, Sir. We'll see ourselves out. Any problems, the Major knows where to find us."

The Major, Philip thought as the door slammed; it was strange to think of Piers in military terms. Even in Germany they had never talked shop; they both had kept their jobs to themselves, and their hours away from the Army were far too precious to be squandered in discussing the firepower of the Saladin Armored Car of possible Russian tank movements along the border. Yet Piers had stayed on. All the same, Major de Salis appeared totally out of context; it was like meeting a girl whom one had only known in a bikini on some Mediterranean beach, coming out of the Ritz in a full-length evening dress; it took time to adjust the two coincident images.

And so the waiting began. The goat was tethered to the stake, only now a second tiger was prowling through the undergrowth.

In the gray morning light all the plans, counterplans and contingency plans that he and de Salis had discussed over the past twenty-four hours seemed futile and pointless; it would need a computer to calculate the possible permutations, but no computer could predict the future and the correct course of action to

76

take. To keep his mind otherwise occupied, he settled down with *The Times* crossword, but soon threw it away in disgust, unable to solve more than five clues. He wandered into the darkroom with the vague idea of getting up to date in filing and cataloguing his negatives, but abandoned that after finding two sheets of contacts gummed together with Morollo's blood. Instead, he took the Walther from the safe, stripped it and reassembled it. Then, as he was shucking the cartridges from one of the three spare clips, the telephone rang.

His hand hovered over the receiver. The moment he lifted it, the radio link would be completed and somewhere in London the tapes would revolve and a man in headphones would start his trace.

He turned the bevel of his Rolex so that the arrow married with the minute hand, then picked up the receiver. "Oh," he said, "it's you."

"Don't sound so depressed." De Salis' voice was cheerful, almost jubilant. "We're beginning to get the breaks. Now listen carefully, as I'm rather pushed this morning. Yesterday afternoon a friend of Thami's spoke to him in Switzerland from Gibraltar and our people there happened to monitor the call. It was in Arabic but the translated transcript came in by Telex this morning. I've got it here." There was a rustle of papers being shuffled. "Here we are," de Salis continued. "Tania Berger's dead. She was picked up by the Moroccans the morning you left Marrakesh and died after five days of interrogation. According to Thami's friend's sources, she didn't talk but I'll come back to that later. The point is that your name came up as a possible courier. She'd mentioned you, an English photographer, to this friend of Thami's. But that's all he knew. Your name, but not the method. For all Thami knows she might've made some kind of deal with you. For example, 'Smuggle this out of Morocco for me and I'll pick it up in London and pay you X hundred pounds or whatever.' That kind of thing." He paused. "Of course, I got on to Rabat straightaway and they confirmed the story of her death. With one rider. The Moroccans didn't kill her, it was your visitor of last night—Papich. He took over the final stages of the interrogation, when she still hadn't broken, and shot her full of some experimental drug that he was trying out. Now Papich claims that she didn't talk; that's the official version he gave. But we know better. Anyway, the Moroccans blew their cool and were getting ready to throw him out when he and Morollo upped and took the evening plane to London. You with me so far?"

"Absolutely."

"To recap then. Thami knows, as of yesterday afternoon, that you've got the diamonds. And it might be an idea for you to approach him. But we can discuss that later. Let him sweat it out for a bit. No, at the moment it's Papich we're dealing with—and he has Jackie. So what I'm working on now is checking him out with his colleagues here. Has he contacted them? And if not, why not?"

"Meaning," Philip was thinking aloud, "that if he is in London officially, then Tania might've hidden something else in the car. And if it's a purely private visit it's the diamonds he's after."

"More or less. But at the same time, knowing what I do about him, if he can deal Chinese heroin in Laos as part of CIA policy and make a killing out of it for himself, he could well be hoping to bring off a left and a right in this affair. But, damn it, he's got to be living somewhere. Just as a matter of routine, I'm having all the hotels checked but I don't think we stand a chance in hell. No, it's when he contacts you and when he drives off in the Porsche that we'll start making some progress."

"It's been a busy morning for the bugger," Philip said.

De Salis laughed. "Yes, hasn't it? The Porsche's all fixed, I'm told. By the way you've got an answer ready for "*Whatever Happened to Baby Wayne?*"

"I think so."

78

"All right then."

"Don't call me, he'll call us."

It was unsettling, Philip reflected, as he opened the refrigerator and took out a can of Heineken, how easy it was to tap a telephone. Until yesterday he had always believed that it needed authorization signed by the Home Secretary, but when he had put it to de Salis, de Salis had laughed in his face. "Legally," he had admitted, "you might have a point. But the Home Secretary's got enough on his plate as it is without having to wade through piles of pink applications and weigh the legal pros and cons of each one individually. My God, if one had to wait for the Home Secretary's O.K. all the time, Kim Philby would probably have been head of the SIS today. And what about the industrial espionage boys: Honestly, Philip, you've got to grow up. And with present-day electronic technology . . ." It was after tea and they were playing a revenge game of croquet. De Salis pointed with his mallet to the elms across the river. " . . . I could have a parabolic microphone in that big tree there that would pick up every word we're saying and relay it back to London. And as for legality, let's face it, it's hardly the name of the game." Then, with a perfect stop-shot, he sent Philip's ball hurtling thirty yards across the lawn into a bed of petunias.

Only rarely did Philip eat a cooked breakfast, and he shuddered at the memory of Lord Ardale's plate piled high with kedgeree, sausages, and fried tomatoes. But today there was no knowing when he would next be able to sit down and eat a proper meal. The sky lightened and the rain had almost stopped by the time he finished his scrambled eggs and bacon. He drifted aimlessly around the flat, constantly looking at his watch whose hands seemed stationary. Maclean, his London agent, called to congratulate him on the Moroccan pictures and to ask him how he felt about a two-week assignment on an oil-rig in the North Sea. Philip said that he would think about it, but he doubted it; it sounded like too much hard work and what he needed was a holiday. Cutting a shocked Maclean off in full spate, no sooner had he replaced the receiver than the telephone rang again, and a friendly American voice was wishing him good morning and trusting that he had slept well.

Chapter VII.

Wilton's

Gray hair pulled back into a bun, breasts ballooning like spinnakers beneath the crisp white uniform, the waitress stood with her head to one side, pencil poised above the pad. Philip smiled at her apologetically; as so often at Wilton's he felt that he was back in the nursery and that if he did not eat a good, wholesome, balanced meal with plenty of cabbage, Nanny's lips would tighten and she would make him go without.

"I think I'll just have some smoked salmon and a green salad, please. I had rather a late breakfast," he explained, as much to her as to de Salis who was sitting opposite him in the alcove.

"Not that it really matters," de Salis said when she had gone. "The bill always comes to the same whatever one has."

"I know," Philip replied. "Astonomical." He sipped at his Bullshot and glanced around the room with its pictures of Edward VII and luxurious elegance of velvet and mahogany. "Still it's worth it once in a while and you can knock it off the croquet money." He

81

selected an olive. "Sorry about the call. And only twenty-five seconds to go, I made it."

"It doesn't matter. It was bound to have been from a phone box."

So his friend in Yorkshire had had a rough night, Papich had said, and wouldn't be able to make it much before three. Well, he'd just have to take a rain check. In the meantime, Jackie sent her love. Sweet kid, wasn't she? Too bad if she happened to walk into a glass door or accidentally set her hair on fire. Philip had asked if he could talk to her; Papich countered by making him speak to Wayne.

Philip was ready for him. "He went out about ten minutes ago." He could hear his heart beating as he geared himself for Papich's reaction.

"He did?" It was more of an exclamation than a question, but Philip could detect no trace of alarm or suspicion in his voice, only curiosity. "He say anything? Leave any message?"

"Something about why sit around here on his ass while you had the girl and were calling the shots. Asked me where Asprey's was and I told him. And for me to tell you he'd be in touch."

"And I'll be in touch with you." And he rang off.

There was a subdued, well-bred stir across the room as a Hollywood actress and her entourage were ushered to a table. As she peeled off her gloves, her fluttering gaze settled on Philip and she waved delightedly. He smiled, nodded, and raised his glass to her, then carefully chose another olive.

"You know her?" de Salis asked.

"Vaguely. I once photographed her. Bottle-blonde and deadly boring. I'll introduce you if you like, but she's only interested in dukes. It's marriage she's after, but if she was really pushed I suppose she might settle for an earl. And the best of luck to him."

"Yes. I see what you mean. And she's not really all that fantastic."

"Then for God's sake stop gaping at her like that, and think about Jackie instead."

"Yes," de Salis said. "Jackie." He studied his nails, then began to fiddle with his knife and fork, arranging them so that they were precisely parallel and pointing at Philip.

"So how are you making out with your friends and allies in Grosvenor Square?"

"Blood out of a stone. Banging one's head against a brick wall. Nowhere. After all this recent publicity they're as tight as a two-year-old's twat. 'No, Major' " he imitated an American accent. " 'At this moment in time we regret we have no current information as to the whereabouts of Mr. Papich. However, if you could obtain the correct security classification, hopefully we might be able to be of some assistance to you.' Hopefully! God, what a foul word. But I'll keep on trying."

"And what about last night?" Philip said slowly. "How much does he know?"

"For God's sake, Philip, I thought I'd explained all that last night."

De Salis sighed. "I told you I was sticking my neck out for you and this should prove it. Nothing, not a thing. That really would've sent him completely round the bend. You, of all people, messing around with the CIA, then knocking off one of their top spooks."

"I see. So we're on our own."

"Far from it. We go ahead as planned. Your car's ready to go—electronic homing device and bugged for sound just in case. The surveillance boys have already been briefed so that instead of picking up the next link in Thami's chain, we latch on to Papich and get Jackie back. And as for Papich, we'll decide what to do with him later. We can always hold him under the Terrorism Act. I'm bored with that bloody desk of mine and it's quite a time now since I've been out in the field. I'm looking forward to a bit of action. Then, when we've sorted friend Papich out, we go back to Thami and what this is all about."

"Bulldog Drummond rides again!"

He smiled at the memory of the books that he had first read by flashlight beneath the blankets in the dormitory at his private school. "Disguised as a typical dockyard worker, no doubt. Or a Black. Or the man who's come to see about the drains."

De Salis knew his Saper, too. "Or Lakington's chauffeur," he smiled. "At last, here come my whitebait. Thank God, I'm starving."

Lunch ended all too soon; they drank sparingly, only one bottle of the house wine between them, and they both refused brandy with their coffee. They parted on the corner of Jermyn Street, de Salis turning east, while Philip found a taxi outside Fortnum and Masons. It was twenty-five past two, and the sun was shining; a time to stroll up to Heywood Hill's bookshop, then wander back through the park, enjoying the scent of the grass after the rain and the girls in their cotton dresses. And here he was, in cab that smelled of wet rubber and stale tobacco, heading for God knew where, off into the unknown. Once again he felt the slight emptiness in his stomach as his nerves tightened; he had already drawn his chips and now all that remained was for the dealer to break out the cards and announce the game.

Sand from the pre-Sahara and yellow dust from the Plateau des Phosphates still lay thick on the dashboard and carpets, and the central console that held the stereo was smudged with fingerprints. There were mementoes of Morocco everywhere: the Michelin map, crumpled and stained; the dog-eared *Guide Bleu;* a packet of Casa-Sport containing three flattened cigarettes; a postcard of the Hotel du Sud in Zagora; a raw lump of amethyst that he had bought from a boy in the High Atlas. He leaned back in the contoured seat and drummed his fingers on the leather-rimmed wheel and flexed the calf muscles of his left leg. The homing device would already be transmitting a signal which, de Salis had told him, had a range of thirty miles and would allow two RDF cars to triangulate his exact position. And then there was the purely visual surveillance. As he drove northwards across Chelsea, he attempted to guess which car was tailing him. The blue Capri with the checkered rally-stripes and a doll dangling from the rear view mirror? The battered white florist's van? The unoccupied taxi with its light off and flag down? He soon gave up the fruitless speculation; it could be one, all, or none of them; and if they were as good as de Salis said, he would probably never know. They could be using perhaps half a dozen cars, passing him from one to another like a football.

Due to a truck that had broken down in Gilston Road, it was five minutes past four when he pulled into the curb outside St. Mary's Church in the Boltons. A man wearing a short black leather jacket and flared denims was slouching in the porch, half his face concealed by huge wrap-around dark glasses. He flicked the butt of his cigarette into a flower bed and strolled across the pavement. He made as if to open the driver's door, then realized that the car had a left-hand drive, and climbed into the passenger seat.

"You're late," he said accusingly. "A bloody spare prick at a wedding." He was in his early twenties and spoke with a self-consciously tough mid-Atlantic accent. Old acne scars pitted his skin and the fringe of blonde hair that curled over his collar could not quite hide an angry red boil on the back of his neck. "Great wheels, though," he said, glancing at the array of dials on the dashboard. "What'll she do?"

"Hundred and thirty, perhaps even forty, given the road."

"Yeah, well, not today you don't."

Philip pressed his foot down on the accelerator and listened to the familiar road as the six-cylinder engine unleashed its power and the tachometer needle sailed crazily into the red danger quadrant. He throttled back and said, "so where are we going?"

"The M40. And don't rap, just drive. I'll tell you when." He pointed a stubby finger at the stereo. "Let's have some sounds."

"What?" Philip said, affecting not to understand.

"Sounds, man, sounds. You know, music, tapes."

"It doesn't work." He rammed the gear level into first and drove off with an unnecessary screech of tires before the man beside him began to fiddle with the controls. He had no idea whether turning on the stereo would jam the signals that he was transmitting or not, and he could have kicked himself for not having asked. But it was a risk that he was not prepared to take; and today, however exaggerated his precautions might seem, he was leaving as little as possible to chance.

The road, now broadened and resurfaced, was essentially the old Western Avenue, the A40 to Oxford which had been the scene of one of the most terrifying drives of his life. As the passenger in a four and one half litre 1929 Red Label Bentley they had left Oxford at five o'clock in the morning and had covered the fifty-seven miles from Magdalen Bridge to Hyde Park Corner in thirty-nine minutes. Now, as always when he passed the neo-Egyptian façade of the Hoover factory, Philip offered up a silent prayer to Simon's ghost; Simon who had killed himself two weeks later, wrapping the Bentley around a tree outside Trumpington while trying to break the Cambridge to London record.

They drove in silence, Philip busy with his own thoughts and paying no attention to the man who was riding shotgun beside him. Now on the new Motorway, they had passed Beaconsfield and he was keeping at a steady eighty in the outside lane up the hill toward High Wycombe when he glanced up into the mirror and caught a flash of British racing green from a car some half a mile behind. Then the road curved to the left and the man beside him uncrossed his legs and said, "O.K., Fangio, this is where we leave the track. Marlow, then Henley." As he took the ramp, the green car swept by with a cheerful double blast of its horn; not de Salis but a tweed-capped young man in an Aston Martin DB5. Dropping down into the

Thames Valley, the road ran parallel to the river where girls in bikinis sunbathed on the decks of garish cabin cruisers and cows browsed in the water meadows. At Hambleden Lock Philip was told to slow down and take the next right. The narrow lane climbed steeply between high hedged banks, its metaled surface, potholed and the edges eroded, entered a wood of towering beeches, then ended at an open five-barred gate. Splashing through the puddles, the Porsche bumped along an unmade track. There was a smell of damp and decay and the bracken steamed in the sunlight that filtered through the spreading canopy of leaves.

The trees thinned and they came over a ridge to a large circular clearing in which stood a cottage. Once, Philip imagined, a keeper had lived there but now there was fresh whitewash on the walls and parts of the swayback roof had been retiled. Chintz curtains hung in the windows and hollyhocks and roses bloomed in the makings of a garden. The track continued on past the cottage and vanished into the trees again. There were no telephone wires. Parked in a dilapidated barn some fifty yards from the house, Philip could make out the trunk of a gray Mercedes with a CD sticker and a Q number plate partly obscured by mud.

"This it?" he asked.

The man in the leather jacket grunted.

Philip stopped the car by the gate in the white picket fence and watched him walk up the brick path. Then he too got out and stood scanning the surrounding woods. The clearing was perhaps a quarter of a mile in diameter, undulating toward the west where the track disappeared, brambles and the stumps of felled trees offering plenty of cover and dead ground. It was very quiet and he could hear no sound of traffic. He glimpsed the flick of a rabbit's tail as it dove into a bank, then a wood pigeon flapped through the branches and sailed up into the cloudless sky. He bent down casually as if to scratch his leg, and adjusted the zip on the inside of his left boot. A turquoise-bodied dragonfly hovered near the car door and he remembered his conversation with Ian in the pub; half an hour at the very least. It was now ten minutes since they had left the main road and he pictured de Salis in rusty corduroys with a shotgun under his arm, or wearing a straw hat and waving a butterfly net, then suppressed his smile as he heard footsteps and turned to meet Papich who was coming down the path toward him. He wore the same loosely cut tweed jacket as the night before and Philip, knowing where to look, could discern the faint bulge that was the Colt Python in its holster under his left arm.

Philip spread his hands and shrugged. "So here I am. One Porsche, mine, as promised. You said half an hour and for half an hour it's all yours. What you're after, I don't know, and I don't want to know. But first . . ."

"The room at the right at the top of the stairs." He looked Philip up and down.

"Makes quite a change doing business with a fellow who keeps his word. Pity we didn't meet sooner." He clapped Philip on the shoulder and treated him to a close-up of smoothly tanned skin and a porcelain smile, the life and soul of the Country Club regretting that it was time to be getting back to the office.

Standing there in the sunlit Buckinghamshire countryside, it was hard to believe that this open-faced, soft-voiced, middle-aged American had once ordered the burning alive of a hundred women and children in a village on the banks of the Mekong River; and then, when the headman had still refused to talk, had lopped off the limbs of his six-month-old daughter, one by one, before his eyes.

"So go on up," Papich was saying. "Take yourself a drink. Maybe I'll join you if I've got the time." He squeezed into the car and started the engine. "Another thing I like about you, son, you don't ask no questions and you do like you're told. Keep your nose clean and you'll die an old, old man."

He drove across the grass and into the barn while Philip pushed open the front door and stepped down into the sitting room. The overstuffed furniture was covered with the same chintz as the curtains; the carpet was green Wilton and the walls hung with horse brasses and hunting prints. The ceiling was low and beamed, and a pair of china dogs stood on the mantelpiece above the wide fireplace in which a fan-shaped spray of pink and white gladioli had been arranged. In an alcove was a tray of bottles and glasses, the plastic ice-bucket disguised as a pineapple.

The young man in the leather jacket was watching a cartoon on television and glanced up incuriously as Philip entered, then redirected his attention to the screen. Taking Papich at his word and although it was really still too early, Philip half filled a tumbler with neat whisky and climbed the narrow creaking stairs. Ahead of him was a bathroom and a door on his right was unlocked. He paused for a moment in the doorway, then drew back the curtains and flooded the room with the golden afternoon sun.

Jackie lay on her back on the old-fashioned brass bed, one arm folded across her forehead as if she were warding off a blow. She was snoring lightly and a dribble of saliva glistened at the corner of her open mouth as if a snail had crawled out of it and down her chin. Her hair was tousled, her lipstick smudged; her thigh was mottled by an angry bruise. The scrap of black lace that Philip had last seen protruding from her mouth now dangled limply from one outflung ankle.

Philip swore softly, then set to work.

He dropped the damp towel on the floor and held the tumbler to her lips, her head resting against his chest. Her eyelashes fluttered, then she retched and coughed.

"It's all right," Philip soothed her. "Everything's under control and it'll all be over very soon." He lifted his wrist and frowned; de Salis was certainly taking his time. He twisted around and peered out of the narrow leaded window. A cock pheasant strutted across the track by which they had arrived, supremely unconcerned. Then, as he heard the faint but unmistakable clatter of a helicopter, his heart lifted. A few seconds later it came into view, a Wessex painted the scarlet of the Queen's Flight, angling down on a course toward the Thames and Windsor Castle.

"Philip," Jackie murmured weakly. Her eyes were clouded and bloodshot, the pupils distended. She blinked and stretched out an unsteady hand. "What happened? Where've you been? You said you'd only be a minute and I thought you were never coming. I'm cold. Make me warm."

Philip bit his lip and fed her more whisky, the glass clicking against her teeth.

Suddenly she sat up straight and stared wildly around her, her nails digging into Philip's knee. "Where am I?" she gasped. "This isn't the flat . . . Philip. For God's sake, am I going mad?"

"It's all right, darling," he said, continuing to stroke her hair. "It was just a bad dream."

She broke away from his arms. "But it wasn't a dream! Those men last night . . . in the flat. Where am I? How did I get here?"

Philip saw that she was starting to panic and was near hysteria and he slapped her hard across the face, twice. Then he held her tightly by the shoulders, forcing her to look at him, and spoke to her, his voice low and urgent. "Now listen, Jackie. Yes, those men last night. They brought you here. They wanted something I'd got and were using you as a hostage, a lever, an insurance policy so that I'd play ball with them. But not to worry. Everything's been fixed now and any minute Piers'll be here and . . ."

Her shoulders heaved and Philip grabbed the towel just in time. The smell of whisky was very strong and as he wiped the traces of green bile from her lips he realized that it was probably the last thing in the world that he should have given her, alcohol on top of barbiturates or whatever drug they had pumped into her. A clammy sweat had broken out on her forehead and, except for the red blotches where he had slapped her, her skin was as white as a fish's belly. Her breath wheezed in her throat and he laid her gently back on the pillow, cursing himself for his crass stupidity.

Philip took a last quick glance through the window, then crossed the landing into the bathroom which faced north. Again he swore. It was now ten minutes since he had entered the cottage, time enough to move a regiment into position, let alone a dozen men. The shadows were lengthening and a few puffy white clouds had appeared high above the beech woods which were as serene and silent as before. Downstairs, some woman on the television was explaining how to make a rag doll and it was then that the nagging doubts at the back of his mind finally crystallized.

Hoping against hope, he would give de Salis one minute more, but he knew with a certainty for which he could not logically account that he would not come. Betrayal was a strong word, but de Salis had betrayed him. He had taken advantage of their friendship to manipulate him like a puppet to play some devious game of his own, and then had coldly and callously cut the strings. Philip's world had been turned upside down. Was anything what it seemed, what he had been told? How did he know that Papich was CIA? That Webb-Walker still craved his pound of flesh for his wife's infidelity almost twenty years ago? That Morollo's corpse was rotting in a silo? That . . . ? Only because de Salis had told him so.

Numbed by the shock of de Salis' treachery, Philip sat on the rim of the bath and watched the seconds tick away. In fifteen minutes Papich would come back to the cottage empty-handed. CIA or not, it made no difference; Papich was out for himself, out for the diamonds. Now he, Philip, understood their myth, had seen the thirteen carat center stone of Corviglia's pendant flashing the purest blue-white fire and lighting up a room, and knew how it felt to hold a fortune cradled in his hand.

The minute had passed. Philip pulled his trouser leg up to the knee, unzipped his boot and took the Walther from its makeshift holster. It was fully loaded, with a round already in the chamber. He thumbed the safety catch forward so that it was ready to fire double action with a single pull through on the trigger. Then, his right hand behind his back, he walked casually down the creaking stairs.

The television was now silent, the screen blank. The man in the leather jacket had removed his dark glasses and was sitting in the same armchair, idly leafing through the pages of *Country Life*, his face was vacuous as the television screen. He looked up as Philip ducked under the beam. The pale eyes blinked; the Adam's apple bobbed; the magazine fluttered to the floor. His mouth worked and when at last he found his voice the mid-Atlantic accent had gone and fear gave an added edge to his native South London whine.

"Now wait a minute, mate," he gulped, pushing himself deeper into the chair. "He didn't tell me nothing about shooters. No way, not for a lousy fifty quid, I mean . . ." He held up a trembling hand as Philip advanced into the room, eyes flicking from the blue-black steel of the automatic's stumpy barrel to Philip's face and back again.

Philip moved a yard to the left so that he could see past to the barn and nodded in its direction. "Who didn't tell you nothing about shooters? Him?"

"The Yank? I never seen him before in my life. Scout's honor, squire."

"Then what the hell are you playing at?" And then Philip had a flash of inspiration. "Brand, Inspector Brand, Special Branch. Associating with known terrorists for purposes contrary to the security of Her Majesty's Government. Terrorism Act of 1975. Sections Nine and Ten," he added for good measure. "So come on, out with it and maybe we'll go easy on you.

Hurry it up, man," he snapped. "I haven't got all day to waste on cut-price yobboes like you.

"Oh Christ," he muttered. "Sod this for a bleeding lark. Well, it's like this, see. Round half-twelve a bloke I don't know as such—friend of a friend more like—gets me on the blower and says how about fifty quid for a nice quiet drive in the country. Money for old rope, he says."

Philip heard him out in silence, a small-time hoodlum on the fringes of London's underworld who had been hired by Papich through a third, or perhaps even fourth, party for the seemingly painless job of show him the way to the cottage. "All right," he said, cutting him off in mid-sentence with a wave of the gun. That's enough. On your feet and over to the fireplace. Turn round and hands on the mantelpiece."

"I'm clean, squire. I told you. I don't hold with shooters."

"Move!"

Reluctantly he came out of the chair and sidled across the room, shoulders sagging, then slowly turned and grasped the mantelpiece.

Philip, knowing the dangers of using an automatic as a cosh, transferred the Walther to his left hand and walked over to the drink tray. He chose a bottle of a bottle of José Cuervo that was almost empty and picked it up by the neck.

"Now listen, squire . . ."

"Some other time," Philip said, and hit him behind the ear. The bottle shattered and he slumped to his knees and pitched headfirst into the gladioli. Wrinkling his nose at the pungent aroma of tequila, Philip took hold of him by the collar and dragged him out of the fireplace and felt, not without a tremor of misgiving, for his pulse. Reassured, after a quick look around the room, he went through into the kitchen. The bolts squealed alarmingly as he drew them back and eased the door open. Squinting into the sun, he estimated that it was some two hundred yards to the shelter of the nearest trees. For a brief moment he hesitated, then a sudden metallic clang of hammering from the invisible barn decided him. This was neither the time nor place for a confrontation with Papich; it would be pushing his luck too far; and one bullet from that Magnum could cripple him for life.

He tried to remember the geography of this corner of Buckinghamshire, a forgotten pocket of woods and hidden valleys. South was the river, perhaps two, three miles away; to the north he would be climbing deeper into the Chilterns. So either east or west and sooner or later he would come across a house with a telephone or one of the minor roads that followed the contours where he could stop a car.

He had never before realized how much Jackie weighed. He had hoisted her over his shoulder in a fireman's lift, his arm clamping her legs to his chest, her dangling head bumping against his back. He paused in the doorway and wiped the sweat from his face with his sleeve. He had already plotted a course toward a tall beech that had been struck by lightning which would keep the cottage between him and the barn. Less than ten minutes now. Giving de Salis one final chance, he paused for a few seconds more, then tightened his grip on Jackie's thighs and started to run.

Chapter VIII.

One-Eyed in Gaza

"Room Service? This is Philip Quest in the small Penthouse. Could you please send me up a bottle of Scotch . . . Yes, Teacher's is fine . . . glasses, ice and soda. And also a couple of toasted bacon and tomato sandwiches, the bacon well done, almost burned. O. K. ? Thank you."

He stepped out onto the narrow terrace and rested his elbows on the grimy stone parapet. The rush hour was over and the street that was used as a short cut between the Old Brompton and the Fulham Roads was now quiet, and the top windows of the houses opposite blazed orange in the setting sun. He watched a woman in a blue dressing gown dry her hair and remembered the last time that he had stood here; a year ago when he had stayed in the same suite for a fortnight while his flat was being redecorated. But then he was enjoying the last days of a stormy affair with the wife of a Peruvian diplomat and the idea that one day, in London, there would be a contract out in his name had never entered his mind.

At first he had refused to believe it. "Come off it,

Charlie. This isn't Chicago in the twenties, or Las Vegas . . ."

"You want to bet? Remember Kenneth Lennon, Easter '74? Dumped from a car in a ditch in Surrey, two in the head, one in the neck. You're hot, Philip," the jeweler had said, "so hot you should be calling the fire brigade to come and hose you down. If I were you, I'd take a trip up the Amazon for the next year or two. Or go up to a copper and kick him in the balls. Get yourself nicked. The grub's not that bad at the Scrubs either."

Philip had listened until he had run out of change, one hand over his ear to block out the shouts and laughter from a group of hearty beer-swilling oarsmen in the Saloon Bar. That had been the second call which he had made from the airless cabin beneath the stairs of the riverside pub in Henley. The first, once again hoping give de Salis the benefit of the doubt, had been to his answering service. A Mr. T. had rung at 5:17, then twice again in the next hour; it was extremely urgent and would he call him back as soon as possible. And that had been all.

Philip pushed his way through the swinging door into the lavatory. He ran a basinful of cold water, took off his dark glasses, and stared at his reflection in the fly-specked mirror. His face was streaked with mud and sweat and there was a dark zigzag of dried blood where a trailing bramble had whipped across his cheek when he had tripped over a root and fallen into a deep gully overgrown. Still, the fall had jolted Jackie back into consciousness. She was still very weak but he had forced her to her feet before the muscles in his back began to stiffen and had dragged her with him through the waist-high bracken until they struck a path that snaked downhill beneath the trees. Several times he stopped to listen; but all that he could hear was the lilting trill of an unseen blackbird calling to its mate. Fifteen minutes later he was sitting in the passenger seat of a Morris Minor as it rattled down toward Henley, explaining to the elderly tweed-suited woman who was hunched over the wheel that it must have been something that his fiancee had eaten for lunch.

He combed his hair with his fingers, then rapped on the thin partition wall.

"Jackie? Are you all right?"

"Better now, much better."

"I'll be in the bar. I'll get the landlord to call us a taxi."

The hearties fell silent as Jackie entered the room. "Looking for me, darling?" one said, while another gave a low whistle of approval. She tossed back her hair and joined Philip at a corner table, their eyes swiveling after her. Their heads bunched together and there was a muttered whispering followed by a great bust of raucous laughter.

"You see," Philip said, "you look magnificent. Even though you've literally been dragged through a hedge backward. Silvana Mangano in *Bitter Rice*."

Her bewildered eyes shaded an even darker blue. "Philip darling, I just don't understand. I mean, what . . . ?"

Philip put a finger to her lips. "Later," he promised. "Not here."

The glass partition closed the driver's head and shoulders a black cardboard silhouette, they were nearing London Airport when Philip finished his story, glad at last to have unburdened himself to someone whom he knew he could trust. He pointed to a TWA 747 lumbering into the air. "With any sense that's where we should be. Off into the blue unknown with a quarter of a million pounds' worth of diamonds in our pockets. Instead of that, here we are in Hounslow or somewhere, with a price of twenty-five thousand on my head. I suppose I should be flattered. But let's face it, I'm just the means to the end."

"But, Philip, these things just don't happen."

"They do. And they are."

"Couldn't your friend, well, have made a mistake?"

"Never, Charlie's never in his life tipped me a loser.

And he knows, Jackie. Believe me, he knows. He knew about Ronald Biggs all the time the police all over the world were chasing around in circles looking for him. And I'll give you odds he probably knows where the rest of the loot from the Great Train Robbery is stashed. No, what Charlie says is strictly kosher." He lit a cigarette and watched the smoke being sucked out of the open window. "So you see the fix one's in. On the one hand, Papich and his gang—now happily minus one—of spooks. On the other, Thami Fouquet and whoever thinks he's good enough to pick up the contract and deliver as per specification. And all the time, lurking in the background, those so-called guardians of the peace, my ex-housemaster, Piers de Salis, and Christ alone knows what they're up to."

"And to think I always thought Piers was a merchant banker."

"And to think I always thought he was a friend," Philip added sourly. "But no doubt time will tell."

"But surely you can go to the police?"

"I thought I'd explained all that. With Morollo's murder—O.K., it was self-defense, but I'd have to prove that in court—on my hands?" He smiled cynically. "Not to mention impersonating a police officer, GBH and God knows what else, though somehow I don't think that cut-price cowboy's going to lay any complaints. Look, Jackie, perhaps I'm getting paranoid but apart from you and Charlie I'm trusting no one. Absolutely no one. Only two people in this whole world know where those diamonds are. Why I didn't tell Piers, I'm not quite sure, but in retrospect I was dead right. And I'm not telling you because what you don't know, you can't tell. What's happened once could happen again. That's why both you and I have got to go to ground and lie low. Now it's not only Papich, and it's common knowledge to anyone who reads Hickey or Dempster that you're what's known as my 'constant companion.' Lie low," he repeated, "and plan the next move. At the moment I don't know if I'm coming or going. But first of all we've got to be practical. Look at us. You doing your *Bitter Rice* bit and me looking like a survivor of the Guatemalan earthquake. All I've got on me is an automatic pistol, a lighter, keys, four cigarettes, and just enough cash to pay for this taxi. I'll have to go back to the flat. It's a risk, but it's a risk I'll have to take."

Philip slid back the partition and instructed the driver to go on past the house and wait on the corner of the King's Road. Before getting out, he surveyed the square through the rear window, but all seemed as calm as a thousand other summer evenings. The barrister who lived in Number 47 was washing his car; the Hesketh twins were bicycling along the pavement; Mrs. Whitworth was walking her Yorkshire terriers in the gardens.

Barry, the Australian architect, answered the door wrapped in a towel, water dripping from his blonde surfer's hair. He was sorry about the racket last night, but Philip knew how it was. Yes, he'd been in all bloody afternoon, working on some plans for a rich bitch's gazebo in Wiltshire. No, not a sound since Philip had left, his ceiling being in the state it was, he could swear to it.

Philip was in and out of his flat in less than ten minutes. He changed out of his torn and muddied clothes, dropped the canvas Vuitton hold-all on the bed and began to pack: dark green gabardine suit, clean levis, shirts, socks, a change of underwear, a black knitted silk tie, a pair of moccasins, a couple of sweaters, shaving tackle. Then he went into the darkroom and opened the safe. From it he took the three spare clips for the Walther and the 6 x 4 brown envelope and quickly checked its contents: passport, international Driving License, various Press passes and letters of accreditation, a thousand dollars in easily changable $20 bills, and a thousand Swiss francs in hundreds. Out of ingrained habit, he found himself considering which cameras to take. Why not? he thought; after all, he was a photo journalist and had taken a camera into tighter corners than this. He picked up his lucky battered black Nikon F with the 80-200 zoom lens and balanced it in his palm, rubbing his thumb over the scratched and dented prism housing, and relived that moment in the crowded Saigon street when the Soviet-made 122-millimetre shell hurled him twenty feet through the air to crash against the mud guard of a jeep. And while he was about it, why not the Leica as well which he could carry in a pocket?

Jackie's case, her handbag, his things, wallet, check book—standing in the hall he ticked them off on his fingers. But he was sure that there was something that he had forgotten. It came to him just as he was about to close and double-lock the door. Of course, the Volkswagen which he had been meaning to take back to Avis this evening. It was still parked in the square and the keys were on his desk.

He had to borrow a pound from Jackie for the driver's tip, then once again he was driving north across Chelsea and there was a weird sense of unreality as he retraced his route of three hours earlier.

"Blake's," he said in answer to Jackie's question. "In Roland Gardens. They know me there and they're used to anything. Actors and musicians mainly. The hamburgers are the best in London and they're past masters at dealing with prying journalists or jealous husbands. We'll be safe there and from now on I'm not letting you out of my sight until we somehow hammer this out and make some sense."

There was a discreet tapping on the door and Philip initialed the bill, then took the tray from the waiter and set it down on the low marble-topped table. It was a small but comfortable room, the walls painted cream, the curtains of thick tobacco-colored tweed, made cheerful by the cushions in bright pink and yellow. Still feeling the effects of the drug (she vaguely remembered the stab of a second injection at the cottage), Jackie had gone straight to bed on their arrival and was now sleeping peacefully. Philip gently closed the door, poured himself a stiff drink and bit into a sandwich.

After his second dark brown whisky, he lit a cigarette and pulled the telephone on to his lap. It was a direct line and first he dialed de Salis' office at the Ministry of Defense. A steady high-pitched whine echoed emptily in his ear. Perhaps he had misdialed; he tried again, but with the same result. Eventually he got through to the operator and was told that the number had been withdrawn from service.

The Egerton Terrace number rang thirteen times before the receiver was picked up. "Piers?" Philip said cautiously.

"Darling! What a surprise! How wonderful to hear your voice again. You don't know how much I've missed you. It seems like a million years. Where are you? In London?"

"Listen, my love," Philip whispered venomously, "and where the fuck were you this afternoon?"

"And how was California?" Then his voice faded and Philip could only just make out what he was saying. "Ex-girl-friend of mine, just back from the States. Haven't seen her in months."

"All right, so I'll do the talking. Is that O. K., or should I call back later?"

"Of course, darling, where were you staying? With the Dunnes?"

"For God's sake, stop hamming it up and lay off the darling bit. I want a straight answer, Piers. Are we both still on the same side?"

"But of course. I know. I'm sorry. I had hoped to come out to Los Angeles and see you, had my ticket booked and everything, but at the very last minute something came up and I had to call the whole thing off."

Philip's brain raced; planning how to phrase his question.

"But I thought you were running the show."

"Yes, I was."

"But not any longer?"

101

"Sadly not. And talking of that, guess who I saw today. An old flame of yours. Remember we were talking about him the day we had lunch at Wilton's when you were leaving for America? When you weren't very hungry and all you had was smoked salmon."

"I'm with you. Webb-Walker?"

"None other. He hasn't changed a bit."

"And he called the whole thing off?"

"Uh, I suppose you could put it that way."

"And is he there with you now?"

"Yes. Just the same as always, even more so."

"Look, Piers, I've got to see you. I managed to get Jackie back but Papich is still on the loose. And to add to that, someone who can only be Thami Fouquet has posted a reward of twenty-five thousand quid for me and the diamonds. The shit's really flying now and I can't think straight anymore. I've moved out of the flat and we're both here at Blake's, Room Twenty-five. So why don't you get the hell over right now?"

De Salis sighed. "Darling, I'm sorry, but tonight I can't. I'd love to see you again, but this evening's out of the question."

There was a brief pause during which Philip could hear the murmur of a man's voice in the background. "Tomorrow morning, then?"

"Absolutely. By the way, did you ever get my letter? As I didn't know your address in California I sent it to your flat, hoping somebody might forward it." And then, as Philip was about to speak, he went on, "Well, darling, I've got to rush. All things being equal, I'll see you in the morning. Good night and God bless."

The dial tone droned on. Philip blinked, unclenched his fingers and slowly replaced the receiver and wiped his damp palm on the coarse beige linen that covered the sofa. He ran and reran the tape of his memory, trying to recapture exactly what de Salis had said, probing after every nuance and shade of meaning. But what disturbed him most were the words, 'God bless.'

In spite of his cheerfulness, there had been an under-
tone of resignation, of stark finality. And then there
was, 'All things being equal.' He felt himself slowly
sinking into a morass and the black mud sucking at his
limbs and closing over his head. Angrily, he told himself to snap out of it and trotted out all the clichés: a
good night's rest; tomorrow is another day; nothing's
ever as hopeless as it seems. But his cigarette tasted
metallic, the whisky of cheap eau de cologne. Massaging the small of his back, he made one last call, to
his mini-cab firm in Earl's Court, then hauled his
aching body out of the sofa and prepared for bed.

Tired though he was, he wanted, he needed Jackie.
She lay on her side, facing away from him, and he slid
under the single sheet and pressed himself against the
silken fullness of her buttocks. He traced his fingers
down the inside of her outflung arm, then cupped her
breast and teased the nipple with his palm. She stirred
and Philip's hand crept down to her hip and he pulled
her closer, the cool skin contrasting with his own
burning body exciting him even more. He nuzzled the
downy hairs on the back of her neck and softly raked
his nails along her thigh. Her legs scissored apart; she
reached to help him, and then he was inside her, hands
locked across her pelvis as together they rolled over
and she clutched at a pillow and worked it down
beneath her arching hips. Philip rode her, cushioned
against the world, their legs entwined, her hair in his
mouth, nothing existing anymore except their two
bodies joined together until he could control himself
no longer.

But still he could not sleep. He lay staring at the invisible ceiling, feeling the soft rise and fall of Jackie's
breathing, and thought of marriage. Here he was, at
thirty-seven, still footloose and fancy free while most
of his contemporaries were on their second or even
third child. It was the trappings of marriage which
disillusioned him. He imagined himself married to
Jackie, deliberately playing the devil's advocate and
picturing the worst: little dinner parties for ten with

an egg dish to start, pheasant in the winter and salmon in the summer; invitations on the mantelpiece addressed to *Mr. Philip and the Hon. Mrs. Quest;* slippers by the fireside, and he had never owned a pair of slippers since he was at school; putting their son down for Eton the day after he was born and arguing about godparents; no more twenty-four-hour poker games and gambling more than he could afford—which was the only point of gambling; cutting down on foreign assignments and working in a studio in London, photographing instant mashed potatoes or parties for *The Tatler;* a cottage in the country on his father-in-law's estate and the frantic rush to get out of London on a Friday afternoon; the unvarying routine of the same woman in the same bed.

God, what a cynical bastard, he told himself; now for the true picture. Smiling into the darkness, he saw Jackie running along an immense bone-white beach to meet him, hand in hand with a little boy, his hair bleached by the sun, and his naked body the color of bronze. Camera slowly pulls back, holding the three embracing figures in the center of the frame; the music swells and a slow dissolve to the words THE END. And Philip fell asleep.

He was awakened by the jingling of bottles as a milk truck hummed along the street, and once again he made love with her, much as a matador will before he struts out into the ring, to seek the cathartic release of tension and to hone his senses to the keenest edge. Leaving Jackie dozing, her lips curled in a contented smile, he kissed her navel and went into the bathroom. A hot, then a cold shower, a new razor blade, and his face stinging with *Eau Sauvage,* he felt ready to beat the world. The sun was shining and it was going to be another beautiful day.

"Sleep well?" he asked as Jackie, wearing cream whipcord trousers and a scarlet silk shirt, joined him on the terrace and squeezed past the white wrought iron table to sit down opposite him.

"Yes and no."

"How do you mean?"

"Well, it's very odd but after all that sleep I can hardly walk."

"I wonder why."

"I wonder."

Philip caught her hand as she picked up the coffee pot. "I adore you," he said. "And if I had my way, I'd spend the rest of my life in bed with you. And not only in bed. In the woods, on the beach, in the snow, on a tiger skin . . ."

"In the sea?"

"Highly overrated. The water gets in all the wrong places, like in the bath. And you know something, I think I've been around in my time but I've never ever once made love in a car. How about that for a confession?"

"My poor darling, you don't know what you've missed."

"You have, I suppose."

"But only in a Rolls-Royce."

"What else?" He grinned at her and passed her the *Daily Mail* and the *Express* and settled back behind *The Times*, grateful that she had taken the hint. He tried to concentrate on the news but found that he had read the front page without taking in a single word. It should be any moment now; the first delivery was remarkably consistent, always between five and a quarter past nine. He turned to the crossword and glanced at the clues: 1 across, *Like Samson in Gaza*. He allowed himself a wry smile; *eyeless*, of course; but at least he was one up on Samson and still had all his hair.

The desk rang through a few minutes after half past nine. There was a gentlemen with a letter. Should she bring it up? If she wouldn't mind, Philip replied and went out to wait for her by the lift.

"What is it, Philip?" Jackie called from the terrace as he came back into the room, ripping the envelope open.

"A letter from Piers. I talked to him last night and

he told me he'd written to me at the flat and I had a mini-cab go around and collect it."

"But how did he get in?"

"You don't think the postman's going to go clumping up all those stairs, do you? He just dumps the lot through the letter box and they're put out on the hall table. I told them to tell the driver to lean on Barry's bell till he answered and to say he'd come for my mail. And I'd also told Barry that I might be away for a while."

He raised an eyebrow when he saw the length of the letter; nine pages of thin airmail paper covered with Piers' neat italic script. The printed heading, *Hôtel de Paris, Monte-Carlo*, had been crossed out and below it was written, *29 Egerton Terrace: 17:45*. The military training died hard, Philip thought, then sat down on the sofa and began to read.

Dear Philip,

I know how you must be feeling as you read this, probably loathing my guts for really landing you in the shit, but, believe me, it was none of my doing. I told you we were sailing in dark and dangerous waters, and that must be the understatement of the year, if not the century. From the very beginning I've suspected that this whole operation has stunk to high heaven, and it was proved this afternoon when I got back to the office.

I was immediately called in by immediate superior and told that as of now I was temporarily relieved of all duties. Just like that. No explanation and he didn't understand it either. I tried to argue, told him I was bang in the middle of an extremely delicate mission, running it myself and totally committed. He sympathized, but an order was an order and that was that. And as to who gave that order, it has to be none other than our old friend W-W.

It's strange and as you know I'm not usually superstitious, but these past few days I've had that same

106

gnawing sense or foreboding I had that winter in St. Moritz. And I was right that time. Remember?

Yes, Philip did remember. De Salis had been selected as the driver of the Great Britain I four-man bobsled team and they were in training for the '68 Olympics at Lake Placid. Philip, who had joined him for a working holiday, could see him now, toying with a glass of apple juice at the Chesa Veglia as he tried, by discussing it, to exorcise his totally irrational fear. Early the next morning he had taken a one-man bob and launched himself, as he had done a hundred times before, down the Cresta Run. Philip, camera already set and focused, was waiting for him at the bend called Battledore, his breath hanging in the sparkling air, stamping his feet in the crisp snow. He heard the roar of the runners, then de Salis hurtled into sight. Even as Philip realized that he was far too high, the bob careened further up the icy wall, then shot from the track at seventy miles an hour. All things considered, he was lucky to be alive; the bob landed on top of him and he had five broken ribs, a dislocated shoulder, and a greenstick fracture of his arm. And his first words when Philip visited him at the hospital were, "I told you so."

"Oh no!" He heard Jackie's sudden exclamation from the terrace. The metal chair scraped back and then she was standing over him, blocking out the sun, dumbly thrusting the folded newspaper into his hand.

"What is it? What's the matter?"

"There." She pointed a finger at a paragraph halfway down an inside page. "I don't believe it! There must be some mistake!"

Chapter IX.

Class and Looks

But there was no mistake, as a call to a friend who worked on the *Evening Standard* confirmed. The midday edition was carrying the same story, the bare facts padded out by biographical details and background color.

"I don't believe it either," Philip said. They were standing out on the terrace and he put an arm around her shoulders and drew her close, feeling her shiver in spite of the warmth of the sun. Up on the Old Brompton Road they heard the donkey bray of an ambulance and caught a glimpse of the flashing blue beacon and the blazing headlights as it weaved its way through the traffic. "That it happened, yes. But not the way they say. Never in a million years. Never," he repeated softly.

"And to think just two days ago . . ."

"I know. It's strange, but for a long time I was utterly convinced that I was going to die on a Thursday afternoon, at exactly four-thirty. For no reason at all; I just felt it. But after a while the feeling suddenly vanished." He snapped his fingers. "Just like that.

Now when I go, I want to go like John Garfield, in the saddle. Or Félix Faure."

"Who?" Jackie asked dully.

"The one who's got all those streets in France named after him." Philip could hear the sound of his own voice very clearly, talking merely for the sake of talking. "He was President just before the First World War and one evening he was found dead in his office with a naked girl who was said to be the best lay in Europe. He had her by the hair and they had to cut a hunk of it off to get her free. She eventually married an Englishman and became Lady Abinger. She only died about twenty years ago. In Brighton, of all places."

He fell silent, picturing the scene in Egerton Terrace with a dreadful clarity.

"No Jackie," he said at last. "It wasn't suicide. They killed him, murdered him."

"They?"

"The faceless ones, the ones he worked with who don't officially exist. The men in the pin-stripe suits with regimental ties, neat little wives and gardens in the suburbs, expense accounts, and pension schemes." He hammered his clenched fist on the parapet. "Held a pistol to his head and blew his brains out. Stuck the gun in his hand and there you are; an open and shut case of suicide. Then tip off the police—because if they don't it might be days before anyone discovers his body—who in their turn tip off the Press. The message reads loud and clear: *Watch it, Quest. This is what happens when you step out of line.* I can hear the coroner now: "While his balance of mind . . . and all that balls. But I know better. I know who was with him last night. And besides, I've got his letter. Some suicide note!" His mouth was full of saliva and he spat into the street five floors below. "But I'll get that bastard if it's the last thing I ever do. I swear it, Jackie, I swear it here and now."

"But, Philip . . ."

"But nothing. Maybe Webb-Walker didn't actually

110

pull the trigger. Knowing him, it would be more in character to have someone do it for him so that he could have him by the balls for the rest of the poor sod's life. It doesn't matter. Piers is dead and Webb-Walker killed him as sure as I'm standing here."

"But why? From what you've told me, Piers worked for him, and they both worked for the government."

"And who do you think Howard Hunt and the rest of the Watergate plumbers were working for? The Martians?" He realized that he was being unnecessarily harsh and softened his tone. "Sorry, darling, but this has hit me worse than anything in years. Be an angel and ring down for some beer. I haven't finished his letter yet. It's like reading a will and pray God I can somehow use what he's left me."

"*But now to business,*" de Salis had written, *though with any luck I'll be seeing you tomorrow, feeling like a complete idiot for letting my paranoiac fantasies get the better of me. But what follows are facts that I've kept in my head and now want to get down on paper.*

A. The go-between/cut-out used by whoever's providing Fouquet with his strike force and hardware has been identified as an English entrepreneur who styles himself Brigadier Talbot. (In fact it's a Congolese rank and he never rose above CSM in the Green Jackets.)

B. Talbot and his wife are the sole directors of a limited company registered under the name of Sunspray Holidays which trades from an office at 167 King's Road, in a building owned by Renton Property Associates. Renton, as you know, is the Ardale family name, although your prospective father-in-law is nothing more than a name on the writing paper, as practically 90% of RPA is owned by a holding company based in Vaduz. This company, Masap S.A., has the minimum two directors required by Lichtenstein

111

law; a local lawyer with one purely nominal share, and J.P.S. Webb-Walker.

C. The only assets of Sunspray Holidays Ltd. are a Land Rover, a converted MTB, and 2,500 acres of deer forest on the island of Moronsay, one of the Inner Hebrides, which they lease from RPA and where they've established a nudist (!) camp in the remains of what used to be a Commando training center during the war.

D. Try, as I did several times under different names, to book one of the Sunspray chalets and "let the heather-scented Zephyrs and the balmy warmth of the Gulf Stream bathe away your city cares" and you'll be told sorry but we're in the middle of extensive modernization and as yet can't give you a definite date for the reopening.

To me, this all adds up—that it's W-W up on Moronsay who's providing Fouquet with a strike force and hardware. In itself it proves nothing—except perhaps a violation of the Foreign Exchange Act—and you'd be laughed out of court, if you ever got that far. But what I like is the blatant simplicity of it all. Who better to provide highly trained private armies on the side than a top-ranking officer in the M of D? Quis custodiet ipsos custodes? If it ever comes to the crunch, he can claim the Official Secrets Act, that he's acting in the interests of HMG, that he's mounting a top-secret operation that's been sanctioned at Cabinet level. And who's to disprove it.

Philip uncrossed his legs and reached for the sweating glass of beer, then took his time lighting a cigarette and stared at his shoes, biting his lower lip as he recalled the jokes about nudists over the port on Saturday night at Rushworth.

Now as to your part in this, the letter continued. *So far none of Fouquet's lot have made a move to recover the diamonds. Why? Because they don't know where they are. And Papich isn't going to tell*

112

*them. And on the other hand, it's not W-W's respon-
sibility to collect from Fouquet, but for Fouquet to
deliver to him. It's also a safe bet that Fouquet doesn't
even know the name of the man he's dealing with. To
him he'll just be the Mister X who can rustle up a
revolution to order—for a price—and whom he contacts through a cut-out—if not a series of them. That's
the way the Arabs like it; the more tortuous the better. It makes them feel safer.*

Here there were two lines crossed out. Then: *W-
W's scretary has just rung and he's on his way round
to see me now. I'd better sign off and get this safely
into the mail. Sorry about this afternoon but I'm sure
you'll have managed.* The next handwriting had begun to sprawl and slope obliquely down the page. *'Re
you and W-W. You're officially in the clear. I've cate-
gorically denied—written report in triplicate, etc.—any
sinister connection between you and Tania B. A
casual pick-up and one-night stand. And as to today's
cock-up, everyone concerned was my own personal
section and I trust each of them to the grave and beyond. Talk to you and see you later.* Here again a
sentence had been obliterated by heavy strokes of the
black felt-tipped pen. *P.S. While I remember, here's
what I owe you for the other day. Take care. Piers.*

Carefully folding the letter and replacing it in the
envelope, Philip picked up the check. Drawn on
Coutts Bank in Park Lane, it was for £80. He looked
at it for a long time and thought of a watch on a dead
man's wrist, mindlessly ticking away the seconds that
no longer existed. Then he tore it into halves, into
quarters, into shreds, and dropped them in the ashtray.

He finally became aware that Jackie was in the
room with him, sitting in the armchair with her feet
curled under her, watching him. He spread his hands
and shrugged. "I think I need a proper drink. It's not
every day your best friend's killed. By the Russians or
whoever, O.K. But your own side . . ." He tossed her
the envelope. "Here, read it for yourself."

113

Although he had never been able to define exactly why, Philip had always felt that there was something unnatural in drinking whisky during the day; like an American naval officer with a moustache, or a French freight train without a caboose, it grated. However, for want of anything else, he poured himself a stiff Scotch and soda and carried it out on to the terrace. There, pacing up and down between the twin tubs of pink geraniums, he alternately drew on his cigarette and sipped his drink, remembering the good times they had spent together. But the past was over and done with; now was now and action was the only answer. In spite of himself, he wished that de Salis had got to the point sooner; reading the letter was like looking into a lighted room across the street, only to see the curtains being drawn when things got really interesting. And not a word about Papich. Still, he must make do with what he had, and always remember that de Salis had paid with his life.

His thoughts were going around in circles and he tipped the rest of his drink into the geraniums. Somewhere at the back of his mind there was a single typewritten sentence in the file on Thami Fouquet which de Salis had shown him on Sunday. The name of the house, Villa something-or-other, had completely escaped him, but the village was on the tip of his tongue. It started with a C, rather like an Italian painter. Canaletto? No, but the right idea. That other Venetian then, Carpaccio? Nearly, but not quite. Caravaggio . . . Yes, that was it! Carabbia."

Moronsay's beautiful in the early summer," Jackie said, looking up from the letter. "The sea's like sapphire, the wild roses are out and there's a mass of yellow irises along the burn. I used to spend practically all my holidays there when I was a child. Fishing, looking for shells, watching the seals basking on the rocks. Once there was a whole family of otters. It's now three years since I've been back. According to Dad, one winter the gales took the roof off the lodge and it'd cost far too much to repair it, having to bring everything in by sea. Then along came the nudists. There used to be a stag, a twelve-pointer, and because he was a Royal of course I called him Monarch. He must be dead by now. I hope so or they'd probably have used him for target practice with their foul machine guns."

Philip nodded and said nothing; let her dream about her childhood. He picked up the telephone and dialed 105. "Directory Enquiries, please. I'd like a number in Switzerland. It's a village near Lugano called Carabbia." He spelled it out. "And the name is Fouquet, Thami Fouquet." He crossed his fingers and touched the veneered side of the television cabinet. People might joke about the stodginess of the Swiss, but at least they were efficient. What other country in the world had the nerve to put sweep second-hands on their station clocks? And Thami Fouquet, according to the file, was a respected resident who paid his taxes.

"I'm sorry, Sir, but there's no one listed under that name."

"Wait a second, it might be under someone else." He rapped his fingers impatiently on the television. What the hell was the old tart's name? "Yes, I've got it, Osborne."

He fumbled in his pocket for a pen, then smiled and jotted the number down on a pack of Gitanes, saying it back to the operator to make sure that there was no mistake. "One can dial direct, right? 010 41 01, followed by the number. Thank you. Thank you very much indeed."

The note of triumph in his voice roused Jackie from her reverie. "What are you doing?" she asked.

"Calling the hounds off. I hope."

"But how?"

"Wait and see—like the pudding. God knows," he remarked as he began to dial, "I usually hate the bloody telephone, but one must admit it has its uses." He gave her the thumbs-up sign. "It's ringing now. Here we go!"

"Hello," he said into the receiver. "I'd like to speak

115

to Mr. Thami Fouquet. I'm calling from London and it's extremely important. *Comment?*" He repeated his request in French and added, "Tell him that it's to do with Philip Quest."

Moments later a new voice came on the line, a soft and gently modulated voice speaking the almost too-perfect English of a foreigner and making Philip think of TV commercials for chocolates or soap. "Have you found him then? Already?"

"Yes. I suppose you could put it that way."

"And er . . . the trinkets which he stole from me?"

"Yes, I've got those, too."

"And Quest?"

"Bright-eyed and bushy-tailed. Alive and kicking. As a matter of fact, you're talking to him right now. I'm Philip Quest and I want to make a deal with you."

"Do you indeed?" Thami Fouquet broke the short silence. "What kind of deal do you have in mind?"

"Cancel the contract you have out on me and you can have the diamonds. But at the same time, I'm claiming the finder's fee and I'd like it in Swiss francs. How about it?"

"I see. But how do I know you're speaking the truth?"

"The truth?" Philip thought for a second. "I took Tania Berger to bed with me in Marrakesh the night before I left for England, the night the diamonds must have been hidden in my car, and she'd shaved her pubic hair in the shape of a heart. I can describe the diamonds, too, if you like. It's a star-shaped pendant, probably Italian and late eighteenth century. All the diamonds are top quality blue-white, all brilliant-cut—i.e. fifty-eight facets—and mounted in 22-carat gold. The center alone weighs thirteen carats and at today's prices is worth something in the region of . . ."

"Thank you, but I am perfectly aware of the state of the diamond market."

Philip could detect more than a hint of suppressed excitement in the calm voice, and imagined the tip of the tongue licking the thick negroid lips. He pressed home his advantage. "I know about this contract because I have some good friends in London. You made it, you cancel it. I'll give you half an hour, then I'll start asking around. If everything's O.K,. I'll call you back and we can get down to business. That's all." And he rang off.

He turned to Jackie. "In the meantime, darling, tell me more about Moronsay."

Charlie straightened his tie and ran a hand over his unruly hair and looked at Jackie in frank appraisal. "Best of the bunch so far. You ought to have seen some of the previous ones he usel to run around with. Right King's Road scrubbers they were. Perhaps he's growing up at last. Class and looks. Very tasty, Philip, very tasty indeed."

Philip sighed. "When you've both finished with your mutual admiration bit . . ." "Lunch!" Charlie exclaimed. "How about the San Lorenzo down in Wimbledon? Day like this you can sit outside and pretend you're knocking back the old Soave in Capri or wherever."

"I'd love to, but we can't. And I'm going there anyway."

"Where? Capri and stay with Gracie Fields?"

"No, Milan, and the plane leaves at two-thirty."

"Just you alone?"

"Sadly, yes. And for Christ's sake stop thinking what you're thinking. Anyway, she's driving me to the airport."

"Who's she? The cat's mother?"

"No," Jackie said with a smile. "Cat Whittington and her Dick."

Charlie gaped at her. "You've got a right one here, Philip."

Then Jackie said that she needed some cigarettes. The door tinkled shut behind her and they were left alone in the cluttered shop in the quiet backwater off the Earl's Court Road.

117

"O.K.?" Philip asked.

"No trouble." He went through into the back room and returned with a soft suede wallet, the size of a tobacco pouch, and handed it to Philip. "I'll be sorry to see it go. Not just for the stones, but the craftsmanship. It's fantastic. I've never in my life seen anything that beautiful. Anyone who messes with it and breaks it up deserves to be shot."

"He probably will be anyway. One day."

"Philip, you sure you know what you're doing?" His eyes were troubled as he watched Philip stow the wallet away in the inside breast pocket of his suit.

"I think so. You said the heat was off and I believe you. So long as some cowboy who hasn't got the message doesn't try and jump me between here and the airport." He bent down and peered at a velvet tray of antique rings in the glass showcase that formed the top of the counter. "That one there," he said, pointing. "The sapphire and the diamonds. How much are you asking?"

"Three and a half, but for you, two-seventy. Lovely setting, Victorian."

"Done. I'll take it on approval."

"Does the gentleman want it wrapped?"

"No," Philip said. "I'll eat it here. By the way Charlie, look after this for me, will you?" He gave me the envelope containing de Salis' letter. "In its own way it's just as precious as the other stuff."

Jackie pushed open the door and Philip turned to Charlie and mouthed, "Not a word about the ring." He glanced at his watch. "We better get going. Christ, back on that bloody M4, I feel I've spent the last ten years of my life there."

"Take care," Charlie said, stepping out from behind the counter.

"You're the second person today who's told me that. Don't worry. I will. See you."

Charlie took Jackie's hand. "If you should feel the need for company while he's swanning round *la bella Italia* . . ."

Philip grabbed her arm and pulled her away. "Tough titty, old sport, but I'll be back tomorrow. So you can wipe that stupid leer right off your face." He grinned maliciously. "Love to Rosemary. His long-suffering wife," he explained to Jackie.

"Below the belt, Philip." He shook his head and clicked his tongue. "Below the belt!"

Inevitably, in the odd ten minutes that it stood in a Resident's Only parking area, the Volkswagen had collected a ticket. "*Jamais deux sans trois*," Philip said as he stuffed it into the glove compartment to join the two others that had been stuck behind the windshield wiper in the past twenty-four hours, one in Paulton's Square, the other outside the hotel. "Rather symbolic of this whole affair. As if Thami Fouquet and Papich weren't enough, we've now got Webb-Walker on our hands. Do you want to drive or shall I?"

"I like your friend Charlie," she said as she rammed the gear level into second and sent the car howling through on the inside of a loitering taxi. "Tell me more about him."

Philip flinched as it seemed impossible that they should not be crushed beneath the tailgate of a vast container truck, then they were speeding through a set of traffic lights on amber and the road ahead was clear. "Well," he began. "Charlie . . ."

A policeman idly glanced their way and started to saunter toward them as they sat parked on a double yellow line outside Terminal 1.

"All right, darling, off I go." He took the almost empty hold-all from the back seat and kissed her hard and long. Standing on the pavement, he leaned down and said, "Straight back to the hotel, and stay there. Just in case." Then, as he turned to go, "a present for you." He passed her the ring through the open window. "It's up to you to decide which finger to wear it on." He raised a hand to his lips, then walked away into the cool of the terminal.

He picked up his ticket at the desk, paid for it with

119

his American Express card, checked in, explained that all he had was hand luggage, and was about to go over to the red-blazered Avis girl, then decided to give Hertz a break for a change. Having made the arrangements, he bought the evening papers and went into the lavatory. Charlie had assured him that there was nothing illegal about it, and it could very well be that he was overestimating the danger; but the metal-detector might pose a problem if it sniffed out the pendant. Security men were no fools and he could envisage the dialogue.

"And what's this then, Sir?"

"Oh, a present for my girl friend."

"Diamonds are they? Mmm, very nice. Fred! Can you spare a minute? And if you wouldn't just mind stepping aside, Sir, and let the others pass."

Carrying both his bag and the two loosely folded newspapers in between whose pages he could feel the outline of the wallet, he presented his passport to a man with a high-domed forehead and a sandy moustache and tried to relax and not to think of Webb-Walker while he riffled through the pages, then handed it back to him with a casual nod. Philip unzipped his bag himself, held up his arms, was waved through, and made his way into the Departure Lounge and headed for the bar where he ordered sandwiches and half a bottle of champagne.

"British Airways announces the departure of flight BE 366 to Milan. Will all passengers please . . ."

The Trident was no more than three-quarters full and Philip had a seat to himself in the tail, conveniently close to the stewardesses. There were the usual tourists and businessmen with Samsonite briefcases open on their knees, but what caught Philip's attention was a group of a dozen or so elegantly dressed Italian woman, chattering away like starlings, all laden with shopping bags: Harrods, he noticed, running a bad second to Marks & Spencer, and one, to his astonishment, had even been to Gucci.

Unfastening his seat belt, he was, as always, fascinated by the number of lakes and reservoirs stretching away into the distance which only existed when they were seen from the air. They were steadily climbing and somewhere down there was his Porsche. From an envelope that he had found in a pigeon-hole in the desk, he knew the address and the name of the owner of the cottage. Probably the simplest thing would be to report it stolen on his return, and let the police get on with it. Unless of course . . . Unless nothing! If Webb-Walker or the Special Branch were cooking up some plot against him, they never would have allowed him to leave the country.

Drowsy with the bright sunlight and the champagne, he thanked the stewardess and shook his head. He tilted back his seat and pulled down the blind. Then, lulled by the steady roar of the three Rolls-Royce engines, Philip Quest slept across France and across the Alps, to awake as the Trident banked and began the descent to the heat-hazed plain of Lombardy.

Chapter X.

Swiss Miss?

At Linate they neither bothered to stamp his passport nor open his bag, now heavier by two bottles of whisky and a carton of Gitanes. In a matter of minutes after leaving the airport he turned off the Viale Forlanini and swung the dark blue Fiat 128 up to the elevated section of the *Tangenziale Est*, one of the two Autostradas that girdle Milan, keeping the city free from all through traffic. Philip thought of London and pressed the accelerator down to the floor. He was one of the few people that he knew who actually liked Milan, having once spent six weeks there doing an in-depth story for one of the color supplements. The Romans and the Florentines might shrug and sniff disparagingly, but there was no doubt that artistically, from the publishing houses of Mondadori and Feltrinelli to the sculpture of Gio Pomodoro, from *haute couture* to La Scala, Milan led the rest of Italy. And also there was the geographical convenience; Venice in a couple of hours, the Ligurian beaches an hour and a half, the Swiss border a mere twenty-five minutes; and Autostradas all the way.

By Italian time it was 5:55 when he passed through the final tollbooth but in Switzerland, as in London, it would be one hour earlier. His instructions were to go to the hotel where he would be contacted at seven o'clock. At this rate, he reflected, he was running well ahead of time, so he decided to stop off in Chiasso.

There was a long line of cars at the frontier, mostly with Milan or Como plates, and the *Finanza* were being very thorough, opening trunks, lifting up seats, checking roof linings, spare tires and tool kits. Feeling Corviglia's pendant against his heart, he could not help smiling at the irony of it all. How many millions of lire were said to be smuggled across this same border every day? Something astronomical; billions probably, especially after the latest crisis in Italy. He took out his passport and displayed it prominently on the sill above the dashboard. All the same, the gray-uniformed corporal gestured at him to get out of the car and open the boot before giving him a cursory *"Va bene"* and passing on to the car behind.

Leaving the Autostrada, Philip had a cup of coffee in the town where every other shop, if it was not selling Japanese televisions, transistor ralios, walkie-talkies and hi-fi equipment, seemed to be either a tobacconist or a grocer, all with signs in their windows announcing CAMBIO-CHANGE-GELDWECHSEL. He then went into a discount camera shop to see if Nikon or Leitz had come up with any new gadgets or lenses.

He took the old road to Mendrisio, then dropped down and skirted the eastern shore of the lake, crossing the causeway and arriving outside the Europa Grand Hotel au Lac a few minutes before the appointed time. Footsteps echoing on the marble floor of the high-ceilinged lobby, he approached the desk and said that he understood that a room had been booked for him; Quest was the name.

A young, black-suited under-manager appeared from the office and took over from the reception clerk. "Yes, Mister Quest. 501." He unhooked a key and said, "Your friend telephoned and said he was

124

sorry but owing to some unforeseen business he would not be able to join you till much later this evening and will ring you at ten o'lcock."

Philip nodded slowly. "Thank you."

They went up in the lift to a room on the fifth floor. Philip walked out on to the balcony and looked down. Then he abruptly moved away from the balustrade. "The only trouble is," he said to the under-manager who was standing beside him admiring the view, "I happen to suffer from vertigo. Now about one of those rooms down there on first floor. The one at the corner, for instance, by the pool?"

The under-manager clicked his tongue sympathetically; he had a cousin in Zermatt who suffered from the same complaint which was very sad because ever since he was a boy he had wanted to be a guide. But yes, he thought that one was free.

It was. Philip turned off the air-conditioning and slid back the French window. The broad terrace ran the length of the building, each room separated from its neighbor by a waist-high white lattice fence. It was no more than a twelve-foot jump down to the lawn dotted with tables and bright umbrellas, and from there over a low wall crowned with oleanders and into the graveled car park. The room itself was extremely modern with a small well-stocked refrigerator and all the switches were on a console beside the bed. By raising a venetian blind and swiveling the set around, one could watch television while lying in the bath. The color scheme was blue and white, and the same patterns were repeated in the windowless corridor. Having discovered the service stairs, he walked down and out through the back entrance, circled the building, and re-entered the hotel through the garden. A fat man in a track suit was waddling up and down the side of the pool where a boy was flailing the water with tired arms, urging him on in some incomprehensible dialect. In a corner of the bar there were two tables of middle-aged American women playing bridge.

Philip played with the loose change in his pocket, at a vague loss as how to kill the next three hours now that he had secured his base. The shadows of the mountains were creeping across the lake and the little electric motorboats and the pedalos were being padlocked for the night. A dinghy with a red-and-white striped sail went about and headed into the shore on the final tack. The stationery shop in the arcade below the hotel was about to close and he bought the Lugano sheet, #1353, of the large scale 1:25000 Swiss national survey. Sitting at a table outside, he drank a beer and studied the map, and wondered which of the tiny black squares on the ridge above Carabbia was Thami Fouquet's fortress. As he was paying the waitress, a large American car drew up to the curb and three Arabs, wearing white kaffiyehs, got out and climbed the steps into the hotel, holding up the skirts of their robes like women going to a ball.

They were Syrians, the friendly under-manager told him, who were with UNO in Geneva and who had come to Lugano for the gambling in the Italian enclave of Campione, where this year the play was very high indeed. Thoughtfully, Philip left the hotel again and walked across the car park; he was hungry and there was no harm in trying to kill two birds with one stone.

One of his favorite restaurants was the Borromeo in Ascona on Lake Maggiore, an easy drive over the pass of Monte Ceneri. After the summit, on a stretch where he could see half a mile in either direction, he pulled into the side of the road to admire the sunset on the peaks above Andermatt. No other car stopped, and at the foot of the pass the road forked, so that for anyone tailing him from the front it would be an unjustifiable fifty-fifty bet as to whether he would turn left for Locarno or head on up the St. Gotthard.

The Swiss eat early and people were already leaving the restaurant when he arrived. He was greeted like a long-lost friend by the proprietor, a Ticinese with flowing white hair who affected cowboy clothes and a sheriff's star pinned to his shirt, and was led to a table in the garden. Trout writhed in a tank and candle-lanterns hung from the palms and the acacias. The waiter scribbled down his order—the raw smoked beef followed by filets of the local Eglifisch—and brought him a liter of chilled white Fendant. Sipping the wine, Philip stretched out his legs and wondered exactly how the night would end.

"*In our mountain greenery, where God paints the scenery,*" Philip hummed as he stepped out of the elevator, unable to get the old Rodgers and Hart song out of his head.

"*Just two crazy people together . . .*" He paused outside the door of 108; an excellent omen, he thought; one and eight made nine and a natural nine at baccarat or chemin de fer was *Napoleon, Le Grand,* unbeatable. Still humming, he unlocked and opened the door. The room gave a sarcastic yawn and he realized that his nerves were tenser than he had imagined. He uncapped a bottle of Perrier water to wash away the heavy taste of pears from the liqueur which had been pressed upon him in Ascona. In the *Evening News* there was a blurred photograph of de Salis taken at some dance, and Philip was thinking about how they would never now race to Monte Carlo when, at precisely ten o'clock, he heard a light tapping on the door.

His hand hovered over the doorknob and he felt a pleasant thrill of anticipation. A tall Chandleresque silhouette with a black felt hat pulled down over his eyes and a .45 in his hand? He twisted the knob and drew back against the wall.

"*Buona sera, amore,*" she whispered throatily, her heavily mascaraed eyes slowly traveling down, then up, his body. "*Che bello che sei! A mi me piace molto un uomo . . .*" She smiled, showing strong white teeth stained with lipstick. ". . . *grande como te.*" She undulated past him, one scarlet-clawed hand brushing his fly, then stood in the center of the room and tossed

127

back her flaming Titian hair. She was wearing a white trench coat, tightly cinched, and black knee-length boots with six-inch heels. "*Bel appartamentito*," she said in her husky sing-song voice. "*Mi dai un whisky, amore?*"

Philip pulled himself together. "I think you've got the wrong room," he said in Italian. "I didn't order any girl."

"I know. Your friend sent me and later we're going to a party. But first we can have our own private party here. At the party there'll be all the other girls and I want you to myself."

"Yes," Philip said. "This . . . er . . . friend of mine. What . . . umm . . . ?"

"Oh yes, I've got a letter for you." She sat down on the bed and undid her bag. Delving into it, she produced a compact, a tube of K-Y, a packet of French letters, and finally an envelope. She smiled archly as she gave it to him and replaced everything except the French letters which she left on the bedside table.

The handwritten note was brief and to the point:

Please forgive this second unforgivable delay, but as you can appreciate raising the necessary finance at such short notice poses certain problems. The bearer, Maura, will bring you to me at eleven. In the meantime, use her as you will, as my guest. She is perfectly clean and I can personally recommend her talents. Her command of her sphincter muscle, for example, is nothing short of miraculous.

There was no signature.

"Yes," Philip said again. "You'd like a drink. So would I." As he was squatting on his heels and working the ice loose, he heard the soft rustle of cloth against naked skin and his heart fell. Making love with Jackie, far from sating his appetite, had only increased it; professional she might be, overscented and over-made-up, but she was splendidly desirable. Then there was the added attraction of the first time with a woman, especially one with a three-star recommendation. '*Vaut le voyage*', as Michelin would say. A foreigner, too. There was something infinitely erotic about making love in a foreign language: *Mi fai pazzire; Bald kommt's mir; N'arretes pas, mon amour.* His trousers were growing uncomfortably tight and he forced himself to think of cricket and who had won the Country Championship in 1956. But that was no good; the only image that came to mind was Laura Webb-Walker in the Royal Tennis court at Lord's.

"My love, what are you doing?"

"Getting some ice." Then, in English, "And wondering how the hell I'm going to stop myself fucking you."

"Fuckie-fuckie? *Si, capisco.* You fuck my pussy and Maura make you go bingo like Gigi Riva."

Philip straightened up and turned around. "Bingo like Gigi Riva?" The moment had passed and he found it impossible not to laugh.

"Gigi Riva famous footballer," she pouted.

"Yes, I know. But why bingo like Gigi Riva."

"He kick ball and BOOM! Thousand kilometers an hour. Maura make you go bingo like that. In pussy, in other place, in mouth—anywhere."

"Some other time," Philip said. He put her glass beside the French letters and stood looking down at her, examining her clinically, all desire evaporated. It was as if she had stepped out of a back page advertisement in a girlie magazine. Heart-shaped holes in the transparent black nylon of her brassiere that was trimmed with red ribbon revealed the rouged nipples of her heavy breasts; she wore a matching suspender-belt and black seamed stockings, and there was no crotch to the flimsy brief in the same material that completed an underwear fetishist's dream of Paradise. With one hand he began to caress her nipples, the other burrowing slyly in between her thighs. Holding Philip's gaze, she formed her mouth into an O and slowly ran a lascivious tongue around her lips.

Philip prodded a finger into her stomach. "I'd go easy on the pasta if I was you," he remarked in Italian. "In a couple of years," he spread out his hands, "pouf, like a balloon."

Her legs snapped together and she jerked upright, anger flashing from her eyes. "Queer, are you? she demanded. And, when Philip made no reply, "I thought so the moment I walked in here. You don't have to pretend with me." She rolled over on to her stomach and thrust her buttocks in the air. "Prefer that, do you?" she mocked him. "Then close your other eye and pretend that I'm a boy. Or perhaps you like the boys doing it to you!"

"Only on Sundays," Philip replied and chose his spot. His palm slapped across her flesh, the force of the blow sending her sprawling headlong from the bed. He went over to the refrigerator to fetch his drink. He raised his glass to her. "Bingo!" he said. "And here's to Gigi Riva."

She was lying supine, her booted legs supported by the edge of the bed, her hair fanned out across the carpet. "Yes," she murmured. "Beat me. Whip me. Anything you like, my love."

"Oh, for Christ's sake! Listen, Maura, I know you've got your professional pride and I think you're very attractive, very sexy, very . . ."

"Very Sophia Loren?"

"Exactly. You took the words right out of my mouth. But unfortunately, I'm feeling rather tired. It's been a long day for me and it isn't finished yet."

He was speaking to her like a child. "And this party you're taking me to isn't all going to be fun and games. I'm here on business and tonight's the only chance I have of seeing your friend, Signor Fouquet."

"Who?" She was sitting up now, adjusting her suspenders.

"Our mutual friend, the Arab gentleman who sent you here."

"Oh, Signor Thami. Are you in the same business as him?"

"Well yes. And what's so funny about that?" he asked as she started to giggle.

"I don't know, but it always makes me laugh. Call it fertilizer or any other grand name you like, but where I come from in Avegno up in the Valle Maggia, shit is shit."

Philip choked on his drink. "One's got to make a living somehow," he said vaguely. "We can't all be film stars."

"I was in a film once," she said with pride.

"I bet. Now why don't you put your coat back on and tell me about this party? I've never been to an Arab party before. I hope there's not going to be any of that nonsense about no alcohol. And where's it being held? At his house in Carabbia?"

"Oh, no! His mother wouldn't approve. She's very strict with him." She shrugged into the trench coat and pulled the belt tight. She looked at her reflection in the uncurtained window. "I'm getting a new one in black leather. Why is it that you English like being whipped so much?"

"Hangover from school, I suppose. Though I personally don't go for it. So where are we going?"

"A friend's flat, here in Lugano, not very far away."

"And when should we leave?"

"We've plenty of time." She inspected her face in the mirror of her compact, pursing her lips and touching up her glitter-green eye-shadow.

Philip was very bad at guessing a woman's age, but she could not have been much more than twenty-five. Jackie's age. He considered ringing her at Blake's, but it would be tempting fate. He had come to Switzerland with a completely open mind, prepared for anything and content to let himself be carried along with the tide, playing it as it came. The lunatic, almost surrealistic, interlude with Maura had amused him and helped pass the time, but any moment now the cast would start assembling in the wings and the curtain would go up for the final act.

They sat together on the bed, drinking Philip's duty-free whisky, while she entertained him with stories of her apprenticeship as a twelve-year-old in a brothel in Zurich. The mythical whore with the heart of gold? Philip wondered. Like hell! And at least he had refrained from the ultimate in idiot questions: "What's a nice girl like you doing in a racket like this?."

She took hold of his wrist and turned it around so that she could see his watch. They ought to be leaving, she said. Philip stood up and collected his cigarettes and lighter. In the bathroom, he could not resist a last look at Corviglia's pendant. The center stone alone was worth more than £50,000 but that was not the point. He held it so that once more he could catch the pure white blaze in all its glory, then returned it to the wallet and clicked the clasp shut.

"Catch," Philip said before he switched out the lights, and tossed her the packet of French letters. "Cleanliness is next to Godliness, especially in your job. And with Arabs one never knows where they've been."

"*Cosa dice?*"

He realized that he had spoken in English. "It doesn't matter. *Andiamo*."

The under-manager's knowing smirk stayed with him as they drove along the lake, the red beacon crowning the black mass that was Monte Bre winking high above them. The town, if not already asleep, was preparing for bed; a group of young men were playing leapfrog on the pavement as they waited for the last trolley bus; a barman smoked a cigarette as he stacked the chairs and tables while his colleague wound back the awning; a few late-night strollers walked their dogs.

Philip parked by the steamer pier and she clung on to his arm, teetering beside him on her high heels, and led him past a chemist's shop whose whole window display was devoted to Geritovital, into a side street of solid gray houses, blank and shuttered. They turned left, right, then left again, at each corner Philip bracing himself as they penetrated deeper into the narrow alleys behind the Municipio.

"*Ecco, siamo qui,*" Maura said as they entered an unlighted courtyard. Then she stumbled, gave a little cry of pain, and let go of his arm.

A hand smelling of grease and garlic was clamped over Philip's mouth; a knee was jammed into his spine and he was bent backwards like a bow. Give the bastards a run for their money, he thought, and lashed out with his heel and elbow simultaneously biting into the ball of flesh at the base of the thumb. He heard a whimper of pain and he gulped in air, but then a second figure looked out of the shadows. Arms and legs flailing, Philip broke the grip of the man holding him and backed into a doorway.

They came at him together and it was all over in a matter of seconds. As he parried one blow with his forearm, a lunging kick caught his kneecap and he tottered sideways, biting his lip to contain the agony, his fingers scrabbling at the rough stone in a futile attempt to keep his balance. The two figures crowded in; a fist drove into his solar plexus and as he gasped for breath the top of his head exploded and he lurched forward and collapsed on the cobbles.

Neither of them spoke. There was a brief tattoo of high heels receding into the distance, then he was rolled over and heavy hands fumbled at his limp body. There was a moment of total silence followed by a muttered exclamation and a short laugh. A hand was thrust into his trouser pocket and he froze as he suddenly remembered the stories of the war in Algeria. He heard the sound of an approaching car. someone whistled; a door slammed; the engine revved and the car drove off.

Philip levered himself up and hopped over to the doorway where he sat down and massaged his knee. Christ, it hurt! But thank God he hadn't laid it on too thick or they really might've worked him over. And as for Maura, she had played her part to perfection. And so had he, for that matter. Still clutching his knee, he hobbled out of the courtyard and set off down the alley. He came to a small piazza with a fountain in the center. He bathed his face, washing away the blood from the newly opened cut above his eyebrow, cupped his hands and rinsed his mouth, then sat down again on a stone bench and lit a cigarette. He reached into his trouser pocket; took another envelope, containing a single sheet of paper, and a $20 bill.

The handwriting was the same:

I trust you enjoyed the pleasure of Maura's company. Sadly that is all I can offer you for your kindness in returning me my property. But perhaps the enclosed will buy you a drink or two and take care of any cleaning bills or doctor's fees.

"Big joke," Philip said. "Ha-bloody-ha!" He crumpled up the note and flicked it over his shoulder. He dusted off his suit and was crossing the road when a car swung around the corner. Forgetting his bad knee, he tried to jump out of the way, but slipped and fell. The car swerved behind him, mounted the curb and came to a halt only inches from the stone bench where he had been sitting. Expecting a volley of curses in any of three languages, Philip scrambled to his feet and spread his hands in apology; it was his own fault and the car had not been traveling more than fifteen miles an hour.

The passenger door opened and a man got out, his eyes gleaming oil-slicks in the medium glow from the starkly modern street lamps. But it was not at his face that Philip was staring. He could almost hear the tumblers of his memory as they spun into action; highly polished black moccasins with a gilt chain across the instep; a pair of argyle socks, the checks three shades of blue. Today, but when? Definitely not in London. The plane? Linate? The hotel? The tumblers fell into place and locked. Outside the hotel, going up the steps. One of the three Arabs from Geneva who had come for the gambling at Campione.

Chapter XI.

The King's Cousin

The handsome Arab with a taste for colorful socks and who was now wearing a beautifully tailored gray flannel suit, was neither Syrian, nor was he attached to the United Nations in Geneva. And later he was to admit that he loathed and despised gambling. The card, enclosed in clear plastic, reminded Philip of one of his own passes; but instead of PRESS printed above the photograph, there was a line of Arabic, and beneath it *de Documentation Exterieure Maroccain.*

"All right, Captain," Philip said, handing it back to him. Their hands touched and Arafa's skin was as dry and as cool as a snake's. "But so what? This is Switzerland, not Morocco. I'm not breaking any law. I'm not even drunk and disorderly. I'm just going for a quiet walk to digest my dinner when you bloody well nearly run me over."

"I would have imagined that the violent exercise that you doubtless took with that whore might have settled your digestion." He called out over his shoulder in Arabic and after a few seconds the driver an-

135

swered. "Though I admit," he continued, "that *Jambon de Grisons* followed by Eglifisch . . ."

"Tell your spook to get his eyes tested," Philip interrupted him rudely. "It wasn't ham, it was beef." They stood facing each other while the water from the bronze nymph's cornucopia splashed merrily into the granite basin. "All right, I'm impressed. But it still doesn't alter the fact that this is Switzerland."

"You read German? If you wish, I can show you a letter from the Minister of the Interior in Bern."

"Don't bother," Philip said. "I believe you."

"Then I suggest we return to the hotel to discuss things in more civilized surroundings. You also need to change your shirt. It's covered in blood."

"Suggest?"

"But of course." He raised his hands like a conjurer demonstrating that there was nothing up his sleeve. "Far be it from me to force you, but it's in our mutual interest. I'll come with you, if I may. My spook—as you call him—has a rendezvous with a girl in a nightclub and I don't want to deny him his relaxation. He's had a very busy day."

"I bet," Philip said. "It really is a nightmare drive to Ascona and back." His sarcasm was wasted, as Arafa had already turned away to give the driver his instructions.

In the car Philip told him how his socks had given him away and Arafa accepted the implied criticism in good part. All the same, Philip agreed, it was a brilliant stroke of double—if not triple—bluff for an Arab to disguise himself in Arab dress. "Of course I noticed you. One couldn't not, the three of you tripping up the steps as if you'd just come off the set of *Lawrence of Arabia*. But I could've sworn that no one tailed me to Ascona. And as for the restaurant . . ."

"You saw the clothes, not the man. And following you to Ascona was simplicity itself, given the cooperation of the Swiss confederates who in their own quiet way are as efficient as everything else in this most efficient and boring of countries." He unfolded the silk handkerchief from his breast pocket and blew his nose. "And where I invariably develop a cold."

"If," Philip said, choosing his words with care, "if they are so efficient and you're all working happily together, why don't you just . . ."

"Go on."

Philip took the plunge. "It's Thami Fouquet, isn't it?" Without waiting for an answer, he continued, "Why don't you just arrest him and lock him up for twenty years, either here or in Morocco?"

"I thought our friend Piers de Salis had explained all that to you."

The car slewed across the road, grazing the bumper of a parked Mercedes before Philip brought it back under control. "Sorry about that," he muttered automatically. Then he slowed down and glanced at the hawk-like profile sharply etched against the light. "Piers? A friend of yours?"

"For more than ten years. Rabat was his first foreign posting and we've kept in touch ever since, both socially and professionally."

"And when were you last in touch with him?"

"Yesterday morning, on the telephone a few minutes before he went out to lunch—with you."

"Then you don't know?"

"Know what?"

"He's dead. Last night. Someone held a pistol to his head and blew his brains out. They're pretending it was suicide, but it wasn't. It was his own chief—the Director, or whatever his official title is." The bland smile had vanished from Arafa's face, and Philip paused, waiting for his reaction.

"Yes," Arafa said at last. "It doesn't surprise me. I never entirely trusted that scruffy little man."

They had arrived at the Europa. Cicadas shrilled in the motionless palms and their footsteps crunched loudly on the gravel. "Your room or mine?" Philip asked, then was struck by the sudden thought that it was three days ago almost to the minute that he had put the very same question to Jackie at Rushworth.

"I've got my own drink so there's no need to pay their ridiculous prices."

"Your drink, my room," Arafa said. "That way we'll be spared any more redheads hammering on the door."

"You know it all, don't you?"

He shrugged. "I try to do my job."

They had been talking now for nearly an hour and Arafa's voice was beginning to crack. He sneezed again and got up to close the window which he had opened to disperse the layer of cigarette smoke that hung in the air. He then excused himself and went into the bathroom. There was the sound of gargling and Philip ran a tired hand over his bristly chin.

It certainly was one hell of a mess. The possibilities of arresting Fouquet had long ago been considered and rejected; three of the best lawyers in Switzerland had all agreed that there was no charge that could be legally brought against him. Certainly, refraining from any foreign political activity was one of the conditions of his Swiss residence. But what evidence—evidence, not suspicion—was there of his involvement in this frankly farfetched and nebulous conspiracy against the King of Morocco? Moreover, he was known to be totally apolitical and since he had been living in Carabbia he had had no contacts of any sort with anyone who might be remotely connected with any of the anti-Morocco revolutionary groups. Nor in Switzerland was the unproven intention to commit a putative crime in a foreign country an offense against any Federal law.

Realizing when he was beaten, Arafa had seriously considered the logical alternative of assassination, an idea put to him, he admitted, by Papich in the bar of the Tour Hassan. But here again he ran into another brick wall. It was three weeks now since Fouquet had left the safety of his mother's villa. How could he keep a squad on permanent standby on the off-chance that one day Fouquet might decide to go to the cinema? Introduce someone into the household? It would take weeks, if not months. And as for an attack on the villa, it would have to be full frontal, probably with anti-tank missiles to blast through the walls, by which time the alarm bells would be blasting off in the Carabbia police station and half of the entire force of the Cantonali would be converging on the villa. So, short of chartering a plane and dropping a bomb, or zeroing in a howitzer from the far side of the lake, that was that. And there was one more factor to be taken into account. If, by a miracle, they did succeed in killing Fouquet, all the various groups who had laughed him off when he was alive would immediately claim him as a martyr, using his death to mount a worldwide campaign against the Moroccan regime.

Then the conversation had veered around to Papich. A fool and a Philistine, Arafa had called him; possibly the most loathsome man he'd ever met. The papers ordering his return to Langley had come through to the Embassy in Rabat the day after he left for London. There was talk of an enquiry into the unaccountable disappearance of laundered CIA funds approaching the $100,000 mark. No doubt this was Papich's final fling to raise the money to buy *haciendas* in Argentina, a country whose praises he had sung so loud and so often that even the Argentinian Ambassador would turn away embarrassed when Papich buttonholed him at a party. No one would rally to the flag for a dead Papich; nor for his catamite, Wayne Morollo. At the mention of his name, Philip had looked up but could detect no quizzical glint of irony in the hooded eyes. So, as they were both putting their cards on the table, he recounted the circumstances of Morollo's death. Arafa nodded appreciatively, but regretted that he had died so quickly.

Thank God, Philip now thought as he walked stiffly to the window, exercising his knee, thank God that he and Arafa were on the same side. Blood would out, and beneath the urbane facade—the European clothes, the fluent English, the polished manners—Arafa was still an Arab with a contemptuous disdain of human life. It was part of the great tradition: Moulay Ismael, who would disembowel a dozen living slaves as an after-dinner entertainment, and built Meknes with the labor of thousands of Christian prisoners whose bodies were used to reinforce the walls; Bou Ahmed, at the turn of the century, ordering the Minister of War to be chained to his brother in a dungeon for ten years, and decorating the gates of Fez with the salted heads of rebel tribesmen; Thami El Glaoui personally executing a man who had made an attempt on the Sultan's life; Oufkir interrogating Ben Barka in a Parisian cellar. He shivered, then started slightly when he saw the reflection of Arafa standing close behind him.

"You're not catching my cold, I hope."

"No, just thinking."

"And there he is," he gestured toward the heights of San Salvatore, "the other side of that mountain, half mad, his brain rotting with congenital syphilis. I can see him at this very moment, drooling over the diamonds that you brought him, sniggering into his beard at his own cleverness in outwitting you and getting them for nothing."

Philip shrugged. "Easy come, easy go. I can't say I'm sad to see the last of them. The responsibilities were beginning to get me down. And there are more important things in life. Still, I did get twenty dollars out of the deal. But what do you intend doing about the girl Maura and the two heavies who jumped me?"

"Nothing," Arafa stated bluntly. "Nobodies." He dismissed them with a wave of his manicured hand. "And I don't imagine that you would want to waste your time in the Piazza Riforma making statements and looking through their collection of picture post-cards." He offered Philip a cigarette, a Casa-Sport, and took one himself, tapping it against the heavy gold case.

And that, Philip realized as he bent his head to the lighter, summed the man up to perfection; searingly strong tobacco in a Cartier case. He then asked the question that had been nagging him for the past hour. "I don't mean to be rude," he said, "but how is it that you've so much . . . well, influence and yet you're still a Captain?"

Arafa smiled. "Not all of us suffer from the same delusions as Field Marshal Idi Amin. And I have discovered that the rank of Captain is usefully anonymous."

"But it's not your real one?"

"No."

"Which is?" Philip persisted.

"Shall we say that I am answerable to one man alone?"

"The King?"

"Yes, the King—my first cousin. Which will perhaps explain the highly personal interest that I am taking in this affair."

"I see," Philip said. "One more question. You said that you weren't—that you couldn't because of Swiss red-tape—that you weren't tapping Fouquet's telephone, so how did you pick me up so easily?"

"Even though Thami Fouquet never leaves the house, they still have to eat. And on his way back from the market this morning, one of his gangsters who pretends to be his butler came here and made the reservation in your name. Very sloppy, I agree, but apparently one of the waitresses at the snack bar downstairs is his mistress so he decided to combine business with pleasure. But *revenons à nos moutons*. But first let me offer you some more of your own excellent whisky."

"Not at the moment, thanks." He sat down on the sofa (on this floor the furnishings were the same as in his room but the colors were red and white) and put his feet up on the fiberglass table. "As I see it, we're aiming at different targets. All right, whatever I might've said earlier, the only reason I came here was to try and get that twenty-five thousand pounds out of Fouquet. And it seemed a fair enough bet. If he was prepared to bandy that kind of money around in

141

London, it must've meant that he wasn't playing silly buggers. Right, so he conned me, played me for a sucker and, as you said, is no doubt laughing his head off at this very moment. So be it. I'll survive." The loosely packed cigarette had stuck to his lower lip and he winced as he pulled it free.

"Yes," Arafa nodded. "Piers told me you were a survivor and now that I've met you I quite agree."

"Now listen, Captain." Philip leaned forward and jabbed his forefinger into the sofa.

"Hamid, please. I feel I know you well enough."

"Fine. Then you'll understand what I'm going to say. I made a vow this morning and it's a vow I'm going to keep. To hell with all that bullshit about turning the other cheek and the meek inheriting the earth! I don't care how, where or when, but sooner or later I'm going to get that murdering little bastard and when I do . . ." He broke off, his anger running away with his words. And then, with a forced grin to cover his embarrassment at his outburst, he said in a calmer voice, "Yes, I think I will have a drink after all."

"You British," Arafa mocked him gently, "are always afraid to show your emotions. But why? You admit love, so why not admit hate."

"But you see what I mean about two different targets. You want Fouquet. I want Webb-Walker."

"So?" He raised his eyebrows. "All that we have to do is to dig a large enough trap and lure them into it together."

The sky was beginning to pale and the stars were going out one by one when Philip returned to his room. He stood out on the balcony, smoking a last cigarette. There had been a heavy dew and the grass below him seemed to have turned silver overnight. A faint breeze rattled the palms and he watched the cat's-paws ripple across the lake. He marveled at Arafa's energy and resilience. When he had left him, he had been ringing Bern and had also booked a call to Rabat. Which reminded him, he had forgotten to ring Jackie. He wondered what they had done with Piers' body and tried to remember if he had any family. There was a sister in Wiltshire, he thought, married to a man who had something to do with films. First the funeral, then the inquest. Or was it the other way around? A man wearing a hat made out of a folded newspaper, his arms covered in flour, trundled by on a bicycle, whistling. It was time to go to bed.

In London, the owl that lives in The Boltons hooted once as it returned from a night's hunting in the neighboring gardens, then glided silently over the rooftops, the broken corpse of a mouse clutched in its hooked talons, to regain its nest in a dead branch of an elm high above the sleeping streets. A quarter of a mile away in the back bedroom of a basement flat in Tregunter Road, Leroy Papich snapped awake, his hand automatically reaching for the butt of the Colt Python beneath the pillow. He thumbed back the hammer, ears straining to recapture the noise that had woken him. A key grated in the lock, and he was out of bed and flattened against the wall by the open door, commanding the passage that led into the hall. Then the light came on and pointing the gun at the floor, he simultaneously squeezed the trigger and gently lowered the hammer.

Papich stepped out into the passage, totally unconcerned about his appearance, spinning the revolver around his forefinger by the trigger-guard. He was wearing lime-green boxer shorts and a pale blue singlet with a picture of David Cassidy emblazoned on the chest, and coarse gray tufts of hair like wire wool spouting from his back and shoulders.

"I thought you were duty officer tonight, Max," he said accusingly. "In my day you didn't come off the graveyard shift till 08.00 hours."

The man called Max, who was a Colonel in the Marines, took off his hat and placed it and his attaché case on the hall table. He was a plump man in his middle fifties, with a scrubbed pink face and pale, slightly thyroid eyes which were magnified by the lenses of his gold-rimmed spectacles. "I've got news for you, LJ," he said in a tired voice as he loosened his tie from his collar. "It looks as if your day has come. And for Christ's sakes," he added sharply, "stop playing with that goddam cannon! Who the hell do you think you are? Wyatt Earp?"

"Rough night, Max?"

"The roughest since Cuba." He took off his glasses and ground his knuckles into his eyes. "Thanks to you. Listen, LJ, tonight you've been burning up more satellite hours than the Olympics. Washington, Langley, the Farm, they've all been on to me. They want to know what I want to know. Why, when you should've been Stateside forty-eight hours ago, are you hanging around here in London? And I want it now, LJ, straight." He turned on his heel and pushed open the door into the sitting room. "And for Christ's sakes put some clothes on!"

"You pulling rank on me, Colonel?" Papich emphasized the last word with an unconcealed sneer. He was lounging against the mantelpiece, wearing a black and gold kimono that reached half way down his thighs.

"In one word, yes." The Colonel sat down at a Sheraton gaming-table on which a chess problem was set out, selected a meerschaum from the pipe rack beside him, and filled it from a jar bearing a view of Windsor Castle surmounted by the Royal coat of arms.

"So what's your grading, Colonel sir? Still GS 13, are we?"

The Colonel was having difficulty in getting his pipe to draw. His knuckles whitened around the stem and he threw it down into the ashtray. "Now see here, Papich," he bit out the words, clenching the muscles of his jaw. "I'm fed to my back teeth with you and your lousy bunch of cowboys. You blast and blunder your way around the world as if you were all directly wired to God. But times have changed, Papich, and your sort soon will be as dead as dodos. And what's this I hear today? The cops fish a car out of the Thames at Hambleden, an orange Porsche with Roman plates. The same car, one of the keepers says, that he'd seen going up toward the cottage—my cottage, damn it, that you borrowed for a quote purely personal matter unquote—twelve hours previously. So you're into the wops, are you now? But which ones? Hardly the SID, knowing your track record, Papich. No, your style's the Neo-Fascists and the Mafia. You're bad news, Papich, the worst since Nixon. You make me sick."

"And when were you last in the field, Colonel? The Berlin crisis?" He raised the hem of his kimono. "Now you see this." He pointed a finger at the welted scar that zigzagged up his thigh and disappeared into his groin. "Four pints of plasma they poured into me. While you were sitting on your ass in Grosvenor Square, passing the canapés and playing footsie with the Brits and telling us what to do, I was doing it. And I'm still doing it and, Colonel, I advise you to step aside."

"Papich, this is an order. Explain your presence here in London."

"No way. Leastways not to a GS 13 with a probable case of piles. That'd be breaking every rule in the book. Now if you were Chief of Station . . . well, that'd be another ball game."

"The Chief of Station's at the conference in Paris—as you goddam well know."

"Jesus, and they leave the likes of you to mind the store!" He burrowed into the sleeves of his kimono and scratched his armpit.

"For the last time . . ."

"Or else what?" He picked up a chair, turned it around and straddled it so that he was facing the Colonel across the table. "Now look, Max, don't let's spoil a beautiful friendship."

"You're too old for the boyish charm bit, Papich.

Save it for your Fulham Road fags. And talking of them, where's friend Morollo these days?"

A dull red flush spread over Papich's cheeks. Holding the other's gaze, he reached out and picked up a black pawn, then snapped it in two between the fingers of his right hand. "I'll remember that, Max," he said in a voice scarcely louder than a whisper. "In fact, I'm remembering it right now. I had hoped to make it easy for you. A nice friendly conversation and we could've come to a nice friendly arrangement." He threw the pieces of the broken pawn on to the board, knocking over the white knight. "Too bad, now we'll have to do it the hard way."

The Colonel pushed back his chair and stood up. "I've had enough of you, Papich. You're out, as of now. For all I care, every paper in the world can plaster your name, your face, your address all over the front page. You'll never work again for any organization. Not even the Formosans will touch you. You talk about friendship. Friendship, shit! I've never liked you, Papich. I've tolerated you, yes, but only because I was ordered to. You crash in here unwanted, unasked for, claiming you're on some mission that's so goddam Double-Red-Alpha that it's a personal secret between you and Richard Helms. Bullshit, I say. And what I say now they'll be reading over their orange juice in Langley tomorrow, confirmation that Leroy J.—and what the hell does the J stand for anyway?—Papich is out. O-U-T, out!"

Papich cocked his head to one side and looked up at him. Then he stuck out his lower lip and nodded appreciatively. "Fine words, Max—fighting words. You've got guts, that's what I like about you. But I've got news for you. You're going to tell them that Papich is in—I-N. I'll draft the signal myself and you'll send it. Because if you don't, that all-American boy of yours at West Point, Maxwell S.—and the S stands for Starr—Donaldson II, is going to find one of these in his mail." He produced a 8 x 10 glossy photograph from his kimono and skimmed it across the table.

"Remember that Christmas Eve party in Tuscarora, Nevada, the year you made Colonel? Some party. But I guess you were too smashed to remember how it ended. So here's a happy snap to remind you of the gleesome threesome. Go on, take it," he taunted the Colonel who stood motionless, the color drained from his face. "Tell me, how does it feel to give head to a nigger while the other one gives it to you in the ass? Shit, what a damn fool question! Of course, by then you'd passed out."

Chapter XII.

The Points at Crewe

Leaning against the Fiat, one arm resting on the open door, Philip watched the single-engined Cessna taxi away from him up the valley. It swung around in its own length and then, without pausing, the pilot opened the throttle and it gathered speed and was already airborne by the time it passed the cluster of low white painted buildings that was both the headquarters of the Aeroclub di Lugano and the offices of Airtaxis Ticinesi. Philip raised a hand in salute and decided, perhaps for the tenth time in as many years, that he ought to take lessons and learn how to fly. He waited until the plane was no more than a speck in the sky as it headed south and then east, climbing all the time to gain altitude before crossing the Alps, then wondered how he was going to kill the rest of the morning. He had already made his two telephone calls: the first to Jackie at Blake's, the second, at Arafa's suggestion, to Thami Fouquet at whom he had blustered and shouted, calling him a double-crossing son of a bitch, only to be told to grow up and be thankful that he wasn't lying at the bottom of the lake with twenty kilos of steel chain wrapped around his neck.

Thinking of the lake, why not take a leaf out of the Sunspray brochure and let it bathe away his city cares? Actually swim in it, never in a million years; it was odd how the Swiss who would fine you for dropping a cigarette pack in the street, still went on pumping their sewage into one of their greatest national assets. But perhaps, like the scampi in Venice, it was sewage that gave the Eglifisch its unique and delicious taste. And it was also about time he gave himself a proper workout.

He drove back over the mountain to Lugano and hired a heavy clinker-built skiff from the man opposite the hotel. He had brought his camera with him and for a while he sculled close inshore on the lookout for any possible pictures that he might be able to sell and so recoup at least some of his expenses. But no one was jumping out of a window or holding up a bank, so he contented himself with shooting off half a roll on a group of nuns, always a good stock subject, then pulled out toward the middle of the lake. Stripped to his pants, he bent to the oars and settled down to a steady rhythm; a hundred slow, sharp bursts of fifty, and then another hundred slow, closing his mind to everything but the squeal of the oarlocks and the water rippling beneath the bow. Rocking in the wash of a passing steamer, he shipped his oars and smoked a cigarette, enjoying the intense feeling of purely physical well-being, of knowing that his body would respond to his commands.

After a shower, he packed his few belongings, signed the bill in Thami Fouquet's name and sat at a table beside the pool, hoping that the fat man in the track suit would slip on the tiles and fall in. Poor kid, he thought, as the fat man yelled at him after he had made a less than perfect turn. He was pouring out the rest of his second Lowenbrau when the waiter told him that he was wanted on the telephone. And three hours later he was sweltering in the departure lounge of Linate. The air-conditioning had broken down and the maintenance men were out on a forty-eight hour token strike.

Philip re-entered England as easily as he had left it, although he had his moments of unease even after he had cleared Customs, half expecting two men suddenly to materialize at his elbow and escort him firmly but politely to a waiting blue Rover. He told himself that he was overreacting, jumping at shadows, that he was in the clear and had de Salis' letter to prove it. Perhaps it was a throwback to his schooldays when Webb-Walker would creep along the corridors in his carpet slippers, listening at study doors. All the same, he seemed unable to shut him out of his mind. He had asked Arafa to describe him; and apparently he had not changed. The lank black hair was thinner now but still as untidy; the same mud-colored suits hung loosely from his narrow shoulders; he still chain smoked and still when concentrating would remove his glasses and pinch the bridge of his nose. But what had impressed Philip most was that, for the last three years, he had won the Peter Ward Cup at Bisley, a pistol-shooting competition open to all senior officers of the various arms of the SIS, consisting of both dueling and rapid-fire at 25 meters with either a standard automatic or revolver. It was the last skill that Philip would have attributed to him, but he had hardly needed it, he thought coldly, in the bedroom in Egerton Terrace. Then there was the problem of his tapped telephone. Somewhere in London there was a potentially lethal spool of tape, and he pictured Webb-Walker hunched over his desk as he listened to the playback of Philip's Monday morning conversation with de Salis. But there was nothing to be done about that now; he just hoped and prayed that de Salis had realized the danger and had managed to erase the evidence.

Leaving as little as possible to chance, he had shaken his head when Jackie had suggested that she should meet him at the airport. And so now, instead of taking the coach or a taxi, he jumped on a bus to Hounslow as it was pulling away from the pavement. At the Underground station he bought a ticket to Piccadilly Circus where he changed trains and backtracked to Earl's Court, then changed again on to the Circle line to Gloucester Road, and walked the last few hundred yards to Blake's.

"Jackie," he called as he pressed the bell. "It's me."

She opened the door and flung her arms around his neck. She had been painting her nails and the heady tang of acetone made him wrinkle his nose. She was wearing her orange bikini and her body was warm from the sun. They kissed, then she linked her arm in his and led him into the sitting room. The sapphire ring, he noticed, was on the third finger of her left hand.

"A surprise for you, darling," she said and with a flourish pulled the napkin off a tray on the table. "The best Beluga and it's a present from me to you. The toast might be a bit cold but . . ."

"To hell with the toast. My God, champagne too!" He spun the bottle around in the ice-bucket. "Saran Nature! Jackie, you're a genius. Wherever did you find it?"

"They had some here. Apparently some film star ordered a case and left half of it behind. And I remember you once saying that much as you like champagne the one thing you didn't really care all that much for was the fizz. So here you are."

"A rare treat," Philip said as he stripped away the foil. "The perfect way to celebrate the prodigal's return."

"So everything was all right?"

"I've made a new friend," he mumbled, his mouth full of toast and caviar. "An Arab gentleman, straight out of *The Sheikh*, who'd swing you across his saddle and gallop off into the desert on his white stallion."

"Another Omar Sharif?" she suggested.

"Not really, and I clean forgot to ask him if he played bridge." He poured out the champagne and held his glass up to the window. "You see, none of those boring bubbles to make you burp. Pure liquid gold, a thousand fine." He smiled across at her. "But yes, everything more or less worked out according to plan—with the added bonus of my meeting Arafa. The Arab or, to be more precise, the Moroccan," he explained and went on to tell her of what had happened on his overnight trip to Switzerland.

"So in fact," Jackie commented when he had finished, "it didn't really work out all that well at all. He conned you."

"In a way, yes. But believe me, I didn't come out the loser." He dug the spoon into the caviar and held it to her lips. "And what's been going on here? Did you fix it with your father."

"Well, yes and no."

"How do you mean?"

"I rang him at home immediately after you'd rung me from Lugano, but he'd gone over to Eggbury to see the Wallaces. Then I started thinking about something he'd said a couple of weekends ago. Do you know anything about birds?"

Philip's hand stopped halfway to the bottle. "What an extraordinary question! But apart from the usual corny jokes about the feathered or the other kind, not really, no. Some one shoots and eats, others sing and wake one up at the crack of dawn. But why?"

"Well, you know how people go on about birds these days, the Royal Society for the Protection of and all that. Surrounding ospreys' and avocets' and golden eagles' nests with barbed wire, alarm bells and students and retired Generals standing a twenty-four hour guard so that no one disturbs them or pinches the eggs. The poor birds," she said with feeling, "they must think they're in a kind of Colditz. Anyway, according to Dad, we've got the same kind of situation on Moronsay this year. Some kind of divers—I think they're called Great Northern Divers—are nesting on the loch and it's all very special as apparently it's the first time they've ever been known to nest in Britain.

153

But what it boils down to is that Antonia wanted to go up there and finish her book. As you know, she doesn't mind roughing it. But Dad said, 'Sorry, no.' To all intents and purposes the island's out of bounds till the end of the month when the eggs hatch." She hesitated. "That's what he said."

"Out of bounds?" Philip repeated with a frown. "But surely you can't stop people landing?"

"But you can. And after all it is private property. You see, there're only two places where one can land. The cove on our side of the island, below the lodge, and the beach on the other side—where the so-called nudies are. The rest is all cliffs."

"Hmm. And who actually is living in the lodge at this moment?"

"As far as I know, just the couple who've been with us for donkey's years, and their idiot son Angus who bumbles around pretending to be a ghillie."

"And in the red corner," Philip said, "a team of mercenaries masquerading as Sunspray's construction crew? Why not?"

"So then I had a brainwave," Jackie's voice cut across his thoughts. "Sandy Glenrannoch."

"What about him?" Philip vaguely remembered a red-faced young man with a ginger moustache who used to amuse himself at dances by throwing rolls at his friends and crawling under tables squirting soda siphons up debutantes' dresses.

"He's got a boathouse that he's converted into a kind of crash pad at Drum. And Drum's the nearest place on the mainland to Moronsay. Any time I want to go there, he said, just ask and if it was free, fine. So I asked him this morning and it's all arranged. The factor's got the keys and we can pick them up any time we want."

"We? Now listen, Jackie. We're not talking about going on a picnic, you know. This is . . ."

"No, Philip. Let me finish. You said you wanted to go to Moronsay. Now Dad's put his foot down and there was no point in bringing the subject up and trying to argue with him. Once he's made up his mind, that's it. Like his panama hat the first of May and the central heating the first of October—even if it's freezing in September. So you can't go as one of us. And you can't go on a Sunspray package either. Right?"

Philip nodded. "Fair enough."

"And you can't very well charter a plane from Glasgow and fly there because the landing strip's also on the nudies' side. So we go to Drum together, you and I. Then I go into Crinan by myself on Friday, the day that Angus does the shopping, and go back with him in the boat. Then—we'll have fixed a time—I'll come over to Drum in the Zodiac, pick you up and smuggle you ashore. There're lots of places if you know where and I do."

"And what," Philip asked, "if Angus refused to take you back with him?"

"Och, come along now, Philip," she said in a broad Scots accent. "Angus McKay saying nae to Miss Jacqueline, the laird's daughter!" She clicked her tongue like a nanny. "What will the world be coming to next?"

Philip considered his glass in silence. "Friday, eh?" he said at last. "Does Glenrannoch have a telephone?"

"Aye, and hot and cold running water, too." Then in her normal voice, "Honestly, darling, anyone'd think you were going to the North Pole."

"Seriously though, what I said just now I meant."

"About not going on a picnic?" She met his gaze without blinking, the dark blue eyes clear and confident. "I know."

"People are going to get hurt."

"I know. But you see, Philip, Piers was a friend of mine, too, and three years ago he asked me to marry him."

Time stopped, a sparrow pecked at the tub of geraniums and the sounds of the outside world echoed loudly through the open windows; a girl laughing, a door slamming, a telephone ringing, a dog barking.

"But you didn't, did you?" Philip heard his own voice say.

"No," She stretched out a hand and touched his knee. "I didn't. Somehow I didn't quite see myself as a merchant banker's wife. Much too dull, I thought."

The station was surprisingly crowded for a Thursday evening in early June. "B 8," Philip said, glancing at the tickets. "There's no point us both sitting here. So why don't you go ahead and book a table for dinner? I'll bring the things." He watched her walk away up the platform, a West Indian porter resting on his broom and giving her an appreciative whistle. Then he returned to the car and again checked the luggage on the back seat, mostly purchases that he had made that morning at the Black's of Greenock in the Grays Inn Road.

Coals to Newscastle, taking camping equipment to Scotland, he had thought as he entered the shop where more than thirty tents, ranging from one-man bivouacs to canvas gin palaces, were pitched on patches of artificial grass. The night before, he and Jackie had made a list, and this he now produced as a bearded young assistant approached. Even pared to the essentials, it seemed endless: first, a waterproof sleeping bag; then a rucksack and a pair of Vibram-soled climbing boots; a hundred yards of nylon line, snaplinks, pitons, and a piton hammer; a tiny stove that burned cakes of smokeless fuel and a canteen that would combine as saucepan, plate and mug; a rubber-encased flashlight; two pairs of oiled Norwegian socks. "Off to Everest, are you, sir?" the assistant had joked as he produced an anorak and matching trousers. But Philip's smile soon vanished when the time came to write out his check; and apart from the expense, what the hell was he going to do with all the gear afterwards? Set up camp in Kensington Gardens and scale the Albert Memorial?

Although he was still staying well away from Paulton's Square, Jackie had gone around to her flat to collect what she needed, and they lunched together at the hotel. Philip then asked the desk for the loan of a typewriter, refusing the offer of a secretary as well, and spent the next two hours crumpling up sheets of paper and tossing them on the floor before he was finally satisfied. He then went to see Charlie Thomas.

It was early closing day so they had the shop to themselves, the steel shutter in place and the blind drawn down over the grill protecting the glass door. They sat in the back room, Charlie full of admiration for Jackie, and Philip let him have his say before bringing him round on course. "I want you to look after this for me, too," he said. "Keep it with the other letter I gave you." He hesitated, only too aware how melodramatic his next sentence sounded. "And if anything should happen to me . . ." he tried to make light of it, "You know, like getting run over by a bus, open them and do whatever you think best."

"Your last will and testament, is it?"

"You could put it that way, I suppose. Though I hope to hell it isn't the last. And something else, Charlie. I hope you don't mind me using you as a letter box but I've given your number to a friend of mine. His name's Arafa but we've fixed a code word to make sure it's all kosher." He laughed. "Hardly the right word in the circumstances. He's an Arab. However, the word's Lalage. So if anyone gets in touch with you about me and doesn't say 'Seen Lalage lately?' or whatever . . ."

"You've gone to Bangkok for a couple of years."

"Exactly. And the number where you can reach me and relay any messages is on the back of that envelope. I'll be there as of tomorrow, but I've no idea for how long. And we'll use the Lalage routine, too. And so will Jackie, which makes just the four of us." A sudden thought occurred to him. "Christ, you don't happen to know any Lalages, do you?"

"What me? You must be joking." He got up out of the old dentist's chair that he had bought in a sale for a pound, and went over to the massive green safe that occupied half of one wall. "Letter boxes, code words, cut-outs," he said over his shoulder. "Real cloak-and-dagger stuff. What have you got yourself into this time, Philip? That pendant I can understand. But this is something else." He tapped the side of his nose. "Arabs, eh? Not planning to knock off Golda Meir, by any chance?"

"Now you must be joking. No, it's just that I've got very personally involved in something that I suppose you could call political. But yes, I am planning to knock someone off, in cold blood and with malice aforethought." His voice rose. "I'm going to cut the bastard into little pieces. And God knows he deserves it after what he's done to . . ."

"No need to justify yourself with me, old son. It's me, Charlie. You've got your reasons and that's good enough for me."

"Thanks," Philip muttered, grateful yet again for his loyalty and his unquestioning acceptance of the facts. "You're a brick."

"A what?" He turned from the safe, the wide grin on his face breaking the tension.

"A brick, you fool! With a 'B.' a genuine Jewish circumcised brick."

The laminated steel door, nine inches thick, swung back and Charlie placed the letter in a metal cash-box on one of the upper shelves. He stood still for a moment, then, as casually as if he were offering him a cigarette, said, "How're you off for shooters?"

"Not too hot, and I was just about to ask you the same thing. You see, this place where I'm going is a small island off the coast of Scotland and there'll be no holds barred. One could blast away all day with a twenty-five pounder and no one would be any the wiser. And at present all I've got's a PPK—the 6.35 one."

Charlie searched his key ring, then dropped to his knees and unlocked a drawer. "How about this?" He cleared a space on the workbench between a miniature lathe and a rack of jeweler's drills, then began to unwind a roll of oil-stained toweling. "Funny, isn't it?" He said as he laid the gleaming blue-black metal bare. "A Jew invents it and now the West bleeding German Army uses it."

It was a weapon that was both beautiful and deadly, an Israeli-made Uzi sub-machine gun, designed to pump out 9mm Parabellum bullets at the cyclic rate of 650 rounds a minute, and lethally accurate at up to two hundred yards. Philip had once test-fired one of the original models on the range near Hanover, and even then had been impressed with its handling. But the one in his hands was lighter, more compact; it had a plastic foregrip and a metal butt that folded under the barrel, making no more than eighteen inches long, and easily concealable beneath a coat; and learning from the ill-omened Sten gun, it was fitted with a grip safety to prevent it firing accidentally when dropped. Philip worked the bolt and checked the firing-pin, then snapped home one of the five magazines, each containing twenty-five rounds, and felt it balancing perfectly and becoming an extension of his arm.

"Nice," Philip said, removing the magazine and laying it and the gun back on the bench. "Very nice indeed. How much?"

"For you, Philip," Charlie spread his hands. "Nothing. You'll be doing me a favor taking it away. It used to belong to a mate of mine who's now blasting the balls off the angels up in The Great Shooting Gallery in the Sky. And if the law ever got it into their heads to turn this place over. Well, hand guns is one thing—I've even got a license—but this is a bit beyond the pale."

Now it, together with the Walther, was zipped into the rolled up sleeping bag which he had stuffed into the rucksack together with his shaving kit, cigarettes and the last bottle of duty-free whisky. The line of cars in front of him began to move forward, and soon the Volkswagen was clanging up the ramp and onto the upper level of the two-tiered line of open wagons. Shouldering the rucksack, Philip left the keys in the dashboard (the car would be unloaded by the railroad staff in Perth) and made his way along the train to compartment B 8 where Jackie was chatting with the attendant who was turning down the beds. Philip asked him to bring some ice and soda, then they sat together on the lower berth until a whistle blew and they pulled out of Kensington Olympia only seven minutes late.

After snaking through the strange hinterland of Northwest London—derelict warehouses and huge piles of eviscerated cars silhouetted against the setting sun—the train joined the main line at Willesden and picked up speed, the cutlery and the glasses in the dining car jingling merrily, the waiters open-legged like sailors as they swayed up and down the aisle. The dinner was excellent and, at Jackie's insistence, he ordered a second bottle of claret. She was on the way to getting rather drunk, he noticed. But then, why not? She slipped off her shoe and wedged her bare foot between his thighs, caressing him with her toes.

"For God's sake, darling," he said in a low voice, shifting uncomfortably. "Behave."

"Why?" she giggled. "Don't you fancy me any more?"

"Of course I do. But this is neither the time nor the place." He broke off as the waiter approached with the coffee pot. "Please, for both of us."

"But it is, darling," she urged him. "The night sleeper to Perth is famous for it. And the one to Inverness, too. The points at Crewe. All that bucketing and jolting around—it's fantastic! It seems to go on forever." An old lady with a cane looked at her askance as she began to croon, "The points at Crewe and I love you."

Philip glanced out of the window as the train hurtled through a station. "O.K., and I love you too. But we're only at Nuneaton and there's sixty miles to go yet."

She giggled again and spilled wine down her chin as she ogled him over the rim of her glass. "Sixty miles to go? Sixty miles you mean to come—at sixty miles an hour. Whoopee!"

By some miracle they timed it right, even though, as Philip brutally told himself as she arched and panted beneath him, her nails digging into his buttocks, his cock might be in it but his heart was most definitely not. Afterwards, while she lay on the narrow berth, sated and drowsy, he slipped on his clothes, took his cigarettes and went out into the corridor. Normally, he loved trains, and had loved them ever since he was a boy during the great postwar days of steam; and as he rested his arms on the brass rail and stared out through his dim reflection into the darkness, long buried memories surfaced: the maroon and gold livery of the Royal Scot; the smell of clinker on a hot summer's day in a freight yard while fussy tank-engines puffed and snorted; the Union Jack and the Tricolor fluttering from the smokebox of the Merchant Navy class streamliner drawing the Golden Arrow; the chocolate-and-white coaches of the Cornish Riviera Express rocketing through Sonning cutting.

But tonight that love had curdled. They had stopped somewhere in the grim suburbs of Warrington and now he wondered if perhaps Piers de Salis had once taken this same train north with Jackie.

Chapter XIII.

Drum

At eleven o'clock the next morning, after breakfast at the Station Hotel and a three-hour drive past Loch Earn and up Glen Dochart to Tyndrum, then dropping down into Argyllshire and taking the minor road that runs along Loch Awe, Philip lay soaking in the peat-stained water in the marbled and mirrored bathroom of Lord Glenrannoch's boathouse at Drum. The house was no more than one floor, built against the face of a low cliff; a wide veranda with a flagpole; a sitting room full of comfortable chairs and sofas and pine-paneled walls hung with a strange mixture of stags' heads and erotic posters; a bedroom entirely furnished in tartans; and a kitchen and a bathroom. Fifty years ago it might have been possible to berth a good-sized boat in what was now used as a cellar. But now a cliff-fall on the south side of the cove had blocked the harbor and a broken line of eroded concrete blocks, protruding from the sand and silt like rotten teeth, was all that reamined of the breakwater.

After his bath, he put on a pair of jeans and laced up his new boots, then went for a walk along the cliffs. There was not a breath of wind and the sun had not yet burned off the mist and the inshore reefs and rocky islets seemed to hang suspended between the sea and sky. Out in the Sound he could hear the plodding thump of a diesel, but the boat itself was as invisible as Moronsay ten miles to the west. He stood on the springy green turf of the point and gazed inland across the peninsula. Hidden from him by the ridge of the heather-covered hillside was the huddle of white-washed cottages that was Drum, the end of the metaled road, nestling in a hollow beside the loch. A line of telephone poles strung together with a single wire marched southward to the boathouse, and on a bluff above it he could make out the overgrown jungle that once had been a garden famous for its azaleas and the blackened remains of Drum House, gutted and to-tally destroyed by fire ten years ago.

On his way back, he paused at the burn to taste the water, sending a blackfaced ewe scrambling up the opposite bank. Jackie was not yet back from Crinan, so he followed the burn down to the cove where it ran into the sea over a bed of scoured gray pebbles. The crushed shell beach danced and shimmered in the heat, a seemingly endless silence between each languid wave. He stripped off his clothes and clambered along a reef draped with great swathes of glistening brown seaweed, poised himself for a second, then dove deep into the clear aquamarine water. Numbed by the shock he burst to the surface. Then put his head down and swam a fast crawl to an islet a hundred yards away, rounded it and struck out straight back to the shore. Teeth chattering, he sprinted up and down the beach until his circulation returned, then stretched out like a starfish taking deep breaths of the clean salty air and letting the sun bake into his bones.

He was thirsty and they had stocked up with a dozen cans of McEwans' Export in Crianlarich. Not bothering to dress, he wandered back to the house, beachcombing along the tideline where the sandhop-pers leaped frantically among the jetsam; a rubber glove, countless round corks that had once buoyed nets, a sheep's skull, an empty tin of Spanish boot polish, and the inevitable amputated limbs of pink plastic dolls. He picked up a piece of driftwood, worn smooth as suede, and used it as a tennis racket, banging pebbles out to sea, thinking of nothing but hitting the rock at which he was aiming.

One of Philip's first acts on entering a stranger's house was to examine the books and now he recalled having seen the blue and gold binding of the *West Coast of Scotland Pilot* on one of Glenrannoch's shelves. He found it sandwiched between Debrett and *The History of Flagellation* and took it out to his deck chair on the veranda. He had been unable to find the corresponding sheet of the Ordnance Survey in London, but Jackie had said that she thought she could get one in Crinan. Still naked, he drank some beer directly from the can, then looked up Moronsay in the index.

The mist had burned off and now, leaning on the wooden balustrade, framed between the rugged northern tip of Jura and the cliffs across the Gulf of Corryvreckan, he could just discern the island's highest peak rising out of the haze on the horizon, a mountain with an unpronouncable name 1,500 feet high. He returned to the *Pilot* which devoted a whole page to the Gulf of Corryvreckan, prefaced with the bald statement: *Caution. When the tidal streams set through the gulf, navigation at times is very dangerous and no vessel should attempt this passage without local knowledge.* He read on, wondering how a twelve-foot rubber dinghy with a twenty-five hp outboard would cope with the whirlpools, overfalls, and currents of up to 8 ½ knots.

He heard the Volkswagen clattering down the unmade track and walked through to the back of the house to meet her.

"It's all arranged," she said, dumping two plastic bags on the kitchen table and brushing the hair out of her eyes. "We leave at two-thirty, after Angus has drunk his lunch. And look," she unwrapped a blood-stained parcel, "I've bought you some steaks—to build your strength up. But sorry, no map."

"Too bad." His gloom of the previous evening had vanished as if it had never been. "Why aren't you wearing a kilt?" he said with a leer. "Then we could have a quickie over a hot stove."

She slapped at his groin with a dishcloth. "Go and put some clothes on. And while you're up, I'd rather like a glass of Sandy's delicious Chablis."

Sitting out on the veranda, he read to her from the *Pilot* and finished by saying, "I hope to hell you've got the local knowledge."

"Don't worry, I made my first solo to the mainland when I was eleven. Admittedly Dad was following in the launch we had then, but I must've made it dozens of times since. It's really just a question of the tides and slack water. And although I couldn't get a map, I borrowed a tide table from the harbor master who's an old friend, and I've got him on our side."

"How do you mean?"

"Well, it was news to me, but they've now got a VHF radio on Moronsay, in the lodge. To call the doctor or whatever. And I've fixed it with him that if I want to talk to you, I call up the Coast Guard Station—Angus may be a bit simple but he knows how it works—and they ring you and either give you a message or say I'll be calling again in half an hour, in which case you jump into the car and beetle over."

Philip had his doubts, but kept them to himself. He thought it highly unlikely that she would be allowed free access to the transmitter, laird's daughter or not. And though it might seem innocent enough, the rea-son that it had been installed in the lodge was because the camp itself was on the low-lying western side of the island where the reception would be poorest. He had always assumed, and Arafa had agreed with him, that there must be a radio link with the outside world, but it was reassuring to have its existence and whereabouts confirmed. Radio had never been his strong suit, but he seemed to remember from a Mediterranean cruise that 2182 kHz was the normal frequency and was constantly monitored by the Coast Guard and other authorities.

"Talking of ringing people," Philip said, "I'd better check in with Charlie."

"Ravioli out of a can, salad and cheese all right? We haven't got that much time before they pour Angus out of the pub."

"Fine," Philip replied. "But the more I hear of Angus, it looks as if you'll miss Moronsay altogether and either run slap into Sgeir something or other, or end up off the coast of Newfoundland."

"No, he's a born sailor."

"So was Christopher Columbus," he retorted. "And he thought America was India."

They went indoors together and Philip picked the telephone off the shelf beside the cavernous granite fireplace. The efficiency of the GPO, or Glenrannoch's clout? he asked himself as he discovered that he could dial direct, and made a mental note to ring up all his friends in America. Feeling more than slightly foolish, he asked to speak to Lalage, then heard Charlie's chuckle as he launched into a rambling story as to how Lalage had been rushed off to St. Stephen's with an infected toe, when he cut in, telling him that a joke was a joke but to pull his finger out and get on with it.

The message was simple and straightforward. Arafa had called from Rabat about an hour ago and would be leaving now for London. Things were hotting up and he had said the next few days should prove crucial. Philip should stand by to move and he would call him at Drum between nine and ten this evening.

Philip lit a cigarette and looked out across the Sound. A crash of breaking china came from the kitchen, followed by Jackie's "Oh fuck!" He found her on her knees, gathering up the remnants of a

167

plate. "Forget it," he said. "I'll do it later. Now what did you do with the tide table?"

Although by sea Crinan was only five miles from Drum, because of the sea loch that sliced deep into the coast, by road it was nearer fifteen. They crossed over the Crinan Canal (which in itself saved ships northbound from the Clyde ninety miles of frequently heavy seas off Mull of Kintyre) and Jackie directed him to the car park beneath the lighthouse from where they could observe the quay which was also the main street of the little resort town.

"There," she pointed to a blue and red broad-beamed fishing boat with a stumpy mast abaft the cramped wheelhouse.

Philip craned sideways so that he could see the name stenciled on her transom. "I should've guessed," he smiled. "No wonder Angus is such a fan of yours. Was it his idea to call her *Jacqueline?*"

"Honestly, Philip! You make me sound like the whore of Bablyon. Just wait till you see him. And over there by the pier is the nudies' boat. I saw a couple of them coming off her this morning, then ran into them later in the butcher's. They were buying a whole side of beef and the butcher made a joke about it being enough to feed an army and I saw them both kind of freeze for a second. Then they laughed, but very fake laughter. And then one of them said it was a man's life out there on Moronsay and the older one looked furious and hacked him on the ankle and he shut up."

"What did they look like?" Philip asked.

"One about forty, the other younger but both rough and very fit. Wearing ordinary working clothes, donkey jackets, and corduroys. "And they both had boots rather like yours. Normal length hair, neither long nor short. And I don't know if it was because I was looking for it, but they definitely had the feeling of soldiers about them. The way they moved and walked, for instance. Sort of relaxed and tensed up at the same as if they expected someone to suddenly shout an order. You know what I mean?"

"Yes." He gazed across the calm waters of the landlocked bay. The ex-MTB was painted a pale blue-gray and large black letters on the bows spelled out SUN-SPRAY. The superstructure had been reduced to the minimum, enlarging the deck space and further accentuating her original rakish lines. Below decks the engines which could probably take her up to thirty knots would occupy most of the sternsheets but she could never carry enough fuel for a two-thousand-mile voyage south through the Atlantic even were she in ballast. Nor did one refuel in any European port with a gang of armed mercenaries aboard. So that put paid to the possibility of her disembarking her cargo on some lonely Moroccan beach.

"There he is now," Jackie nudged his arm. "You'd better come and meet him."

A stocky figure wearing a tweed cap and a navy blue sweater was lurching along the quay, paying no attention to the car that was hooting behind him. In his own good time he crossed over to the *Jacqueline* and let the sack that he was carrying over his shoulder drop the ten feet down on to the deck.

"I hope those aren't the eggs," Philip said and hauled Jackie's duffel bag out of the back.

A week's growth of black beard and rolling whisky-red eyes gave him the appearance of a mad pirate but when he spoke his voice was as soft as burn water, and he stammered. He was older than Philip had imagined, in his forties, and three fingers of his left hand were missing. Philip made some small talk about the weather, then Angus, with a sideways glance at Jackie, took two paces backward, collided with a bollard, shook his head violently from side to side and said that if Miss Jackie was ready they ought to go.

"He likes you," Jackie whispered as they watched him lower himself down the rusty ladder. "I can tell."

There was a loud thud as Angus joined the sack on

169

the deck. Philip peered over the quayside to see him crawling on all fours toward the wheelhouse. "I doubt if he'll even remember me in the morning."

"Wait till we get under way. You'll see."

"Until tomorrow then. Take great care, Jackie darling. And if things don't work out or you have to change your plans, just jump into the Zodiac and you know where I am."

"Tomorrow," she promised, then broke away and slid nimbly down the ladder.

The engine coughed and started, then settled down to a steady throb. Only the wheel seemed to be holding Angus upright, but as Philip cast off and Jackie coiled the lines, the boat moved slowly away from the quay in a perfect quarter-circle before he eased the bows around and headed toward the open sea. The note of the engine quickened; Jackie waved; and Philip saw from the foaming white wake that Angus was steering a course as straight as an arrow.

An air-conditioned coach from Glasgow pulled up on the quay and disgorged a group of American tourists, the courier announcing that they had half an hour for a cup of tea. Secure behind his dark glasses, Philip mingled with them as they descended on the souvenir shops like locusts, and he was in the tobacconist's revolving a rack of postcards when the two men from the *Sunspray* entered. One look was enough to prove Jackie's point; and even though Germany was a long time ago, Philip clearly remembered a combined exercise with 45 Commando, and the older man reminded him of one of their sergeants who had set a haystack on fire with a Very pistol. He edged nearer the counter. The younger, a Londoner by his accent, was flirting with the blonde assistant, while the other, an Irishman, was reading from a list, buying cigarettes of various brands by the carton. But if Philip had hoped for any indiscreet remark or a chance slip of the tongue, he was disappointed; and no doubt the big Irishman had already bawled out his companion for his carelessness in the butcher's. He watched them leave and walk toward the pier, then he left, too, and returned to the car beneath the lighthouse.

Back at Drum, he steeled himself for another swim, again regretting that he had not thought of buying a wet-suit in London. According to Jackie, the Sunspray brochure was right about the Gulf Stream warming the waters off Moronsay. But, as he had pointed out, they were talking about the west coast, not the eastern side with its precipitous cliffs falling five hundred feet into the sea. Searching among the girlie magazines and the soft-core pornography, he found a paperback of Alan Williams' *Long Run South* and took it down to the beach where he spent the rest of the afternoon. As evening came and the screaming colonies of gannets returned to their nests, a chill crept into the air and Philip put on a sweater and decided to light a fire. There was a stack of logs downstairs in the cellar and as he loaded the basket it crossed his mind that it would make an excellent shooting range. The idea triggered off another, so he unpacked the Uzi and descended to the beach where he climbed around the headland to a secluded bay. He set up a tin can on a rock, then paced off fifty yards, pulled back the cocking handle, and set the selector lever to R for single shots. The butt pressed into his shoulder, he aimed and fired. Nothing happened. "What the . . ." he muttered, then the metal flange of the grip safety caught his eye. The spring was stiff and he had to squeeze it tightly with the soft pad of flesh between his thumb and forefinger. Thank God he had found it out in time, he thought as he squinted along the barrel. The bullet struck the rock and whined off out to sea, low and six inches to the right. He fired again and the can leaped into the air and clattered over the pebbles. Not risking a burst—and anyway on automatic the only thing to remember was to hold the muzzle down—he repeated the process at a hundred and at two hundred yards until he was satisfied that he had got the feel of the gun, then picked

171

up the ejected cartridge cases and dropped them into a deep crevice in the rocks.

The sea turned to orange as the misty red sun sank behind the truncated peak of the mountain with the unpronounceable name. There was a stalker's telescope hanging behind the kitchen door and he took it from the scuffed leather case and braced himself against the flagpole. For a while all that he saw was darkness. He checked the elevation and the angle and moved a fraction to the left. A faint glow appeared and as he adjusted the focus it became a tiny square of yellow light. It flashed three times, and Philip went indoors to light the fire. As the kindling crackled, he poured himself the first whisky of the evening and turning toward Moronsay raised his glass and drank to Angus.

A quarter moon hung low over Jura and Philip wondered where he would be this time tomorrow. But better to enjoy the creature comforts while they lasted. The pine logs were blazing happily and the curtains were drawn; there was a vast collection of tapes and records and he had found a bottle of '64 Romanée-Conti in the cellar. He had hesitated before bringing it up, but then had thought, what the hell! From what he remembered of good old Sandy, a great Burgundy or Algerian plonk was all the same to him so long as it was red and liquid.

As he grilled his steak he could hear Neil Diamond blasting out *Cracklin' Rose*, a song that took him back to the first night that he had slept with Jackie. It was toward the end of last September and he was staying with friends at Cap d'Antibes. He had had a modestly profitable evening at the Casino and when he got back to the house he found an impromptu party in full swing. A yacht belonging to friends of his friends had just come in from Sardinia, and Jackie was one of the girls on board. He had seen her around London often enough practically always with a man, and although he used to dream of possessing her magnificent body, he had never made a pass at her, knowing as surely as the sun rose in the East that one day they would make love. *Mektoub*, it was written. The music was deafening and in the center of the room, black with sun and wearing a long white dress, she was dancing barefooted by herself. Someone passed Philip a gold snuffbox full of cocaine. He accepted, and even before he looked up he knew that the dark blue eyes were watching him. He rose to his feet, crossed the floor, took her by the hand and led her into the garden. Neither of them spoke. Then they were rolling on the coarse damp grass beneath an olive tree, her thighs locked around his leg, while up in the house the stereo slammed into the opening bars of *Cracklin' Rose*. Later they went up to his room; and in the morning both she and the yacht were gone. Without bothering to shave, he drove straight to Monte Carlo. Everyone on board except the Captain was still asleep. And twenty minutes later they were breakfasting together in the Hotel de Paris, her bags already packed and loaded into the Porsche.

The smell of burning brought him back into the present. His steak was ruined, one side charred to a cinder.

The second steak was more successful and he ate it in front of the fire, trying to avoid constantly glancing toward the telephone. He asked himself why Jackie's admission that she had an affair with Piers, that he had asked her to marry him, should have cut so deep. After all, it was three years ago and her life was no one's but her own. As it was now. He and she had never exchanged vows of fidelity; they didn't need to. It was damn nearly nine months now, a record that he had been faithful to her. Then he thought of Marrakesh; not that it really counted technically as he hadn't actually got it in. No, that was balls, complete and utter sophistry; he had tried and failed. But the fact that he felt guilty and ashamed was a good sign; he cared for Jackie, didn't want to hurt her—loved her, in a word. But still her affair with Piers rankled. Because neither of them had told him? Perhaps. He looked around the room with its antlers and erotic posters; the cuckold's horns, he reflected grimly, and the remembrance of joys past. Then a dreadful image flashed across his brain, of Sandy Glenrannoch's hairy pink buttocks pumping into Jackie's receptive loins, and he hurled his wineglass into the fireplace with all his force.

The physical act and the shattering of glass had so released his tension that he found himself laughing aloud for having let his paranoid fantasies take control. But then waiting, sitting around doing nothing, always set his nerves on edge. The wine hissed in the fire and he went to fetch another glass, thinking that if the French got to hear how he had treated one of their greatest wines, they would probably ban him from the country for life. Stretched out on the sofa, he began planning the trip that he would make with Jackie when all this was over. Monte Carlo? Why not? And pretend that Piers was racing them in his green Morgan and so lay his ghost forever and a day.

The bottle was empty, the ashtray piled high with stubs. The hands of his watch showed that it was three minutes past ten. He rang Charlie but the line was permanently busy. He did the washing up and was about to try again when he glanced out of the kitchen window and saw twin beams of light stab the sky. The cart track led to nowhere but the boathouse and the car would be less than five hundred yards away, coming over the ridge any second now. He ran through the house, fumbling for the unfamiliar switches. The factor, paying a courtesy call to see that everything was all right? Maybe, maybe not. In the dim red glow of the firelight he searched for the Uzi, picked it up, put it down again, stuffing it beneath a cushion. Where the hell was the Walther? Still in the sleeping bag inside the rucksack. He blundered into the bedroom, flicked the light on for an instant, then brought the rucksack back into the sitting room. He heard the car change down into first to negotiate the last steep hairpin bend. Too late he remembered the Volkswagen, parked outside the kitchen door; it would've been too late anyway. It would be either that door or the flight of wooden steps leading up to the veranda. He chose the kitchen and flattened himself against the wall so that he could see around the edge of the uncurtained window, a dishcloth draped over the pistol in his hand.

A rabbit was caught in the tunnel of the headlights and it jinked and swerved down the track before diving into the heather. The car turned into the roughly leveled space that had been hacked out of the cliff, and Philip drew back into the corner as the headlights swept the kitchen. The car stopped, the engine was switched off, the lights remained on.

An elongated shadow moved over the row of pots and pans on the far wall and the bolts of the door rattled in the sockets.

"There's some steps over there, sir," a woman's voice called.

There was the faintest scrape of shoes against rock as the shadow disappeared, and Philip tiptoed through into the sitting room, the safety catch off and the gun warm in his palm. He crouched on the floor and eased one of the heavy curtains back no more than an inch and waited as the steps creaked and a slim figure came into view. He was wearing a dark topcoat and a scarf was wound around his neck. As he turned toward the French window a glimmer of moonlight reflecting off the sea caught his profile, and Philip released his breath and straightened up.

Obviously Captain Arafa's cold had got worse, not better.

Chapter XIV.

The Gulf of Corryvreckan

"Your friend was going to pass the message on." Arafa took off his scarf and unbuttoned his Loden coat, revealing a light tweed suit of Glen Urquhart check. He caught Philip's glance and said with a smile, "I thought I had better dress the part as one of my ancestors came from Scotland. She was shipwrecked off Asilah and captured by pirates who sold her to my great-great-grandfather." He crossed over to the fire and stood there warming his hands.

"I've been out quite a lot," Philip explained. "But what are you doing here? And how did you find this place?"

"That was simple, as I had your telephone number. And I'm here because what I have to tell you is for your ears only and if one talks on an open line, one might as well shout it from the rooftops with a loudspeaker. But first, do you think we could have some coffee? It's been a long day and I'm sure my driver would like some too. Don't worry, she can make it."

"Where have you come from? I thought you were in London."

"I was. Then I flew to Prestwick where a helicopter met me and took me over to Campbeltown. It would have attracted too much attention continuing on up here so the DNI had very kindly laid on a car for me." *

"The DNI?"

"The Director of Naval Intelligence. But more of that later. The poor girl must be freezing. I hope I haven't given her my cold."

Arafa's driver from the base at Campbeltown was a very pretty WREN with short golden curls bunched over her hat, the length and elegance of her legs further emphasized by the black uniform stockings. "Mary, this is Philip." Arafa introduced them and she disappeared into the kitchen, refusing Philip's offer of help and closing the door behind her.

"It was proved in the war," Arafa remarked, "that women are much better security risks than men. They never feel the need to boast and show off how important they are. And your WRENs are the best of all. But tell me how matters stand with you."

Philip told him. "So by six o'clock tomorrow morning," he concluded, "I should be on Moronsay, all things being equal as long as we don't get drowned in the Gulf of Corryvreckan. I've also got this." He reached under the cushion and brought out the submachine gun. "Just in case."

"Suppose for a minute these Sunspray—as good a name as any—people catch you. It's a fact that has to be faced. What's your cover story?"

"Why not these birds, these Great Northern Divers? I'll take my camera with me and say I'm an ornithologist who's on to the scoop of the century. After all, Ardale put the story around and for all we know it might be true."

Arafa fingered his tie and nodded. "Yes. Excellent."

Mary came in with two cups and coffee pot on a tray. "It's only Nescafé, I'm afraid. But I couldn't find any proper coffee." She smiled, her eyes only for Arafa. "I hope you don't mind, sir."

"The best cup of coffee that I've had in my life was in the *bled* above Foum-Zguid. It was half acorns and half sand. And after that I can take anything."

"Yes, sir." She returned to the kitchen with a provocative roll of her hips.

But Arafa was elsewhere. "Yes," he said to Philip. "I was seventeen and had just killed my first man. We had some properties there and this man was causing trouble. It was my first year at Le Rosey and my father thought that life in a Swiss boarding school was making me soft. So he sent me to deal with him. And I dealt with him—with one of my father's matched pair of Purdeys. It was very messy and I was sick. Then I had that cup of coffee."

Philip blinked and threw another log on the fire. "While my only worry in the world was how many runs I'd get in the match against Eton—and whether Laura Webb-Walker would be able to get away from her husband and meet me behind the pavilion." He had told Arafa that story in Switzerland.

"But now it's the husband whom you're wanting to meet." Arafa put down his cup and his lips twisted into a cynical smile. "The worthy Webb-Walker, the pillar of the Establishment, waiting for his knighthood, while all the time he has one hand in the till while the other goes through the motions of ensuring his country's security, a jackal creeping on his belly while he scavenges for what he can find. In my country we have ways of dealing with vermin like him but here," he raised a hand and let it drop back on his thigh, "you think differently. So be it." He glanced up at Philip who was poking the fire with his toe. "I'm sorry," he said with his old urbanity. "I let myself be carried away."

"I quite understand. My dear Hamid, I wouldn't have your job for all the money in the world."

"But I have. And to tell the truth, I enjoy it. But sit down and listen to what I have to tell you." He frowned into the fire, collecting his thoughts. "More times than not, coming to a working arrangement

179

with the British Secret Service is like picking your way through a maze blindfold. The SIS, the Special Branch, Naval Intelligence, RAF Intelligence, the Foreign Office Intelligence, the various MIs and DIs of the Ministry of Defense—all of them keeping their own secrets, hatching their own schemes and each one bitterly resentful of the others. There was a classic example only last year when one of the MIs paid a freelance $100,000 in gold for a piece of information that the RAF already had on their files. But for once this compartmentation—a very popular word in Washington these days—is paying dividends as far as I'm concerned. For reasons that would take far too long to explain . . ."

"Meaning," Philip interrupted him, "that you wouldn't tell me even if we were marooned together on a desert island."

"I suppose that's one way of putting it. Anyway, the present DNI is not only a very close friend of mine but also a man with whom I've worked before and whose professional qualifications I rate second to none."

"Hence the car and the helicopter and no doubt an aircraft carrier if you need it."

"Yes," Arafa replied seriously. "I imagine that could be arranged."

Philip got up from his seat on the leather-topped club fender. "How about a drink?" He nodded toward the door, "And what about Cinderella? Or isn't she allowed to drink on duty? Queen's regulations and all that."

"I've no idea. Ask her."

She was sitting at the table poring over a book, forehead furrowed in concentration as she chewed the end of a pen, an open notepad at her elbow. She should really be getting on with her homework, she said, and held up the book so that he could see the cover. It was a Russian grammar. But perhaps a small whisky and water would help.

Philip returned to his place by the fire. "I have a

feeling we ought to drink to something. Death and destruction to our enemies. And talking of enemies, what news of Papich? I keep on dreaming of that bloody gun of his, of being swallowed up by the barrel and falling faster and faster till wham—he pulls the trigger and I wake up."

"He's keeping a surprisingly and, to my way of thinking, suspiciously low profile. When I first spoke to the DNI after you had gone to bed in Lugano, I asked him to set up a twenty-four hour surveillance. They had no trouble picking him up. The tenant of that cottage near Hambleden is a CIA Station Officer who lives in Tregunter Road and it was there that they found Papich. However, that very same morning he packs his bag and goes straight to the embassy where he's been ever since. And what's going on inside there, I have no idea. Nor does the DNI's man in the Embassy. A debriefing? A court of inquiry? Have they retired him and are they holding him on ice before sending him back to the States? Or what? I don't know. But when I flew into Campbeltown he was still there. However, that's . . ." He sniffed loudly and his head bent backwards and his shoulders rose as he fumbled in his pocket.

It seemed that he was about to explode, but at last the sneeze came and once he had started he could not stop trumpeting into his handkerchief, his body jack-knifing with each fresh spasm.

"Gesundheit," Philip said. "You ought to be in bed."

Arafa dabbed the tears from his eyes. "Exactly what the King told me this morning. But the final countdown has already started and if we pull out now we will have lost a unique opportunity. An opportunity for me to rid my country and the world of Thami Fouquet, and for you to make good your vow to avenge Piers de Salis' death." The hooded eyes glinted in the glow from the fire, unwavingly holding Philip's gaze and boring into his brain. "No cold feet? No second thoughts?"

181

"No," Philip replied. "None. Otherwise I wouldn't be here."

"I thought not. So now let me tell you that the trap is about to be sprung, and that some time within the next seventy-two hours the first and last meeting will be arranged between Thami Fouquet and James Webb-Walker. Here, as we planned, on Moronsay."

During the night the weather had broken. It had already been starting to cloud over when Philip said goodnight to Arafa and watched the lights of the Daimler vanish over the ridge. Now the wind had veered round to the southwest and was freshening every minute and squalls were darkening the ice-gray waters of the Sound. Force Four gusting to Five, Philip guessed, as a splatter of rain whipped across the veranda. Moronsay was totally invisible, and Jura and Scarba were no more than sudden glimpses of black rock as the clouds fleetingly lifted. He consulted the *Pilot* again; it might be worse, if the winds were due West, and at least they would have the current with them; but all the same it was an ideal day to spend indoors.

To help pass the time, he stripped and cleaned the Walther, then did the same with the Uzi, experiencing a moment's panic as he dropped the retaining pin of the extractor and saw it roll beneath the stove. He then packed the rucksack and put it inside a large plastic bag and measured off a length of line to secure its neck, leaving the running end free to tie around his waist.

He played three games of chess against himself, but each time black won. There must be a moral in that somewhere, he reflected and reached for the pack of cards, shuffled and cut them, and dealt himself the most complicated patience that he knew. After a while he threw the cards down in disgust and sat and listened to the waves rolling into the beach and the grinding of the shingle as it was sucked back out to sea. The contours of the shoreline had completely changed; much of the sand had been scoured away and jagged new fangs of rock exposed. He thought of Tania Berger and Jackie, of Webb-Walker's face when they confronted each other after almost twenty years, of what would happen to Piers' de Salis suits, of the pre-set walkie-talkie that Arafa had given him, now safely stowed away, in a pocket of the rucksack.

An old scarlet Land Rover, traces of the Royal Mail insignia still showing, splashed down the track and the factor picked his way through the puddles, the wind tugging at the skirts of his coat. He was a pleasant young man of about Philip's age, a lowlander by birth, and he had called in to show Philip how to change the Calor gas cylinders. Philip made a show of interest, then offered him a drink and relaxed over a jug of Bloody Marys while the factor—glad, as he said, to have the chance of a decent chat that wasn't about sheep or cattle—talked about cricket and the fantastic massage parlor with genuine Siamese "Body Mousse" that he had discovered on his last trip to London. He invited Philip to lunch, to come and take potluck with him and his wife, but Philip refused, saying that he was expecting an important telephone call.

In the event, the telephone never rang; but he had not expected it to, and no news was good news. As he would probably be living on Spam and baked beans for the next couple of days, he decided to cook himself a proper meal and again raided the cellar, this time bringing up a bottle of Batard-Montrachet, as red wine in the middle of the day invariably made him want to go to sleep. He started with a Salade Niçoise, followed by the inevitable steak which he doctored with a sauce consisting mainly of Lea & Perrins and mustard, and it was already three o'clock by the time he put the water on for the coffee.

The windows no longer shivered so violently in their frames and the seas were breaking more gently over the reefs as the tide rose. The sky was still overcast, but the visibility had improved. He stripped to his shorts and rolled up the clothes that he had been wearing, a pair of Levis and a black polo shirt, and stuffed them together with his boots into the plastic bag, then put on the dark green and brown camouflage anorak and trousers. He made one final check; the only thing that he had forgotten was a can opener. He bolted the windows and hid the key of the kitchen door beneath a stone, and slithered down to the cove, the mud squelching between his toes. He found a sheltered hollow and sat with his back against a lichen-covered rock, his feet wedged under the plastic bag for warmth. Asshole little town, he thought, blaming Crinan for not having a sporting goods shop or a ship's chandlers where he might have bought a wet-suit.

The bright yellow pinprick became a dot, then slowly resolved itself into a sou'wester and oilskins as the dinghy zigzagged in toward the shore. Jackie raised an arm and pointed, glanced over her shoulder, and came swooping in like a surfer on the crest of a wave and with a sudden burst of speed roared into the heaving but unbroken waters of the inlet, whose entrance was no more than five yards wide, where Philip was waiting knee-deep in a floating carpet of wrack.

She rammed the gear lever into neutral and Philip grabbed the lifeline that was stanchioned into the stubby bow and manhandled the dinghy around. "What's it like out there?" he shouted as he threw his bag on to the bottom boards beside the red fuel tank around which at least three inches of water slopped.

"Fantastic! Really great!" Her cheeks were flushed and her eyes were alive and dancing. "We must've been doing all of thirty knots through Corryvreckan. We were planing!"

Philip heaved himself over the side and fended off with his feet. The gray Zodiac was steered by a wheel and not by the tiller mounted on the outboard, so he squeezed his legs under the rudimentary wooden dashboard beside her as she re-engaged the gear, her hand poised over the throttle as she waited for the right wave. Then the engine screamed up to full power, the bow seemed to rise vertically and he clung on for dear life as he was blinded by a sheet of spray and they lurched with a sickening crash into a trough between the combing breakers.

"Whoopee!" Jackie yelled. "Ride 'em cowboy!"

Philip raised his head and wiped the spume from his face. "You know something?" he shouted. "You're fucking mad!"

Her only answer was a wild grin as she spun the wheel and then they were out into the deeper waters of the Sound where nothing worse than a heavy swell was running. They skimmed and bounced across the waves until they came into the lee of Scarba when Jackie glanced at her watch and throttled back and steered toward a crescent-shaped islet where there was a tiny strip of white sand beach.

"*Sgeir Dubh*," she said, throwing out the anchor and cutting the engine. "Black Rock to you."

"Bad day at," Philip replied limply, looking up at the cliffs soaring above them a mere fifty yards away. "What do we do now? Go ashore for a cup of tea?"

"Darling, didn't you enjoy it? You've gone quite pale."

"Like hitting yourself on the head with a hammer. It's wonderful when you stop. But I'm not so sure." The water was ominously still and he was very much aware that there was nothing between him and the sullen black sea but a sheet of plywood and a microscopically thin layer of rubber; and he could have sworn that the cliffs had moved, were bulging outward and had already started to fall. "This place gives me the creeps. Why don't we get on with it?"

"We've got to wait for the ebb." She pointed at a great skein of slimy brown seaweed that festooned a rock. "You see, it isn't working. Slack water. But to get the best out of the stream, we'll have to give it another ten minutes." She pushed back the sou'wester and shook out her hair.

They sat in the fragile dinghy and looked at each other, the only living beings in the dark desolation of sea and rock; even the gulls avoided the southern tip of Scarba. Her lips were cold and tasted of salt; her oilspins creaked as she held him tight.

Philip broke away and took his cigarettes from the chest pocket of his anorak. "Arafa came last night."

"Lucky old him."

"No. Seriously. His devious Arab plot is working out and Webb-Walker should be here either tomorrow or the day after to collect the loot from Fouquet. So what's the situation on Moronsay? How are famous nudies getting on?"

"I went to look at them this morning, but nothing special seemed to be happening. I couldn't get very close as they've got a twelve-foot wire fence surrounding the camp and the whole bay. To keep the deer out, so they say. But there's an old croft on the hill overlooking the camp so I went up there with the binoculars. But they weren't sticking bayonets into sacks or marching up an down and forming fours—or whatever soldiers do. But they weren't getting the place ready for the summer season, either, and it's a dreadful shambles. In fact, they hardly came out at all. Look, I've made you a map." She unfolded a sheet of paper and spread it on her knees. "The main building's here, right in the middle. It's got a brown corrugated iron roof. And down here by the jetty there's a row of cottages that was a shark fishery years ago."

"And this is the landing strip?"

"Yes. And the only gate in the fence is here. I didn't see it open as no one came in or out. But it's got one of those intercom things on it like Paulton's Square."

"Right." Philip zipped the map into his pocket. "Now what about this radio in the Lodge?"

"It's not actually in the house itself but in an old pillbox up on the cliff. There was someone there last night and just as I was leaving now I heard the Land Rover. They'll have seen me, but it doesn't matter.

After all, it is my island. Angus will tell them who I am—and that will be that."

Philip believed her; she would draw herself up to her full five-foot-nine, the nostrils would flare, the eyes harden, and the victim would touch his forelock and humbly beg her pardon before retreating with his tail between his legs. "And the electricity," he said, thinking aloud and remembering what she had told him in London, "comes from a generator in the camp."

"A present from the Army during the War. Though I think Dad had to pay something toward it. It's in the last of the cottages down by the jetty."

"And Angus and his parents?" He dropped his cigarette into the sea. "How do they get on with them?"

Jackie smiled. "There's hardly any contact. His father's bedridden now and his mother's as deaf as a post. But when it's necessary, yes. Like last month when Angus wanted a spare part for the boat and they went and picked it up for him at Crinan. And a couple of times they've radioed for the doctor, much to Jamie's—he's the father—disgust. He doesn't believe in doctors and wants to be left alone to die in peace. And he is nearly ninety."

"And how many of them are there?"

"About thirty—at least that's what Angus says. But he's not very reliable about things like that. As you saw, he doesn't think much of people and all he really cares about are the deer. And so long as they don't start poaching . . . Well, why should he worry?"

The cigarette butt had drifted out of sight and the submerged tendrils of seaweed were beginning to wave languidly as the current swelled into the cove, sucking and gurgling around the rocks. All they needed now, Philip thought, was a flat battery or water in the carburetor. But the electric starter fired the first time, the rasping whine of the outboard echoing eerily back from the hollow cliffs.

"You wait," Jackie said as he hauled in the anchor. "You've never seen anything like it." And once again

187

Philip had to cling on to prevent himself falling backwards as she opened the throttle to the full.

"Christ!" Philip shouted as they cleared the cove. We're not going through that!"

"Oh yes we are! It's beautiful!"

Then the polished black basalt walls of the cliffs were rushing past them, so close that he could reach out a hand and touch them, and he shook his head in sheer astonishment, gasping like a schoolboy at his first naked woman. To the left, a milling expanse of boiling white water seethed and churned, foaming and swirling, as the smoking overfall raced westward through the straits, head on into the wind. But in the ten yards separating the roaring maelstrom from the base of the fissured cliffs, some freak of nature had created a channel as calm and as smooth as glass where not a single eddy or ripple disturbed the surface of the translucent green depths.

He saw Jackie glance at him, her face triumphant; her lips moved but the wind and their speed tore the words away. He cupped his hands around his mouth and bawled into her ear, sharing in her intense exhilarations. "You're right, it's beautiful! Fantastic! We must do it more often! And to hell with Scylla and Charybdis, give me Corryvreckan any day!" Then he settled back, reveling in the sting of salt on his cheeks, and marveling at the phenomenon which caused the magically precise dividing line to be drawn between the channel and the raging overfall.

All too soon the straits widened and the twin headlands of Jura and Scarba fell behind them as they pitched and rolled in the open sea. The visibility was still no more than five hundred yards and Philip could see nothing but waves and cloud when Jackie eased the throttle right back.

"Another three or four minutes," she said. "You'd better get ready. That is, if you're still sticking to the plan."

"Absolutely," Philip replied as he wriggled out of his trousers. "I'm taking no risks at all at this stage of the game. And especially as they saw you leave. Laird's daughter or not, someone'll be waiting for you." Then he shivered as he removed the anorak and turned around and dragged the bag through the water that now covered the bottom boards.

Suddenly the wind died away and he could smell the tang of heather.

"There's quite often this mist here," Jackie said in a low voice, "and we've got a quarter of a mile to go. But it breaks up just like that. One minute you're in it, the next you're out in the open. Good luck, darling. I'll tell you when, and see you tomorrow."

"Tomorrow," Philip repeated, making sure of the knot sealing the plastic bag, then looping the running end of the line around his waist and tying a bowline. He crawled into the stern and pulled a sodden sheet of tarpaulin over him, then felt the vibration as Jackie increased speed for the run into shore. "A rock like a face that's come away from the cliff," was how Jackie had described the only possible landing place. "There's a rowan growing out of the forehead and the cave's directly above it."

"Philip," he heard her say. "There's a man watching us. You were right."

"Then wave to him. What's he doing?"

"Waving back. We're almost there. He's out of sight now."

"For Christ's sake don't forget to put the bloody thing in neutral." He clutched the bag tightly to his chest, bracing himself for the backward roll over the Zodiac's clammy side.

"Go! Now!"

He took a deep breath and pushed aside the tarpaulin, then the icy waters closed above his head and he was kicking out toward the cliffs of Moronsay whose coastline, in the micro-second that he had glimpsed it, was the most inhospitable that he had ever seen.

Chapter XV.

Jackie's Delight

The first disaster of the day occurred early in the morning on the second pitch, while he was negotiating a delicate traverse along a hairline crack that slanted across the tilted slab a hundred feet above the sea.

Philip had been taught to climb in the Lake District while still a boy, and at Oxford he had graduated to the Alps, spending three consecutive seasons there, concentrating on rock and tackling the great granite climbs on the Aiguilles above Chamonix and the vertiginous limestone pinnacles of the Dolomites. But one day in Glencoe while he was leading up the West Buttress of Buachaille Etive Mor, his second had come off, swinging like a pendulum in space, and Philip had only managed to hold him by a miracle. His palms had been burned raw by the rope and they still had had to complete the climb as there was no simple way down and they had reached the point of no return. But although his second was unhurt except for a few cuts and bruises, his nerve had broken and it had been the nightmare day of Philip's life as sometimes losing his temper and cursing him into moving, he had nursed him to the summit. From that day on, Philip's love affair with rock for rock's sake had begun to wane; he had continued climbing, proving to himself that he had not lost his nerve, but the passion had gone.

And so it was that in the dank gloom of the previous evening he had come face to face with his first major climb in ten years. The cave which Jackie had discovered when she was a pig-tailed schoolgirl of thirteen was warm and dry, with a sandy floor well above the high water mark. Outside the narrow entrance, an uneven turf-covered ledge, the size and shape of a tennis court, ran along the foot of the cliff, and he stood on its edge, head craned back as he considered the possible routes and planned his attack. The first pitch would be nothing more than an eighty foot scramble up the vestiges of a gully, but then the overhangs began and they would have to be turned. Once past them, there was a crack which broadened into a chimney that looked as if it led to a saw-toothed buttress which curved away out of sight. Any route to the right was unthinkable; the rock was arched like the nave of a cathedral and not even a Joe Brown or a Walter Bonatti would make that go. The left-hand buttress, then. He grinned wryly as he remembered the story of the over-ambitious climber trying to persuade a Swiss guide to accompany him up a notoriously difficult climb. *Es geht*, he kept repeating; and the guide nodded his head. *Jawhol, mein Herr, es geht. Aber ich gehe nicht.* He made a preliminary sortie; the rock was good solid schist, the holds excellent. The worst problem would be the exposure, and climbing solo he would have to protect himself as best he could.

He spread out the sleeping bag near the entrance of the cave, then drank some whisky and heated up a tin of beans. Night came and he might have been the last man left alive in the world. The sea rose and fell, only fractionally blacker than the starless sky; and there was not a single light to be seen. He rested the flashlight on a ledge and for a time dealt out hands of poker as if he was sitting round the table in his flat with four other players, but the game soon palled and he thought himself to sleep, wondering what methods Arafa had used to snap the weakest link in the chain, the bogus Brigadier.

He was woken by the gruff barking of seals and yet again the Western Highlands had lived up to their reputation for ever-changing weather. The sea was as blue as Jackie's eyes, sparkling in the warm sunlight. He scooped some rainwater from a pitted rock and while it came to the boil stood reconsidering the cliff now that the sun had brought it into relief. A gray Atlantic bull seal was basking on the rocks below. Philip nodded to him. "*Es geht*," he said. "*Und gehe Ich*."

Now he could see the same seal framed between his boots as he adjusted his balance and slid his left toe an inch further along the crack. This was the crux. Above him protruded another huge slab, sloping downward like the eaves of a roof; six feet away in a groove made by an obtuse angle of the rock was the vertical crack, wide enough for an arm or leg, that led to the chimney. But to reach it he would have to step out over the void, committing himself to holds that were no more than minute wrinkles. With a second belaying him, he would not have hesitated; nor if he had the mechanical aids—the *étriers*, the sophisticated ironmongery, the adjustable slings and ladders—of modern solo climbing. But he had not. And, he told himself, it was a poor climber who relied to much on fiberglass and aluminum. Men, not machines, climbed mountains.

Slowly and cautiously, the fingers of his left hand wedged in a waist-high crevice, he felt for a snaplink and unclipped a piton hanging from one of the home-made slings that draped his shoulder. Reaching as far and high as possible to the left, he inserted the metal tip into another hairline crack, then drew back to his stance and took the piton hammer from his chest pocket. He hammered the piton home and selected one of the longer slings and clipped it to the ring in the slender piton. He then took up the slack and knotted it around his waist. He rested, his forehead pressed against the rock where the gleaming specks of mica seemed to leap and dance. His heart was pounding, and a drop of cold sweat splashed from his armpit and trickled down his ribs. The muscles of his left leg were beginning to throb and twitch and the knee that had been kicked in Lugano felt numb and cramped. It was now or never. He gave a tug to the doubled rope stretching above him and inched out again onto the sheer smooth face, clinging to it partly by the friction of his body, fighting against the counterbalancing weight of the rucksack that was dragging him off the cliff. Now his whole body was damp with sweat. And then he heard the soft scrape of his boots and the rasp of his anorak against the schist as the whole slab seemed to lurch upward. Then, clawing at the rock with both hands in an instinctive futile effort, he fell.

The world somersaulted, the small of his back crashed into the side of the cove, he bounced off a ledge, then there was a jerk that forced all the breath from his body as the double loop cut into his stomach. The rope sprung, tightened again, and he spun around and swung slowly to a halt, dangling free above the void. Grabbing the rope with both hands, he painfully hauled himself up to a triangular niche where he could stand and loosen the constriction from his chest. If he rested again now, the reaction would set and perhaps his nerve would be gone forever. He could already feel a tremor starting in his legs. Gambling everything on the piton—it had held him once, it would hold him again—and refusing to speculate what stresses his eleven stone falling a clear twenty feet might have caused, he kicked off from the niche, developing an ever-increasing arc until he was carried clear across the grove, and jammed his left leg deep inside the crack. He climbed the next fifteen feet to the bottom of the chimney in a dream. Then, as he felt the tug of the line belaying him, he wriggled into the protection of the dark slimy walls and collapsed face down, his check cushioned by a blessedly cool patch of emerald green moss.

At last he stirred himself and sat up, his hands shaking as he lit a cigarette. Severe to Extra Severe, he thought, grading the final crucial stages of the traverse; on the Continent V or VI. And there was still another four hundred feet to go. He unknotted the thin nylon rope that had saved his life and let it fall free, "Fuck that," he said, remembering the old convention which dictated that climbers should remove their pitons and all traces of their climb from the rock. The seal had gone and as he munched a bar of chocolate he looked up the chimney to the wedge of bright sky no more than sixty feet above him. Although the walls were wet, they were only a yard apart and bridging up them with alternate thrusts of his back and feet against the two opposite walls would be child's play compared to the last pitch. He shrugged out of the rucksack, preparing to sling it across his chest. As he did so, he heard a faint metallic sound, like the chink of loose change. Even as he unbuckled the flap of the outside pocket, he knew what he would find.

The walkie-talkie had taken the full impact of his fall and after staring numbly at the shattered remains of the black plastic casing, he hurled it out to sea and followed its parabola until it splashed into the calm blue water.

Philip forced his way through the tangled mass of briars guarding the lip of the cliff, and the climb that he had christened Jackie's Delight after a prominent pinnacle half way up the buttress was over. The descent, if indeed he had to return to his camp in the cave, would be easy; there were enough stances and he had enough rope to enable him to abseil down all the way. Unburdening himself of all the climbing equipment, he buried it in a sandy bank, then allowed himself a cigarette while he studied the lie of the land.

The island of Moronsay was shaped like a fat figure-of-eight, tilted on its side and some six miles long on a northeast-southwest axis. It was narrowest at the waist, where a steep ridge cleft by a miniature pass separated the Lodge on the rocky east coast facing the mainland from the sandy bay where the Army had built the original training camp in 1941. The ridge formed the spine of the island, reaching its highest point at the truncated peak of the mountain on the northern headland, a bare two miles from the hollow where Philip lay.

Shredding his cigarette and letting the welcome breeze whirl the scraps away, he set out over the springy turf, keeping a constant watch on the skyline to the left. The going was easy, the ground rising gradually and the turf giving way to heather. There were no trees, no bushes to break up the expanse of green and purple; only outcrops of rock and naked slopes of gleaming shale. He was stopped in his tracks by a brace of grouse getting up from almost under his feet; and once he had dropped to the ground and froze as he sensed, rather than saw, a movement in a clump of bracken only fifty yards ahead and a stag rose to his feet and bounded down the empty hillside. He paused well below the summit of the ridge to consult Jackie's map, then bore south and west on a course that should bring him out above the corrie and the ruined croft which overlooked the camp. Now he could see the tract to the Lodge, descending the pass and the roofs of the Lodge itself and beyond them a vast gold and blue panorama stretching from the mainland to the mysterious Paps of Jura.

Worming between two rocks, Philip gently parted the heather and gazed down into the corrie. Gullies of white scree scarred the semicircular bowl scooped out of the mountain and were mirrored without a ripple in the clear green surface of the loch beside which a small herd of hinds with their calves were grazing like cattle. So this was the loch where the famous Great Northern Divers were supposed to be nesting; the loch was scarcely larger than the Round Pond in Kensington Gardens and the only sign of birdlife was a pair of hooded crows pecking at the water's edge. The croft stood on the far side of the loch where the burn started on its course down the valley at whose seaward end the camp must lie. It was almost midday, another hour before Jackie would bring him his lunch and the latest news of anything that might have happened.

Damn the deer! Somehow he had to persuade them to move without panicking them, especially as they were with their calves. The camp was no more than a mile away and even if they were all townsmen they were also professional soldiers, and a herd of deer galloping down the valley would be sure to arouse suspicions. It was ironic, but whenever he had been out stalking, the stag had always been downwind and he had to crawl miles through the heather in great circles before he could approach within range. Now the situation was reversed and the breeze was bringing the odor of deer to him. He was contemplating a slow flanking movement around the rim of the corrie when one of the hinds raised her head and sniffed the air. She walked daintily to the bank of the burn and the others followed. They stopped once more, heads lifted, then one by one trotted through the shallows and were gone. Philip gave them another few minutes and launched himself down the slope.

As an observation post the croft was ideal. Protected from the rear by the hillside, it lacked only a roof. With a small mortar, Philip thought, one could destroy the camp within minutes. It was a measure of their confidence that they had left it unguarded. But then what had they to fear on a private island ten miles out in the Atlantic, inhabited by two cripples and a drunken half-baked ghillie? The odd repressed Scotsman sneaking ashore to gawp at the nudists?

Hardly any problem there, as the camp always seemed to be closed.

Keeping well back in the shadows, he clambered over the fallen beams and edged through the knee-high nettles and positioned himself in a corner from which he could look out through the frameless window at the bay spread out below. For a moment he frowned as he seemed to recognize the long white beach and the chain of rocky islets, like basking whales; and then it came to him, it was the beach along which he had been running to meet Jackie in his dream. He grimaced and turned his attention to the northern end where the burn meandered across a marshy field and into the sea. It was here, on a slight rise, that the camp had been; some twenty innocent-looking chalets in a neat line in the dunes, the beach, a row of stone-built cottages near the jetty, from one of which came the hum of the generator, and the largest building of all, a hangar-like structure with the brown corrugated iron roof. The jetty projected fifty feet out into deep water and was made of metal girders surfaced with wooden planks; at the T-shaped seaward end the *Sunspray* was moored. There was no sign of the Land Rover; and in reality the landing strip was nothing more than the field that was dotted with grazing sheep. There was certainly more than enough space to bring in light aircraft, but not for anything larger, such as a Dakota.

There was some sort of activity outside the main building and Philip took Glenrannoch's telescope and focused it, careful to keep the lens out of the sunlight. The scene that met his eye could only mean one thing: Phase One of Arafa's plan had been completed; the strike force was preparing to strike.

Now the journalist in him took over. Thank God the cameras hadn't gone the way of the walkie-talkie! He unwrapped the Nikon from its protective sweater and glanced up at the sun. A thousandth at f 11 should eliminate all risk of camera shake. He would have preferred a longer lens, but the all-purpose 85-

200 mm zoomed out to its full extent would work perfectly well. Of course the blow-ups would show the grain, but that should add even more drama to the pictures. He was already imagining the captions: *The latter-day Spartans,* or *The Dogs of War get a crew.* He ripped open a fresh box of film and got to work.

A table and a wooden chair had been placed in the sun outside the main building. Standing in line was a queue of a dozen men, some wearing full camouflage uniforms, some just the trousers, others shorts, smoking and talking among themselves as they awaited their turn. The tall Negro puffing a cigar made a final flourish with the clippers, then pulled away the towel and shook it out while the man who had been sitting in the chair rose to his feet, rubbing his hand over his freshly cropped skull and the next man took his place.

Then Philip changed focus and finished the film on the Irishman whom he had seen in Crinan, who was now perched on a packing case cleaning a submachine gun. And through the telescope he saw that it was the standard British Army issue Sterling, the L34A1 model that was equipped with a silencer that slowed the bullets in subsonic speed and made it a truly noiseless weapon; a gun that was virtually unobtainable on any black market in the world. So perhaps de Salis had been right and the poor bastards weren't in fact mercenaries, but serving soldiers who believed that they were off on a secret mission for Queen and Country. And why not, with the present British involvement in Oman and the other states around the Persian Gulf? If it was so, he wondered what the cover story was. A lightning commando raid to free a political prisoner or a high-ranking hostage held to ransom? Or perhaps just a simple assassination of some anit-British troublemaker and blame it all on the PLO or Black September. For obvious security reasons they would have no idea of their true destination or target; and one deserted beach at dawn was very much like another. For it was at dawn, a week from today, that

199

Captain Arafa, after calculating a minimum five days for the voyage, had plotted the assassination of his cousin, King Hassan II of Morocco.

Phase One was how Arafa himself had described the first state of the plot to lure Thami Fouquet out of Switzerland. One of Fouquet's go-betweens in Morocco was a carpet dealer called Kitani, and it was to him that the secret had been leaked with sufficient evidence to substantiate it: that the King would spend the following weekend incognito at his aunt's villa near Barga, on the Atlantic coast between Larache and Moulay-Bousselham, where, because of the Princess' eccentric insistence on the traditional values of the desert, there was no telephone or even electric light.

The bait had been swallowed greedily, and had brought Phase Two into play. This demanded the kidnapping in London of Brigadier Talbot and its purpose was double-edged. The first essential was to persuade Talbot to contact Fouquet with the news that his strike force was ready to sail as soon as the outstanding $5,000,000 had been paid. This included the charter of a tramp steamer sailing under a Liberian flag, and his principal wanted cash this time, and not a certified check on a Swiss bank—in American dollars as the notes were smaller and easier to carry.

His principal also thought it quite in order that Mr. Fouquet might want to check on the quality of the goods before he took delivery, so he suggested that they should meet on the island where they could exchange contracts, as it were, and the same means of transport as before had already been arranged at Shannon.

And so now only Thami Fouquet's arrival was needed to complete Phase Two. Philip had not asked questions as to who had actually kidnapped the Brigadier, nor how he had been persuaded to comply with Arafa's wishes. But since Arafa had come to Scotland before the start of Phase Three, evidently his talents were no longer needed and the Brigadier was now a totally broken man. And Phase Three was simply the Brigadier telling Webb-Walker the same story in reverse: that the money would be on Moronsay by Saturday midnight and that Fouquet would deliver it to him personally and to no one else.

There was one minor embellishment, a matador's flamboyant *adorno*, that had made Arafa smile when he had told Philip the story at Drum. It concerned the charter of the ship, and its purpose was to make each man believe that he had cheated the other out of $30,000. Apparently $50,000 was the previously agreed price for the charter; but the Brigadier had told Fouquet that he had arranged it privately for $20,000; not a word to Webb-Walker and they would split the difference. And to Webb-Walker he would say that he had managed to squeeze Fouquet for $80,000, making them both a fat profit for nothing. "Perhaps it's gilding the lily," Arafa had remarked. "But quite in character."

Typical of Arafa's character, too, Philip thought as he swatted away a fly; he enjoyed his little games. But now there was the little problem of the smashed walkie-talkie. He would just have to take his chances with the radio and 2182 and trust that the DNI's people were listening.

An air of relaxation now hung over the camp. The Negro had shut up shop; some men were swimming, while others played football on the beach, their shouts as a goal was scored clearly audible to Philip sweltering in the croft. None of them wore any badges of rank and the Irishman whom Philip guessed to be their commander was checking a pile of kit bags and stores, ticking the items off on a clipboard and drinking from a can of beer. The sight of him increased Philip's thirst all the more and after unpacking the Leica and taking some general views of the camp, he left the croft and walked across the burn. The water was achingly cold and stunned his sinuses. The pair of hooded crows were still scavenging along the loch and a buzzard circled high above the jagged rim of the corrie. It was not yet half past twelve and time dragged.

Back in the croft, he munched some dates and watched a tiny brown lizard flicker up the sunlit wall. As there was nowhere else to go, he imagined that the Land Rover must be up at the Lodge. He wondered what Jackie was doing and how long it would take her to cover the three miles of moor to the croft. She had probably left by now, and he smiled as he pictured her striding through the heather, hair blowing romantically free in the wind and whistling *The Road to the Isles*, her kilt swinging around her knees, an adman's dream for a "Visit The Inner Hebrides" campaign. The reality was much more likely; back to her old stalking life, khaki jeans and face down in a bog, invisible on the hillside.

Hull down on the horizon, a ship trailed a smudge of black smoke. Even with the telescope he could see little through the haze. The Navy standing by, the old wartime Q ship sailing under false Liberian colors? It was then that he heard the Land Rover and saw it come jolting down the tract and stop at the gate in the high metal-mesh fence. One of the two men got out and spoke into the red box on the gatepost, then the sheep scattered as the car drove across the field and over the bridge spanning the burn to halt outside the main building. The Irishman tucked the clipboard under his arm and came to meet them. He nodded and looked up into the sky, shading his eyes with his hand, then pointed directly at the croft.

Even as he shrank back Philip heard the roar of the engine as the aircraft swooped low over the corrie, skimming the waters of the loch and passing no more than twenty feet above his head. He could distinguish the individual rivets on the white fuselage and the treads of the tires as his hair was blown forward and the nettles flattened by the slipstream. It headed out to sea, waggling its wings, and as it banked and turned south he saw that it was a single-engined Piper Cherokee with a British G registration. The pilot brought it in very fast, then it merged with its shadow and taxied to the very edge of the burn, the door near Philip already opening as it slewed around.

Then Philip had his first sight of Webb-Walker in twenty years. He jumped from the aircraft and the Irishman ran toward him. They talked animatedly for a few moments, Webb-Walker gesturing back toward the ridge. The pilot cut the engine and in the silence a whistle shrilled. The football bounced into the sea as the game was immediately abandoned, and everyone sprinted toward the Irishman, some completely naked, others hurrying from the main building, buttoning up their shirts. The Irishman was barking orders, towering above the diminutive figure of Webb-Walker by his side. The group broke up as ten of the men who were fully dressed were selected. Less than a minute later they were piling in and on to the Land Rover which had already been turned around. They all carried Sterlings. The Land Rover accelerated, the Irishman jumping on to the running board. The gate swung open, then closed again as the overworked engine screamed away up the hill.

The guns, Philip thought sickly, off for a quick drive before lunch; only the Glorious Twelfth was still two months away. That bloody little shit must have spotted her from the plane. Now Webb-Walker was talking to someone hidden by the fuselage and for an instant Philip saw red. He was ramming a magazine into the Uzi and already unfolding the butt when he came to his senses. At four hundred yards it was a lottery, and alerting the island would help nobody at the moment, lest of all Jackie. What was more, they hadn't caught her yet; and she knew the terrain like the back of her hand. So all was by no means yet lost.

The pilot climbed out of the cabin and at the same time the man to whom Webb-Walker had been talking stepped from behind the aircraft, and Philip's newly rebuilt morale collapsed like a house of cards. There was no mistaking the loud checks of the loosely cut tweed jacket, nor the man who wore it: Leroy J. Papich.

An hour later, the third disaster struck. The Land Rover returned, with Jackie in the back, the Irishman's arm clamped around her waist.

Chapter XVI.

Dead Ground

Although the door and the windows were wide open to try to catch what little there was of the onshore breeze, the heat inside the two-roomed cottage was intense. Now that loading had begun, the room was empty except for a truckle bed and a rickety wooden chair on which Papich had hung his jacket and shoulder holster. The bare stone walls and lack of air combined to remind him of the basement in the tree-lined street behind the Cité Universitaire in Rabat. He had succeeded there and saw no reason why he should not succeed now on this Godforsaken island. This one might have more class than the Kraut, but like Gertrude Stein said, a cunt was a cunt was a cunt.

Outside on the jetty, there was a resounding crash as a crate was dropped and the Negro supervising the loading swore for a full fifteen seconds without repeating himself. Papich turned to look at him, casting a speculative eye over the hairless deep pectorals and the muscled thighs. Too bad he would soon be steaming off into the wild blue yonder; he even moved like

Wayne and now that Wayne had gone wherever good old boys go, it was time to start seriously considering a replacement. In a way he supposed he theoretically owed Quest a vote of thanks; lately Wayne had been getting far too uppity, always on the make, demanding more and more. Golden Boy, they had called him; they should've seen him after two days under fifty tons of shit. But they had had some good times together, especially in Vientiane, and the old rules still held good, an eye for an eye, a tooth for a tooth. Which made two scores that he had to settle with Quest; that, and the time and effort he had wasted chasing round in ever-diminishing circles after Corviglia's pendant, and having had to parlay himself into the present asshole situation. He ground out his cigarette on the wall and unlocked the connecting door.

This room was totally bare except for a 1975 calendar advertising a Glasgow garage hanging from a nail. She was standing by the barred window, staring out at the beach where a team was deflating the four large black rubber dinghies and removing the outboards to be cleaned and greased.

"Look," she said, eyeing him contemptuously up and down, "I don't know who you are or what you want, but I'm warning you. This is private property and if you think . . ."

"Shove it, Duchess. You lost the colonies two hundred years ago. And as to all that," he mimicked her voice, "we-haven't-had-the-pleasure bit, you know too fucking right who I am, Sunday night, a flat in London. Remember now?"

"Me?" she arched her eyebrows in disbelief. "In London on a Sunday? You must be joking. Now go away and bring me whoever's in charge here. That little man with glasses." And she turned her back on him.

"Now you just listen to me, you . . ."

"Oh, go away," she said wearily. "Piss off."

"Now look . . ." Papich took a step toward her.

"Come any closer and I'll scream."

"Then scream, baby, scream."

She opened her mouth before he could reach her and the scream was still ringing in his ears as she bounced against the wall and slumped to the floor. There was the sound of running footsteps and the Negro's face appeared, pressed between the bars.

"Hey, man, what's going on?" he demanded in a flat Birmingham accent. "You killing a pig or something?"

"You mind your own goddam business, nigger," Papich snarled. "And get back to work."

"Since when are you giving the orders round here?" he paused and bared his teeth in a watermelon grin. "Whitey."

"Now see here, you black bastard . . ."

The Negro shrugged his shoulders and threw him a mock salute. "Yes, sir. No, sir. Three bags full, sir. I'm looking forward to seeing you on board, sir. On a coal black night, a hundred miles from land." He hitched up his shorts and strolled away, whistling.

"Son of a bitch," Papich muttered, unclenching his fists, then squatted down on his heels and grasped Jackie's chin, forcing her face up to his. Her eyes remained closed and blood trickled from one nostril. He shook her and dug his fingers into her skin.

"Now look, Duchess, that's just for starters. You want me to get real mean? Like me and you taking a walk over to the workshop? They've got some real fancy equipment there. Like blowtorches," he touched her head, "for your hair." He pulled her lips apart. "Power drills for your teeth. Maybe even a compressor for here." He thrust a hand between her thighs and squeezed her brutally hard. Her whole body jerked and she gave a low moan. "Because you see, Duchess, in my book coincidences don't happen. There ain't no such thing. So why not save yourself a load of trouble and tell us what you're doing here? And where's your one-eyed friend? Saddling up to come galloping out of the sunset again?"

207

Then he reeled back cursing as Jackie moistened her lips and spat into his face. He was wiping his cheek on his shirtsleeve, poised above her and already swinging his heavy oxblood Cordovan brogue at her ribs, when a mild voice behind him said, "That's quite enough, Papich. I don't believe in coincidences either, but as I happen to be an old friend of this young woman's family, I would prefer to handle it my way."

The scream had carried clearly up the hillside, piercing the sound of rushing water, and Philip had winced and bit his lip, powerless to help her, his decision made for him by the two men who by now would have reached the croft and would be lighting up to enojy a surreptitious cigarette as they waited for their comrade to join them. It was now over three hours, he realized, since he himself had smoked.

The sun formed a rainbow over the leaping spray that clouded the bubbling surface of the pool that lurked deep in the naked black rock. He was soaked to the skin and only the rucksack which he had held above his head as he plunged into the pool was remotely dry. Shivering violently, he crouched on the mossy ledge and peered out through the milky green curtain of the waterfall, hearing the clink of metal striking rock as the third man threaded his way up the rim of the miniature gorge. A shadow fell across the water and there was a clatter of a dislodged stone. Then the shadow moved silently away and Philip breathed again.

He had ducked out of the croft after the dummy assault run when he had seen the men lined up on the beach, excluding the loading party and the coxswain who were dismantling the dinghies, and formed into eight three-man teams, all in full combat order. Two of them had driven off in the Land Rover while the others had spread out and started to move up through the heather, beaters stalking the birds. Perhaps it was no more than a routine exercise to keep them from going stale before the embarkation, but he had not waited to find out. The waterfall was some thirty yards below the croft where the burn kinked and was joined by a minor gully; and once the line of beaters had passed he would take this gully which snaked south of east toward the Lodge.

He gave them another ten minutes, trying to control his chattering teeth, then waded into the pool and three quick strokes which seemed to last an eternity as he braced himself against the bullet plowing into his spine took him to the bank and the shelter of the overhanging branches of an alder. Halfway up the gully, he crawled into a clump of bracken and looked back across the burn. As he had expected, a sentry had been posted at the croft. He wouldn't last long in this kind of warfare, Philip thought, unless someone told him to wear his watch with its face on the inside of his wrist; which was why he had taken off his own Rolex on the stainless steel bracelet, a potential heliograph that could reveal his presence with a single flash of reflected sunlight, and stowed it in his pocket.

The gully finally petered out into the hillside and by then his back was almost dry. The only alarm had been the click of stones when he had edged around a rock to come face to face with a fawn that could not have been more than a day old, as dappled as the shade in which it was lying. The fawn had gazed at him without the slightest fear in the liquid eyes, but Philip had hurried on, once having seen a hind rearing and slashing at an eagle with her hooves to protect her calf. A flat trough of dead ground between two ridges stretched eastward and he rose from his crouch and broke into a run, the sun hammering on to the back of his neck, the tangled heather clutching at his ankles. Again he put up some grouse and lay panting with his face pressed into the damp earth, but no one shot at him or shouted. Once he heard the shrill blast of a whistle, but it was behind him and far to the north. Anyway, he reasoned as he jogged on, wiping the sweat from the stubble on his upper lip, the ruck-

209

sack grinding a groove in the small of his back, he was through the eighteen-man cordon in the immediate vicinity of the camp sweeping up and across the island. That left the six who had gone off in the Land Rover; either they had joined up with the others or were at the Lodge. He tripped and stumbled into a small ravine. There was a pool of muddy water and he lay on his stomach and lapped it up, oblivious to the foul and brackish taste. Surely the next ridge must be the last.

It was, and a smile of relief cracked his lips as he looked down on the pseudo-Chinese facade of the Lodge. After returning from a visit to Sicily, the same Lord Ardale who had built Rushworth at the height of the family fortunes had decided to enliven the barren landscape of Moronsay with a smaller and more personal version of La Favorita in Palermo. He made the drawings himself, complete with a belvedere and minarets, scalloped cornices and Gothic arcades, left everything in the hands of his architect, and departed for Russia. Luckily he died before he saw the architect's interpretation of his dream. It had even been sited wrongly, Jackie had said, facing north on the south side of the bay; and to Philip it resembled nothing so much as a cross between the Brighton Pavilion and a derelict suburban cinema. There was no doubt that it certainly deserved a full-page color spread in the book on follies, but not now with the Land Rover parked by the twin flight of steps leading up to the *piano nobile*.

From the saddle on which the house was built, one path wound down to the foreshore and a breakwater alongside which the *Jacqueline* was docked; the other slanted up the side of the headland to a grassy hummock above which showed a flat gray concrete roof and a tall aerial that was heavily guyed.

Philip backed a few feet down the ridge, took out his watch, and was amazed to see that it was already past six o'clock. A bank of cloud was building up on the western horizon and as he loaded and cocked the Uzi he decided to take the Lodge first. His eye-patch had been dangling around his neck all day, and coming out of the sun, his filthy clothes indistinguishable from the uniforms that they all were wearing, only the length of his hair would betray him. But that was a detail not worth worrying about; the element of surprise was his. He stood up and slung the submachine gun over his shoulder, the breech bumping against his hip, then stepped out smartly and began to descend the slope, digging in his heels and letting his momentum carry him down to the track.

He walked straight up the steps and hesitated a moment under the portico, ears straining to catch any sound, before twisting the tarnished brass handle in the shape of a dolphin and pushing open one of the tall double doors. The hall had a floor of black and white marble squares and was backed by a horseshoe staircase which led up to a colonnaded gallery that ran along three sides of the lofty room. There were five doors to choose from, but the nearest one on the right he could eliminate; he had looked in through the window and it was the dining room. But the dining room should lead into the kitchen, and in the kitchen, unless he was out, he should find Angus. There was a serving hatch above the sideboard and he gently slid it back and found himself looking across a stone-floored pantry at a green baize door on the other of which a radio was playing.

The green baize was soft beneath his hand. The door swung back on well-oiled hinges and by the time Angus' red-rimmed eyes had blinked and focused, Philip was already running the Uzi's muzzle into the pink nape of the newly shaved neck of the man with whom Angus was sharing a bottle of Islay Mist, and sweeping his Sterling off the table into a corner by the sink.

"Sorry to break it up, gentlemen. But the party's over."

"Smith, F. J. Corporal. 76903 . . ."

Philip Quest lost his temper. "Say that once more," he shouted, "and I'll blow your bloody balls off! You're not in some lousy B-movie trying to impress the Gestapo. This isn't a game, it's for real. So just shut up and answer my questions. And you, Angus, keep out of the bloody way. Go and sit down before you fall down."

Angus was gaping at Philip as if he was a visitor from another planet. Since Philip has burst into the kitchen he had not uttered a single word, but had stood gently swaying backwards and forwards, slowly swiveling his head from Philip to the Corporal and back again, as if he was watching a game of tennis in slow motion. Now he threw out his chest and walked stiffly toward the dresser and lowered himself with the utmost dignity into a chair.

"Right," Philip said. "Now stay there."

The chunky young man who called himself Corporal Smith was sitting squarely at the table, his hands laid out in front of him. His ears stuck out from the blonde remnants of his hair and he had a round smooth face with a countryman's high complexion. He stared stolidly at a point in the wall above Philip's shoulder, the gray eyes totally blank.

Philip saw that he was getting nowhere and changed his line of attack. "Now listen," he said in a confidential tone. "Whether you know it or not, you're in trouble, big trouble. All of you are. As I said, this isn't a game or some exercise dreamed up by the War Office. It's deadly serious. Tonight you think you're smiling, but you're not. The party's over and God knows what's going to happen to you. I don't. Probably nothing if you cooperate. It's not your fault you've been conned, taken for a ride. All right, I appreciate your loyalty to your mates but you won't be selling anyone down the river, that's been done months ago. No one's going to put you on a charge or send you off to Northern Ireland. And I've got nothing against you personally. Fine, so you've proved how tough you are. You've proved you weren't asleep during the lectures on interrogation techniques. So perhaps they'll make you a Sergeant next week when this is all over. I'll see if I can put in a word for you. O.K.? Now I'm not going to make any idle threats of kneecapping and you never play football again—it was a great goal, that second one your scored. So let's just take it nice and easy and you tell me the orders of the day, and more specifically your orders here."

But even as he stopped speaking, Philip knew what the answer would be; and short of beating him into submission, which might take hours and was not guaranteed to succeed, there was nothing he could do about it.

"Smith, F. J . . ."

"Don't tell me. Let me guess."

Rousing Angus to go and find some rope was an equally thankless task. Having made the Corporal lie face down on the floor, Philip drained the jug of water standing on the table, then poured out half a tumbler of whisky and luxuriously lit a cigarette. He retrieved the Sterling and considered taking it with him instead of the Uzi, but then decided that the advantages of a silencer were outweighed by the superior firepower and the compactness of the weapon that he had now got to know. But where the hell had that drunken fool got to? Over to the mainland for a piece of rope?

Finally Angus returned with a length of clothesline, muttering darkly beneath his breath. Either Philip had to give him the gun and do the job himself, or trust that Angus still could tie a knot; he just prayed that he would think that he was on board the *Jacqueline* and he was lashing down the hatch.

"Well done," he said as Angus rocked back on his haunches before pulling himself upright. He prodded the Corporal to his feet and tested the rope that bound his hands behind his back. "Splendid. Now where can we put him where he'll be out of the way in case any of his friends come to call. Is there a cellar or somewhere like that?"

Beneath the week's growth of heavy black beard, Angus' face lit up with a knowing grin. "A cellar? Aye, there is. An' guess who's got the key?"

"Oh, for Christ's sake." Philip wiped the back of his hand across his mouth. "So let's the three of us go down there and get another bottle."

"Aye, that's no such a bad idea."

"Then let's go and get this bloody farce over with! You show us the way and the Corporal and I will follow."

"You know, Corporal," Philip said as Angus produced a huge key and eventually unlocked the low wooden door at the bottom of the stone steps that led down from the pantry, "when I die, they'll probably find your name, rank, and number engraved on my heart. Much as I appreciate your stubbornness, this time you've carried it too far. Right, in you go. I'm rather inclined to forget things, so you'd better keep your fingers crossed that I remember to tell the Navy you're here when they move in to clean up the mess. Still no comment? Too bad." He pushed Angus aside, switched off the light, and turned the key.

In the kitchen Philip took what was left of the Islay Mist and put it in the rucksack, then pulled on the Corporal's khaki knitted cap that was lying on the table. Leaving Angus crooning some Gaelic dirge as he opened the new bottle, he left the Lodge and removed the key from the Land Rover's ignition and tossed the bolt of the Sterling over the cliff as he forced his aching legs up what he prayed was the last hill that he would have to climb that day. Once again the Atlantic breeze had freshened with the evening and the bank of clouds was rolling further up the sky above a livid sea. The sun went in for a moment and even though the airstrip was equipped with a rudimentary lighting system, he wondered about night landings if the cloud closed in and the ceiling dropped.

The wind whipped at the aerial and sang in the wire guy-lines, flattening the tussocks of coarse grass that crowned the rim of the hollow mound in which the pillbox had been sited to command the eastern approaches. Over the past thirty years the weather had eaten away at the cement and even a child would have found the entrance low. A new padlock hung from a rasp beside the dull gray steel door which Philip eased open. He then descended the four steps into the circular bunker where he could stand upright. There were two light sources in the bunker; a single bulb protected by a metal cage set in the ceiling, and an Anglepoise lamp on the wide shelf on the seaward side which threw a concentrated cone of brightness on to the sand and pen of the man in headphones who was sitting in a canvas chair, writing jerkily on a yellow pad. He must have noticed or felt the momentary draft before Philip had closed the door, as he raised his left hand and said distractedly, "That you, Fred? Be with you in a minute." Then, into the mouthpiece of his headset, "Zulu Tango, confirming ETA 22:30. Two-two-three-oh. 'Bye. Roger and out." Dwarfed by the gleaming bulk of the transmitter, a field telephone stood at his elbow. He cranked it as he removed his headphones, repeated the time of Tango Zulu's estimated arrival, then replaced the receiver in the cradle and pushed back the chair.

"Fred's not feeling too well," Philip said, moving into the light. "So I thought I'd save him the trouble and relieve you myself."

Some twenty minutes later, Philip had locked the thick cellar door behind him. Angus had passed out on the kitchen table and he had not bothered to tie up the radio operator; even if he freed the Corporal they would need explosives or a pneumatic drill to break out of the cellar. There had been one heart-stopping moment when he had thought that the bullet ricocheting around the cement walls of the pillbox must cause some irreparable damage, but his luck had held.

And that one bullet, searing past the radio operator's ear, was all that had been needed to persuade him to carry out Philip's instructions. Philip had stood over him as he pulled switches and turned knobs until the two fluorescent green fans met in the center of the tuning panel and formed a single brilliant line. He had written down the call sign that Arafa had given him, and he drummed his fingers on the plastic casing of the Uzi's barrel as an age passed before the shaking hand gave him the headphones and the word "Lalage" crackled in his ear. There was an extended pause of total silence and the absence of any static made him think that they had lost contact, then suddenly Arafa's voice was coming through loud and clear.

Now he sat on the steps of the Lodge and washed down the last of the ham sandwich with the last of the Islay Mist, waiting for night to fall. The thought occurred to him that matadors never ate before a fight to make the surgeon's job easier, then he pushed it away to the attic of his mind and ticked off the points on his check list one by one. The field telephone was out of order; the orders of the patrol that had set out from the Lodge were to join up with the others and return to camp after the search had been completed; the radio operator and Corporal Fred Smith would not be relieved till midnight; the password for the gate was "Wellington." It was the last piece of information that had boosted Philip's hopes the most. Although the fence had seemed innocent enough from the croft, it was wired to alarm all along its three-mile length and he had already considered, and rejected as impossible because of the massive overhang, the one theoretical weak point where it ended on the cliff below the croft.

A light came on in one of the upper windows and a lavatory flushed. In their flat, Angus' mother would be preparing for bed, while her son slept off his stupor. And when would he be going to bed, Philip wondered as he ground his knuckles into the empty socket of his eye? And where? He clipped his watch back on to his wrist and walked down the steps to the Land Rover, telling himself not "Waterloo" or "Napoleon," but "Wellington," like the boot.

Chapter XVII.

"The Prize, Gentlemen . . . Mam'selle 69!"

For a full sixty seconds the water beneath the *Sunspray*'s transom boiled white as the deep-throated roar of her engines rose to a crescendo, then they were throttled back and stopped, and there was silence except for the hum of the generator and a burst of laughter and applause from the main building. The coxswain who would take her out to the rendezvous in the deep waters of the bay where she would be hoisted aboard the freighter, checked the cargo on her foredeck, then climebd up on to the jetty and made his way across the camp to join the others at the farewell dinner.

A few minutes earlier, after being introduced to the assembled men as an observer from the Pentagon and making a brief speech on the importance of Anglo-American relations, Leroy J. Papich had left Webb-Walker to tumultuous applause and had walked over to his temporary quarters in one of the chalets.

He now drew the tartan oilcloth curtains and sat down on one of the two flimsy beds and placed beside him the present that Wayne had given him to celebrate their first Chinese heroin deal, an alligator overnight bag from Mark Cross. He checked on the hair that he had moistened and laid across the tongue of the zip; it was still there. Not that he had anything to hide, but it was good to know they trusted him. He took out his nail file and broke open a fresh box of .357 Magnum shells, selected six and filed a deep cross in the soft lead nose of each bullet. He then drew his Python, swung out the cylinder to eject the shells, and reloaded with the dum-dums that he was now forced to make himself as their commercial manufacture was banned throughout the world. The last time that he had fired it had been in the confined space of the Marine Corps range in the Embassy basement, so now he used the blunt end of the nail file to adjust the screw of the rear sight for long-distance shooting at up to fifty yards. Okay, so he'd never won any half-assed competition blasting the hell out of a piece of cardboard. Who cared? At that distance he'd blown a VC's belt buckle clean through his spine.

It was Octopus, the newly installed computer at Langley, reputed to be the most sophisticated in the world, that had finally given Papich the lead for which he had been so desperately searching. Thanks to the cooperation of Colonel Maxwell, he had been assigned an office on the top floor of the Embassy where he had shut himself away from the clatter of the teleprinters and the hurrying clerks and cipherines and had ordered coffee, a bottle of Old Grandad, and a carton of his filter-tip Camels. He had then sat down to make a list of every name that could possibly be connected with the case in hand, rejecting no one however remote, outdated, or trivial the tie-in might seem; his own colleagues, officers of foreign intelligence Services, barmen, informers, bankers, concierges, even the owner of the restaurant at Temara Plage where he and Wayne used to swim and pick up the doe-eyed Lebanese. His list consisted of more than seventy names, ranging alphabetically from Arafa to Zander, a French SDECE agent whose cover was a toy shop in Lugano. Then he asked for, and his request was cleared through Washington, computer time on Octopus. One printout, pairing two of the names, stuck out like a sore thumb. Webb-Walker and Renton, Quest's girl friend. From then on in it was merely a question of delegating the legwork. Renton was also the name of a property company and that same evening Papich picked up the telephone, dialed Webb-Walker's number in Whitehall, and said, "This is Leroy Papich. Long time no see. Washington '75, that Angolan fuck-up. But this is more of a personal matter. I'm interested in going into the vacation business and they tell me you might have some shares to sell in an outfit called Sunspray. So let's meet and talk it over. Like now." In the plane coming up from London, Papich again repeated his demand for a fifty-fifty split, but only because he knew that Webb-Walker expected it of him; just as he expected Webb-Walker to refuse and tell him that he was lucky to be cut in at all, and thirty percent was better than fifty percent of nothing.

But best of all was one hundred percent of everything, and that was the Ace pot that he was going to scoop tonight. The Piper had already been refueled for the return trip in the morning, but there was no way he was going to wait that long. He had been trained to fly after Korea and in a couple of hours he would be high above the Irish Sea, holding a course of one-hundred-thirty-five degrees for London and the Embassy, alone with half a million dollars on the seat beside him.

And now for the floorshow that he had promised the boys at the end of his speech. Webb-Walker had looked fit to bust a gut, but the cheers and the wolf whistles, the fists thumping on the tables and the banging of plates had forced him to realize that he could easily have a riot on his hands if he did not comply. "So what's it to you?" Papich had shouted above the din. "I know you didn't get anything out of her, but why make these guys suffer? And how would you feel if some killjoy civilian you didn't know from Adam gave you the thumbs-down at a moment like this? Jesus, these boys are going off to fight and ain't seen a woman in weeks. And Quest's girl—it's beautiful! It's poetic justice. She's got to go anyway, and baby, what a way to go!"

One of the first lessons that Philip had learned at the poker table was that once you had made up your mind to bluff there was no going back; you played the worthless pair of twos you were holding as if they were invincible, betting and raising the maximum whatever the opposition. And so he came down the hill with the headlights on full beam, flashing them impatiently as he approached the fence. Leaving the engine running, he said, "Wellington" into the intercom, then turned on his heel and was already engaging first gear as the gate swung open. With a gun at his head, the radio operator had eagerly explained the geography of the camp, filling in the details on Jackie's map. The chalets were unoccupied; the men both ate and slept in the main building; the command post was the first of the six two-roomed terraced cottages; the second was Talbot's quarters, now occupied by the civilian gentlemen; the third was the armory and workshop; the fourth and fifth store rooms to one of which Jackie had been taken; the sixth and nearest the sea housed the generator and the fuel supply.

As he bumped across the edge of the field his headlights caught the white paintwork of the Piper lurking like a giant moth at the end of the strip. The landing lights had not yet been switched on; there was an hour to go and whatever happened he must ensure that Zulu Tango touched down safely; losing Thami Fouquet now would bring Arafa's whole career to a sudden and inglorious end. He crossed the burn and parked in the appointed place, an open shed fifty yards from the main building, and sat for a moment listening to the music and raucous laughter. Apparently this was the only occasion that alcohol had been permitted on the island and they would have five days on a dry ship to sober them up; Saturday night at the pub, Philip thought; the Duchess of Richmond's ball on the eve of Waterloo; the last supper. So let them enjoy it while they could.

A figure swayed down the elongated rectangle of light that poured from the door and was noisily sick. He was in his shirtsleeves and Philip realized that tonight of all nights each man's weapons would be safely locked away in the armory. He folded the stock of the Uzi and carried it against his thigh like a pistol, then made his way across the grass toward the three lighted windows which marked the landward end of the row of cottages, leaving the rucksack beneath the seat.

The command post was his first objective. He walked warily on the balls of his feet, more or less secure in the knowledge that he had the run of the camp, but always alert for a chance encounter in which case he would play drunk or open his legs and start to undo his fly. He circled around and approached the cottage from the side. There was no need to go any nearer; from where he stood in the shadows he could see enough. The room was furnished in Civil Service green: two metal tables, chairs, a filing cabinet and screwed to the wall a large panel whose switches were all neatly marked with red Dymo-tape. An electric kettle was steaming and as Philip watched, the man sitting by the telephone reading *Playboy* got up and made himself a mug of coffee. As he stirred it, he stared sourly out of the front window, and Philip ducked down and moved silently away.

His right shoulder grazing the wall, Philip crawled beneath the sill, then held his breath and carefully rose to his feet on the cracked flagstone that was the threshhold of the second cottage. And then, without warning, he was swallowed up by a warp in time and it was 8:25 in the morning of the day after he had accidentally blown up a corner of the gymnasium, and

223

he was standing in the drafty corridor while the bell rang and boys shouted, summoning up courage to tap on the dark brown door of his housemaster's study. The same butterflies were fluttering in his stomach, but now he tightened his grip on the Uzi and walked straight in, not bothering to knock.

Nor did anything about Webb-Walker's appearance dispel the illusion. He was wearing the same nondescript clothes, a brownish sports jacket and gray flannel trousers; the same lock of hair drooped over his pale forehead. Hunched over the table, he might have been correcting the same Latin unseens; even the same dirty cough was the same as he cleared his throat, stubbed out his cigarette, and then removed his glasses and pinched the bridge of his nose.

"Ah, Quest," he said in his mild and pedantic fashion. "Older and certainly dirtier, but essentially the same lecherous adolescent. Surprised, yes, but not amazed. And no doubt you recall the circumstances in which that famous *mot* was made. I admire Miss Renton for her spirit, if not her honesty. Unfortunately I cannot say the same of you. Evidently you have lost none of your arrogance and at last you have gone too far. I trust you realize where your greed and meddling has led you. You will be charged under the Official Secrets Act, trespassing on Government property being the most minor of the counts, and the trial, of course, will be held *in camera*. Then there will be the illegal possession of a firearm with intent to endanger life, but undoubtedly as far as you are concerned, the *bonne bouche* will be the murder of a certain Wayne Morollo." He clicked his tongue regretfully. "For an experienced officer of de Salis' rank it was a rare mistake of judgment to believe that personal friendships carry that much weight in his profession. A reliable witness will attest to his last seeing Morollo alive in your flat in London and forensic tests will certainly reveal traces of blood and other evidence." He reached out a delicate hand for the pack of Craven A beside the ashtray.

"No," Philip said. The same cigarettes; he had thought they'd stopped making them years ago. Leaning against the door, he had listened to Webb-Walker with a perverse amusement, spellbound by what he had to say. And why not? He had all the time in world before Zulu Tango landed. But now he had heard enough.

"You seriously believe that one of them might contain an explosive device of some kind? Or a nerve gas that can paralyze you in half a second? Come now, Quest. Or should I call you Biggles? Be your age."

"And you know what we used to call you at school?" Philip said venomously. "Wanker and Creeping Jesus. You can take your pick. But that's all over now, washed up like you. Kaput. Finito. You bored on about me being tried but it's your own trial you ought to be worrying about. This isn't a personal vendetta any more. It's the big time, the official time. You've been rumbled, Webb-Walker, and it was Piers de Salis who rumbled you. And it's because of Piers that I'm here. I came here to kill you, to snuff you out like you killed him. And don't waste your breath trying to deny it. But looking at you now, you're not worth the bullet. It'd be much too easy, too kind and I want you to suffer, you bastard. And don't you think you can flannel your way out of this one. It's all down in black and white. You sneered at Piers' lack of judgment and perhaps you were right about your own shitty profession. But he trusted me and wrote it down and that's it. That message from Talbot was a fake. And so was the one to Thami Fouquet. Oh yes, he'll be here all right, but five minutes after he touches down so will the Navy—Her Majesty's Navy with a landing party under the temporary command of an old colleague of yours who loathes your guts almost as much as I do, a certain Captain Hamid Arafa. And you can blather on till the cows come home, but there's no way you're going to wriggle out from this one. Neither you nor your psychopathic sidekick, Papich. And what's he up to, by the way? Lining them all up for a blow job? And Jackie, where's Jackie?"

Philip's mouth was dry and he longed for some water, but he was not going to take his eye off the motionless figure crouching behind the table, and he knew from Arizona that it was the small pale scorpions that were the most poisonous of all.

Two spots of color stood out on Webb-Walker's hollow cheeks, but his expression of an understanding doctor humoring a lunatic had not changed. "By Jackie I presume you mean Lord Ardale's daughter?"

"God, you're a snob as well!" Philip said disgustedly. "How the hell did Laura ever come to marry you? Pregnant by some other man?" He saw Webb-Walker flinch as his words hit home, the first sign of any feelings that he had yet shown. But his reaction took him completely by surprise.

A thin smile played on his lips and his eyes gleamed happily behind the thick lenses of his glasses. He put the tips of his fingers together and leaned back in his chair, then quoted Byron. "There was a sound of revelry by night."

Philip shrugged helplessly. "So what? As a matter of fact, I thought that, too. The ball before Waterloo."

"I'm glad that the thousands of pounds that your parents spent on your education were not entirely wasted. And how well do you remember your Burke? His speech in 1783 on Fox's East India Bill."

Philip stared at him. "Look, it's no good you trying to pretend you've gone mad, because you haven't."

Webb-Walker ignored his interruption. "Then let me refresh your memory as to his happy choice of phrase. 'Licentious soldiery.' You asked me where Miss Renton was and now you have your answer. At our American friend's suggestion, she will now be entertaining the troops, Burke's licentious soldiery. And I leave it to your imagination as to precisely what form of entertainment that will be. Hardly conjuring tricks, I should think, or a selection from *South*

Pacific. And judging by the noise, her act is going down extremely well."

At that moment there was no force in the world that could prevent Philip's involuntary glance over his shoulder toward the window, and it was then, with the speed of light, that a tiny black gun appeared in Webb-Walkers' right hand and he fired three times in quick succession, the shots making no more noise than the bursting of a balloon. Champion as he was for the past three years, at the range Webb-Walker grouped all three bullets in an area the size of a matchbox in a direct line with Philip's heart.

Slammed against the door by the impact, Philip felt his feet skid from under him. The sub-machine gun hit the floor, the back of his head the wall. Temporarily stunned, his glazed eye saw a smiling Webb-Walker rise to his feet and walk toward him, a wisp of smoke rising from the stubby barrel of the pistol. He neither breathed nor moved a muscle until Webb-Walker peered down to verify his marksmanship, then he grinned and kicked out with all his strength, his boot rocketing into Webb-Walker's groin, lifting him off the floor and sending him crashing into the wall.

The horn-rimmed glasses crunched beneath his feet as he bent over the spread-eagled body and picked up the gun, a .25 Beretta automatic that he had worn in a spring clip in the sleeve of his jacket. Jesus, he thought, that had been the closest yet. Thank God for German workmanship! He unzipped the chest pocket of his anorak and took out the Leica. Two of the metal-jacketed bullets had drilled neat holes through the lens cap, smashed the lens and now rattled in the body of the camera; the third had been stopped by the self-timer. He stood still and listened; the only sound was the racking wheeze of Webb-Walker's tortured breathing, and thank God, too, for solid Scots building.

Switching off the lights and silently closing the door behind him, Philip broke into a run and then as the hangar-like outline grew clearer he realized that he was acting out of pure instinct and that his mind was a complete blank. Had it been just a trick of Webb-Walker's to distract his attention for that vital instant? A bluff to send him blundering into a roomful of drunken soldiers? No, that gloating voice had been in deadly earnest; at last he was getting his revenge for that day at Lord's now twenty years ago. Philip forced himself to slow down and think rationally, unnerved by the sudden silence. Door or window? Door. Why should anyone peer in through a window? And when the man had staggered out to be sick, he had caught a glimpse of a curtained vestibule shutting off the door from the main body of the hall.

In spite of the dank sea air, the sweat was pouring from his face; the wooden floor creaked beneath his weight and the dingy velvet curtain smelled of stale tobacco, and then, over to his right, the dreadful silence exploded into sudden pandemonium as a man's voice, an American voice, announced, "And now gentlemen, a big hand—and I know you know what I mean—for our star of the evening . . . none other than Mam'selle Soixante-Neuf herself . . . The Duchess!"

Entangled in the snagging folds of the curtain, Philip swore and ripped it free. The door by which he had entered was in the center of one of the longer sides of the building. To his left he could see rows of books, ahead of him were the showers and lavatories. He turned right down the short corridor and pulled aside a second curtain. The hall was blue with smoke that swirled below the three powerful lights that hung from the evenly spaced girders bracing the arched corrugated iron roof. The thirty-odd men crowded around the trestle tables were cheering and stamping their feet, all heads turned toward the low platform at the far end where Papich was holding up his hands, vainly appealing for silence. Beside him, flanked by two tall grinning men, her face hidden by her long black hair as she tossed and ducked her head. Jackie writhed and struggled to break their grip on her arms. She was naked, and a man at the front table jumped up to try to embrace her, only to be hurled back by a boot in his ribs to a renewed burst of cheering and a roar of obscenities.

At last Papich could make himself heard. "Thank you, gentlemen, thank you." He raised his clasped hands in triumph, a boxer acknowledging his victory. "Like they say, first served, first come." He paused, laughing, as he waited for the din to subside again. "Now so's you all don't get trampled in the rush, we've got to be fair. And so the Duchess here has very kindly agreed to judge who'll be the lucky man to have first bit at her cherry. The prize, gentlemen—wait for it, wait for it—will go to the guy, Jew or Gentile she don't care, will go to the guy with the fattest, thickest, longest . . . That's it! You've guessed it! So let's hear those zippers zip and see what men are made of!"

After the initial paralyzing shock, Philip's first reaction had been to cut down Papich there and then; at fifteen yards he could hardly miss. But then, as Papich continued with his hideous parody of an MC in a sleazy downtown nightclub on Fremont Street in Las Vegas, reason had returned. Even with the element of surprise and the sub-machine gun he could hardly hope to hold a mob at bay until Arafa's landing party arrived. Then the leer on Papich's shining face triggered off an image of Wayne Morollo in the darkroom. He squinted up into the glare and traced the wires to a junction box on the wall high above his head. He let the curtain fall and backed down the corridor. So where the bloody hell was the fuse box? There must be one. But there was not. The panel in the command post? Too far, and first he would have to deal with the man on duty. He tried in vain to shut his ears as he stood helplessly in the entrance hall, desperately searching for a positive course of action. The switch by the door? It was metal, and besides he had no screwdriver; and the wires were encased in a metal tube. The light hanging above him was out of reach. The washroom, then? He flicked the switch down, then up again, and felt the adrenalin pumping through his veins. He swung himself up onto the central row of basins, his feet slipping on the porcelain, and jumped. His outstretched hands caught the plastic shade and for a moment he swung in midair, but then the cable ripped free from the girder and both the shade and the bulb smashed beneath him as he fell and landed on the bare boards. He stamped on the bakelite fitting and tore out the two wires which he twisted around the nearest tap. He ran back to the door and pulled the switch, shading his eye with his hands. The room exploded as if a charge of magnesium had been fired, then he was sprinting down the corridor as the laughter turned to jeers and booing catcalls.

Philip plunged straight in, lashing out wildly with both fists, bludgeoning, elbowing, and kicking his way toward the platform. Within seconds he had caused total chaos as the fighting spread like wildfire. The noise was appalling as he plowed through the shouting, cursing, grunting pack. A falling bench barked his shin; a flying plate caught him on the ear and sent him crashing into a corner of a table. A beery face breathed into his, and there was a scream of agony as he bit the hand that was clawing at his mouth. Glass broke, and he fell over a flailing leg. A chair bounced off his back and a wild swing jarred his whole arm as his knuckles connected with a shaven head.

"You bleeding pack of animals!" an Irish voice bawled inches from his ringing ear. "You cunt-struck maniacs! Mackenzie, Ingram! Get some bleeding lights in here!"

There was a sudden spurt of flame as a lamp flickered and went out. Philip had lunged toward the platform and was already leaping on to the khaki-covered back of the man who was pinning Jackie to the boards. He locked his fingers around the gulping throat, thumbs seeking out the pressure points, and forced the chin back, then threw the limp body aside. As he reached out blindly he felt a searing pain where Jackie's nails raked his cheek. He seized her wrist and pulled her toward him, ignoring her screams. "It's me, damn it," he panted into her ear as she fought him off and they rolled together across the platform. "Jackie, it's me!"

Then the blast of a whistle pierced the pandemonium and praying that he was where he thought he was, Philip dragged her unresisting toward where one of the two doors behind the platform should be. A moment later he was slamming it shut and groping toward a rectangle of paler darkness. The whistle shrilled again as he fumbled with the catch.

"Mackenzie! where those bleeding lights? Mother of God, the bastard who started this, I'll have his guts for garters!"

Now for the $64,000 question, Philip thought as he manhandled Jackie over the sill and swung down after her on to the damp grass. Had he blown all the fuses, too? He ran to the corner and felt his heart lift as he saw the light still burning brightly in the cottage. He raised his wrist to look at his watch, but the crystal had been smashed and only the hour hand remained, pointing uselessly at six o'clock. He ran back to Jackie who was leaning against the wall, shivering, her arms clasped across her breasts. He peeled off his anorak and forced it over her head. She made no effort to help him, looking up at him with vacant eyes when he asked her how she was. He had seen cases of shock like this before, and realized that he was only wasting time. He grabbed her hand and trailing her after him like a recalcitrant child dragged her down toward the beach.

Philip pulled her into the narrow gap between two of the chalets and down on to the soft drift of wind-blown sand. "Now you just stay right here and don't move till I come back."

"The American, he . . ."

"Forget him. He'll be taken care of, don't worry."

231

He, too, was beginning to feel the cold now that his sweat had dried. He rose to one knee and peered around the blistered paintwork of the chalet. A faint orange glow showed in one of the windows of the main building and a man's silhouette passed across it, but whether he was inside or out, Philip was unable to tell. Order seemed to have been restored, but soon they would discover that Jackie was missing and the search would be on.

Jackie tugged at his shirtsleeve. "Philip," she said in a voice that was far away. "Where are you going?"

"Any minute Thami Fouquet'll be here and you can't land a plane in the dark. God knows what's happening, but if no one else is going to turn those lights on, I'll have to do it myself. Remember now, just sit here and wait. There's nothing to worry about. Webb-Walker's all safely tucked up under his bed with what looks like, among other things, a fractured skull and as soon as Fouquet arrives Arafa will move in with the Navy. So that's it. Now you just take it easy and I'll be back for you."

He stepped over her huddled against the wall and slithered down to the firmer sand of the beach. Protected first by the chalets and then by the dunes, the longest way would be the quickest and he would not have to waste precious seconds in scouting out the land and constantly looking over his shoulder. The breath rasping at his throat, he drove himself on up the beach, setting his pace to the muttered rhythm "ETA 22:30, ETA 22:30," trying to rub away the stitch that was lancing into his side. He glanced up and saw that he was almost at the jetty and as he bore to the right up through the dunes, the twin rows of lights that marked the landing strip silently stabbed the sky and he slowed to a walk, then sank to his knees in the sand. Christ, all that effort for nothing; but he had completely lost his sense of time and it was his own fault for starting to panic. He was nearly level with the end of the runway where the Cherokee was parked and he settled down behind a hillock of silky grass where the burn flowed out into the sea.

The low clouds reflected a strange luminescence and the receding avenue of lights formed an effective curtain between him and the rest of the camp. The water lapped at the *Seaspray*'s hull, and listening to the soothing hum of the generator he realized that in effect he had now been called off the field and would spend the rest of the same sitting on the touchline, wrapped in a blanket, waiting for the final whistle while the professionals tidied up.

The distant drone of an aircraft grew louder. By now, as it lost height for the final approach, the blip would have faded from the radar screen and Arafa would be strapping himself into the helicopter as the rotors began to whirl and swish. Philip scanned the sky, but could see nothing. And then, directly overhead, a flashing red beacon dropped out of the clouds and Zulu Tango made a perfect three-point landing halfway down the runway, the pitch of the engine changing as the pilot applied his brakes.

"Go!" Philip said into the imaginary walkie-talkie. "It's all yours, Hamid." He stretched his bruised and aching limbs and reached for a cigarette, then remembered they were in his anorak. A bulky figure moved out of the darkness beside the Cherokee, the ground level lighting making his face a grinning skull. It was Papich and he was unbuttoning his jacket. From where he crouched, Philip could see the uncertain frown as he looked toward the cottages, then back to the far end of the runway where Zulu Tango was already turning.

Philip, too, was watching the aircraft taxi back up the field when he caught a sudden movement on the edge of the dune to his right. A sheep, he thought, but an instant later there was a spurt of flame and the crack of a shot, followed by a second, and a third. Then, to his horror, Jackie was stumbling across the runway, straight into the path of the aircraft bearing down on her, the Walther that he had left in a pocket of the anorak blazing in her hand.

Leaping to his feet, Philip yelled to her to get down and fired blindly from the hip, the stammering roar drowning his words. He saw Papich kneeling by the Cherokee's undercarriage, saw his head swivel round, saw the Python braced in both hands. He fired again. A tire exploded. Zulu Tango was now swerving toward him and as he dove to avoid the scything wing an iron fist struck his shoulder and lifted him bodily from the ground, spinning him around and hurling him face downward into the grass. The world lurched sickeningly as he rolled over onto his back. His right arm refused to work and a gale was blowing in his face. A hugh shadow was shutting out the sky and his last conscious memory of Moronsay was his left hand somehow gripping the Uzi and emptying the magazine into the belly of the eagle as it reached out its talons and snatched him away up into the blazing, roaring orange night.

Chapter XVIII.

Of Pelicans and Pendants

"Up, up and away," Mrs. T. warbled in the kitchen where she was defrosting the refrigerator. "In my beautiful balloon."

"Mrs. T.," Philip called from the bedroom. "Can you tie a tie?"

"Coming, dear." She bustled into the room, wiping her hands on her flowered apron, and clicked her tongue approvingly. "You do look a treat," she said. "It makes such a nice change to see you in proper clothes. This tie, dear? One of my gentlemen used to have one just like it. Old Harrovian, he was. Are you one too?"

"Watch it," Philip said. "Duels have been fought for less. No, as a matter of fact it dates from the days when I was in the Army. My old regiment, and as I've got rather an important appointment this morning, I thought I ought to wear it—for the first time in years." He sat down on the bed while she buttoned his collar and slipped the knot into place.

"And what does the doctor say about your poor

shoulder?" she asked as she helped him into the coat of his dark blue suit.

"Apparently it's healing nicely but I'll have to keep the sling till the end of the month. Which is a bore as I can't drive or . . ."

"Or I know what, dear." She giggled and winked. "Still, there's ways and means of overcoming one's deformities."

"Thanks a bunch," Philip said. "Now do you think you could kindly get some ice?"

"Bit early, isn't it?"

"You don't know where I've got to be at midday. And if I told you, you wouldn't believe me."

"Not the Palace, dear? Making you an OBE, are they, like the Beatles?"

"Ice, Mrs. T."

A Bloody Mary in his hand, he wandered into the darkroom and gazed sourly at the enlarger, thinking of the negatives that he would never print, had never seen, the scoop of the century that had either been destroyed or locked away in a safe at the Admiralty. Ten, perhaps twenty thousand pounds down the drain. At least they might have made him a token offer, even if it had only been enough for a new Leica. And then there was the Porsche, and the insurance people cutting up rough, demanding in exactly what circumstances it had come to be lying in the mud at the bottom of the Thames, the interior vandalized. He wondered about his next car. Rolls-Royces were all very well, but unless one was over forty they smacked of property speculators and asset strippers, pop stars and fashionable hairdressers. Anyway, for the time being he was perfectly happy with the Mini-Cooper and Jackie as his driver. He scraped his toe over a stain on the linoleum; coffee, not Morollo's blood. And another example of petty officialdom was the fuss they had made over the unlicensed Walther, confiscating it and implying that he was lucky not to be fined. He glanced automatically at his wrist, then up at the darkroom clock; Charlie would be bringing him a new watch at lunchtime, one that had no doubt fallen off the back of a truck.

It was too fine a day to waste indoors and he decided to wait for Arafa in the gardens. After Mrs. T. had flapped around him like a mother hen with a clothesbrush, he stood for a second on the pavement watching a telephone engineer sitting in an open inspection hatch pump up a blowtorch, smiling at the thought that a week ago he would have instinctively marked him as a watchdog, but today was like walking out of prison. As he was unlocking the gate, he met Barry wearing his Hawaiian shorts and glistening with oil, returning from his morning sunbathe with the au pair girls and their charges.

"Have a good holiday, Philip? Though I must say, you're looking a bit rough. What happened to your face? And your arm? Not another jealous husband?"

Philip touched the scabs on his cheek. "No, not this time. As a matter of fact, it was one of your lot who did my arm. But it was about a girl."

"Disloyal things! I don't know why you bother. As you can't beat us, join us. You know where to find me. Just stamp your tiny foot. *Ciao, bello.*"

"It's first on the right for Bondi," Philip called after him. "And you've forgotten your surfboard." And he was rewarded with an outthrust flip of the gaily patterned buttocks.

Philip sat down on a bench in the sun and winced as he jarred his elbow and set the pain throbbing in his shoulder. Papich had only fired once before one of Jackie's wildly inaccurate shots had hit the Cherokee and exploded the fuel tank, and the bullet, so the Lieutenant-Commander in the sick bay at Campbeltown had told him, had by some miracle missed both the clavicle and the scapula as it plowed through his trapezius, leaving an exit the size of a fist. In time the muscle would heal, but he owed his life to the immediate transfusion of three pints of plasma that he was given on board the helicopter and the use of his arm to the skill of the Surgeon-Lieutenant on board the frigate who had just returned from a course on gun-shot wounds.

But Philip had known none of this; and for forty-eight hours he had inhabited a strange twilight world, obsessed by a single question which, try as he might, he could not answer. Why, when he did not own one pair, was he wearing pajamas? On the fourth day he was sitting up and receiving visitors. Arafa was the first, and he brought with him a bottle of champagne; Thami Fouquet was in the top-security military prison outside Beni-Nellal, and his cousin sent him thanks and best wishes for Philip's recovery: Phases Four and Five completed. Leroy J. Papich had ended up as he deserved, an overcooked hamburger, but both the CIA and the Embassy in London was strenu-ously denying that they had ever heard of him and were refusing to claim the body, which was beginning to irritate the Admiral who had commanded the Na-val side of the operation. The twelve Marines who had landed from the *Wessex* had secured the camp in less than five minutes without firing a shot, their only casualty a broken ankle when a private slipped on the *Sunspray*'s deck. The men of the strike force had still been blundering about in the darkness and were to-tally bemused by the Marines' arrival. An officer from Naval Intelligence had begun his preliminary interro-gations that same night in the camp. In every case the story was the same; Philip's theory that Webb-Walker was using the Army was right and wrong. They were all ex-members of the SAS who had re-ceived official papers from an office in Whitehall, of-fering them excellent pay and added bonuses to join a specialist commando unit that was being formed to combat terrorism, and in signing on they had believed they were re-enlisting. And as Arafa said, if Webb-Walker could put together such a scenario, the possi-bilities were terrifying. Backtracking from de Salis' letter, the DNI had mounted an in-depth investigation into Webb-Walker's activities over the past years and had already uncovered evidence of his involvement in

Argentina, Angola, Rhodesia, and the Lebanon. But that was all that Arafa had been told; after all, he was a foreigner. And as for Webb-Walker himself, the doctors admitted that they had absolutely no idea when he would, if ever, come out of the coma.

That same evening, after a long session with a bearded Commander and a stenographer, he saw Jackie for the first time since she had made her wild avenging dash across the landing strip. "Look," she said, her legs flashing as she pirouetted like a mannequin. "The kilt, especially for you." She, too, had brought champagne, from Glenrannoch's cellar at Drum where she had gone to close up the house, and they drank to each other, neither of them raising the subject of what had happened during those last fifteen minutes on Moronsay, though Philip knew that one day they would have to exorcise the devils that lurked in the dark corners of her memory.

And then, yesterday, they had left the base at Campbeltown, driven to Perth, and had put the Volkswagen on the day train to London. After a few words in the right ear and a few pounds in the right hand, Philip had secured a compartment to themselves, and a few miles north of Crewe Jackie told him not to move and got up to pull down the blinds herself. And by now—damn not having a watch!—she should be leaving Rushworth where she had gone to break the news to her unsuspecting father that Sunspray Holidays were closing down its camp on Moronsay and would not be renewing the lease.

How the hell had he managed that? Philip asked himself as he saw the shining black Daimler purr to a halt outside the flat. He kicked a bouncing rubber ball back to a laughing French girl in an indecent brown bikini and let himself out of the gardens. The street smelled of hot tar and the inside of the car of new leather.

"Good morning," the driver said, a smile dimpling the pretty face framed by short golden curls.

"Hello," Philip replied. "But what about your Russian grammar."

"She decided Arabic might come in more useful," Arafa said. "Language of the future, she calls it. Don't you, Mary?"

"Quite right, too," Philip said.

The usual knot of sightseers loitered on the pavement and Philip could see them whispering among themselves, asking who he was, as the door closed behind him and the policeman at the top of the steps raised his hand to his helmet. The Daimler was parked across the street and Philip shook his head as Mary looked up. They'll be hours yet and I think they'll probably ask him to stay to lunch. They're on about phosphates now and God alone—or rather Allah—knows what Hamid knows about phosphates. Still, as we both know, he's very plausible about most things. Well, Mary," he straightened up, "it was nice meeting you. See you in the Casbah sometime."

"You're sure I can't drop you anywhere?"

"I'm only going round the corner. And you'd better keep your station—or whatever the correct Naval term is." He walked away toward St. James's Park where the office workers were eating their sandwiches on the grass and the tourists were feeding the ducks and pelicans on the lake. When he arrived at Wilton's Jackie and Charlie Thomas were already there, sitting opposite each other at the same table in the alcove where he had last lunched with Piers de Salis. Charlie was wearing his black and white pinstripe Al Capone suit and Jackie a yellow silk dress and a broad-rimmed floppy straw hat. They were talking animatedly and it was Charlie who saw Philip first.

"You know what your bird's been telling me? You've been to Number Ten."

"Quite true." He slid in next to Jackie and squeezed her thigh.

"Well, stone the bleeding crows," Charlie said at last.

"How was it?" Jackie asked. "What did he give you to drink? HP sauce?"

Philip smiled. "I was wondering about that, too. But no, he had everything. But I thought I'd have one sherry as a kind of test, thinking it was bound to be Cyprus the way he and his colleagues are always hanging on about fascism and the lack of democracy in Spain "Uhuh." He wagged his finger. "Honest-to-God Tio Pepe, chilled as well. There's politics for you."

"Probably got a villa in Torremolinos, too," Charlie said. He beckoned to the waitress with the ballooning breasts who bore down on them like a clipper under a full press of sail and ordered three Bloody Marys.

"So what actually did you talk about?" Jackie said.

"Nothing, really. All that bit about Queen and country, averting a potentially dangerous situation—the usual blah."

"No medals?"

"Just a manly handshake. By the way, darling, the King's invited us to his birthday party in July. That's one in the eye for Billy Paterson who's always trying to finagle an invitation. But remembering Skhirat '71, I think we can plead a prior engagement."

"I thought the dashing Captain Arafa was having lunch with us today," Jackie said.

"Affairs of state."

"A pity. I would've liked to see him again."

"At least you met him," Philip said. "Which is more than I did with Thami Fouquet. And let's face it, we owe it all to him."

The waitress brought their drinks and the menu.

"Tell me, Philip," Charlie rubbed his chin. "That quarter of a million quid that Fouquet brought from Switzerland. Who ended up with that?"

Philip opened his hands and looked from one to the other. "Search me. Your guess is as good as mine. I was out cold and never saw a thing. The Navy never mentioned it. And unless Jackie darling," she looked at him with wide-eyed innocence, "has stashed it away in the heather, that only leaves Arafa. And he swears that Fouquet was trying to pull a double-cross and that all the notes were fakes. But at least he admits to seeing the money, so fake or not, it did exist. And good luck to him. Why should we care? Right, Charlie?"

Charlie reached into his pocket and produced two packages which he handed across the table. Undoing the smaller one, Philip held out his arm for Jackie to clip the new Rolex Submariner around her wrist. "You open that one," he said and sat back and watched her face as she pulled off the paper and tipped the contents of the chamois leather bag onto the crisp white tablecloth. He winked at Charlie and stirred the dazzling river of gold and diamonds with his finger. "So now you see, darling, why I wasn't too worried about being conned in Lugano. Everyone was boring on so much about the pendant that they forgot the chain—22 carat gold and twelve and one half carat Blue/Whites worth about thirty thousand pounds. A fair return, I think on one's original investment. Expenses paid, a new car, trips . . ." He fell silent, suddenly ashamed of himself as the ghost of Piers de Salis passed through the room.

"All those carats," he heard Charlie Thomas say, "Enough to feed all the bloody rabbits in the world."

THE PENETRATOR
by Lionel Derrick

Mark Hardin is a warrior without uniform or rank, pledged to fight anyone on either side of the law who seeks to destroy the American way of life.

Over 2 million copies in print!

☐	40-101-2	Target is H	#1	$1.25
☐	40-102-0	Blood on the Strip	#2	1.25
☐	40-422-0	Capitol Hell	#3	1.50
☐	40-423-9	...king Manhattan	#4	1.50
☐	40-424-7	... Massacre	#5	1.50
☐	40-493-X	...kyo ...	#6	1.50
☐	40-494-8	...lo P...	#7	1.50
☐	40-495-6	...rthwest Co...	#8	1.50
☐	40-425-5	...ee City Bombers	#9	1.50
☐	220690-2	...libomb Flig...	#10	1.25
☐	220728-0	...er in Taos	#11	1.25
☐	220797-5	B...y, Boston	#12	1.25
☐	40-426-3	Dixie Death S...	#13	1.50
☐	40-427-1	Mankill Sport	#14	1.50
☐	220882-5	Quebec Connection	#15	1.25
☐	220912-0	Deepsea Shootout	#16	1.25
☐	40-456-5	Demented Empire	#17	1.50
☐	40-428-X	Countdown to Terror	#18	1.50
☐	40-429-8	Panama Power Play	#19	1.50
☐	40-258-9	Radiation Hit	#20	1.50
☐	40-079-3	Supergun Mission	#21	1.25
☐	40-067-5	High Disaster	#22	1.50
☐	40-085-3	Divine Death	#23	1.50
☐	40-177-9	Cryogenic Nightmare	#24	1.50
☐	40-178-7	Floating Death	#25	1.50
☐	40-179-5	Mexican Brown	#26	1.50
☐	40-180-9	Animal Game	#27	1.50
☐	40-268-6	Sk...igh Betrayers	#28	1.50
☐	40-269-4	...rjan Onslaught	#29	1.50
☐	40-270-9	Computer Kill	#30	1.50

PINNACLE-BOOK MAILING SERVICE
P.O. Box 690, New York, NY 10019

Please send me ...ks I have checked above. Enclosed is my check or money order for $_____ (Please add 50¢ per order and 10¢ per book to cover postage and handling. New York State and California residents add applicable sales tax.)

Name _____

Address _____

City _____ State/Zip _____

Please allow approximately four weeks for delivery.